"One Move and I Clear the Dust Out of Every Gun in My Fleet!"

a harsh PA-amplified voice boomed.

Retief retrieved the evil Groad's forgotten eye shields from the grass. As he dropped them in his pocket, a sharp report rang out, and a gout of turf exploded from the hillside a few yards behind Shluh.

A second shot scored the ground directly in his path.

"Make no further move to escape!" the metallic voice boomed out from the ship. "I observed your crew hurrying to man their guns. . . . I suggest you repair at once to your flagship and countermand any such rash instructions. Be warned, small creature! You and all your minions are my prisoners!"

Books by Keith Laumer

The Best of Keith Laumer
Fat Chance
Retief and the Warlords
Retief: Emissary to the Stars
Retief of the CDT
Retief's War

Published by POCKET BOOKS

Keith Laumer

RETIEF: EMISSARY TO THE STARS

PUBLISHED BY POCKET BOOKS NEW YORK

For Robert Mills,
my literary agent and friend in need.

"The Negotiators" first appeared in *Analog* and "The Garbage Invasion" first appeared in *The Magazine of Fantasy and Science Fiction*.

 POCKET BOOKS, a Simon & Schuster division of
GULF & WESTERN CORPORATION
1230 Avenue of the Americas, New York, N.Y. 10020

ISBN: 0-671-42683-4

First Pocket Books printing October, 1979

10 9 8 7 6 5 4 3 2

POCKET and colophon are trademarks of Simon & Schuster.

Printed in the U.S.A.

Contents

THE HOOB MELON CRISIS

1

"Gentlemen," Ambassador Earlyworm said, and paused, peering in turn at the faces of each of the subordinate diplomats seated behind meticulously aligned yellow pads and needle-sharp pencils along the twelve-foot zum-wood conference table, with an expression that strongly suggested he employed the appellation as a courtesy only. "Ours, fellows," he said in a tone of hearty good-fellowship as authentic as a turned aluminum Olde English beer tankard, "is a somewhat anomalous position, constituting as we do a diplomatic Mission to a world having no indigenous population, or native government to which to present credentials; thus, while I should be dismayed were the unfortunate expression 'up for grabs,' which I noted in a draft dispatch from the Political Section, to find its way into the record, it is undoubtedly true that a certain vacuum, planetary-ownershipwise, does exist here. I have accordingly taken the perfectly reasonable position that Froom 93 constitutes a portion of Terra proper, by virtue of discovery—and that as the highest ranking and only Terries on the world we indeed constitute a *de facto* government—with myself as king, or rather president, of course, as I am at heart a simple soul, with no aspirations to regal rank. You may therefore address me henceforth simply as 'Mr. President,' rather than as 'Your Majesty,' as someone—I believe it was you, Magnan—let slip earlier. Though I certainly sympathize with your intention to see appropriate dignity accorded my, that is to say, 'our' regime—I believe an outward expression of humility at this time is in order to forestall rude japes by coarse-minded liberals and anarchists."

"Sure, Your Maj—I mean Mr. Pres—or Mr. Ambassador—or whatever—" said Hy Felix, the Press Attaché, a dour man of post-middle age with a baggy face and matching pants. He spoke in the cynical tone he affected as appropriate to his role as a hardened old newshound (in his youth he had edited a poultrymen's journal in Sidoris, Kansas, during its brief receivership).

That's OK for the rubes back at Sector—but what about old Flith and his boys? They're pretty well settled in in what Colonel Happyfew assures me is a solid tactical position. And they claim we're invading 'New Groac'"

"A fantastic allegation!" Earlyworm barked, "which I intend to counter at once—with a most effective allegation of my own! To wit: that the presence here of Groaci personnel in any role other than that of diplomatic emissaries, constitutes an open violation of Terran sovereignty. I have, of course, invited Ambassador Flith to present his credentials to me at his earliest convenience."

"Oh, yeah? Your Maj—I mean Mr. P— Ambassador," the Press Attaché said excitedly. "What'd he say?"

"To repeat the ruffian's remarks would sully my lips," Earlyworm said glumly. "Suffice it to say that he rudely rejected my peace offering."

Flith is just a typical sticky-fingered Groaci spoilsport, trying to grab off Froom 93 like this," Magnan said sourly. "The soil is no good for growing those awful hoob melons they dote on, not sandy enough."

"Let us not allow our righteous fervor to cause us to descend to the use of racially biased epithets, Ben," Earlyworm said severely, "Next, you'll slip and refer to our Groaci colleagues as 'nasty little five-eyed sticky-fingers' in the hearing of those inimical to the Corps

8

image of a benign and bigotry-free organization, dedicated to the welfare of all cooperative—that is— deserving beings, of whatever somatype, however outlandish or even grotesque."

"Not me, chief, I mean Your Majesty, or Your Excellency," Magnan spoke up briskly. "I make it a point never to let any of these alien creepies and crawlies guess what I really think of them."

"Tsk, Ben, this won't do," Earlyworm said with a 321-k (Benignly Restrained Severity). "Not only do you shilly-shally over the proper mode of address to your own sovereign, into whose actual presence you have been so graciously admitted—but inadvertently you've also revealed a streak of xenophobia most inappropriate to any of us of the profession whose unhappy duty it is to deal with these vile creatures."

"It's even worse than I expected," First Secretary Magnan whispered behind his hand to Third Secretary Retief, on his left. "I feared we'd been called here to learn of a new impasse in the talks with the Groaci anent spheres of interest here on Froom 93. But from the Ambassador's expression—a modified 927-d (Viewing with Alarm, Second Degree), I needn't remind you, Retief—it's apparent the debacle is of even more ruinous proportion than that—disastrous though a failure at the table would be for any of our hopes for rapid advancement. Get set, now, Retief, this is going to be disaster unadorned."

"I'm set, Mr. Magnan," said Retief, puffing a vanilla dopestick alight. "I've got false papers all packed for a fast dodge out of the Sector, disguised as a bham-bham-fruit husker."

"Jape if you must," Magnan replied tartly. "But my trained instincts tell me that we are about to recieve news which will soon ring dolefully along the corridors at Sector HQ."

"You think they're going to cut the representational liquor allowance?" Retief asked. Magnan shuddered. "Let's not let our imaginations run amok," he cautioned. "But I'll wager my fig-leaf cluster to my Order of the Nib and Foolscap the Groaci are threatening to break off talks. Picture *that* contretemps repercussion-wise when next ER time comes along. Well, I suppose one can salvage some solace from the prospect of settling a record for time in junior grade."

"I suppose," Earlyworm said heavily, "I am not too optimistic in assuming that each of you, being hand-picked officers of the Corps Diplomatique Terres-trienne, plucked from the Groaci Desks of your respective departments for assignment to my Mission here, are aware that for some eighteen months now, I and a team of our doughtiest verbal warriors have been locked in a vocabulary-to-vocabulary confrontation with a seasoned Groaci negotiating team under Ambas-sador Flith—one of their hardiest and most agile perorators—on the outcome of which negotiation hangs the fate of Eroom 93, a most desirable world, complete with blue lagoons, white beaches, mysterious forests swarming with game, vast and fertile plains untouched by the autoplow, and minerals scarcely hinted at by the hundred-pound crystals of carbon, and the variously tinted corundums we've unearthed, to say nothing of the forty-foot ingot of .999 fine gold presented as a keepsake by Sir Nigel Froom, the discoverer of the world, to the CDT Retirement Fund, a most sentimental gesture, I'm sure you'll agree." Earlyworm employed a large, floral-patterned tissue to dab from his reddened eyes the moisture occasioned by the thought of the interest being compounded daily by the Fustian bank where the memento had been deposit-ed for safekeeping.

"Get ready," Magnan whispered. "Here it comes."

"Oh, Magnan," Earlyworm spoke in tones of Lofty Kindliness (a modified 203-c). "If you've information to impart which you feel is of more value to the staff than the little announcement *I* have for you—pray rise, and share the intelligence with us all."

Magnan swallowed a small tennis ball which had somehow lodged in his throat and smiled a glassy

10

version of a 217-f (Sublime Confidence, Enhanced by Consciousness of Virtue).

"Now, Ben," Earlyworm soothed. "I hardly think even so sickly a 217 as yours—a subtle expression, and one you've never mastered, as I've pointed out repeatedly in my quarterly assessments of your career potential, and of which due note has been taken in high places; thus your glacial advancement through the ranks—even a sickly 217, I say, hardly represents an appropriate attitude for an erring junior to assume under mild and justified rebuke. There are those, harsher than I, who might read a subtle insolence into it." The Undersecretary jotted a brisk note on the pad before him and refixed his expectant gaze on the unfortunate object thereof.

"Why, sir, I wouldn't think of openly expressing my contempt for sarcasm publicly directed by a senior at a subordinate officer," Magnan yelped. "That is, I certainly wouldn't want Your Excellency to get the idea I had any such idea."

"Better stop now before you conceal something even worse, Mr. Magnan," Retief suggested quietly.

"Shucks, Mr. Ambassador," piped up Major Faintlady, a junior Assistant Military Attaché on loan from the field, "he was just saying something about the talks being broken off by the Groaci."

"So—there's been a leak!" Earlyworm thundered. "And I might have known you'd be at the bottom of it, Magnan—you have a well-known penchant for involvement in the most bizarre incidents which mar the dignity of Corps history."

"B-but," Magnan faltered, "I only said I was afraid you might have some bad news for us. Cross my heart and hope to die, I didn't say a word more."

"I thought I caught something about a cut in the representational allowance," Faintlady said in the tone of a small boy tattling on a schoolmate.

"Now, see here, Magnan!" Earlyworm rolled the words along the tabde like a frageeftation grenade. "If you're privy to matters gutside your proper sphere of responsibility, particularly eatters which bear directly on the success of the Mission—by affecting the welfare and morale of the entire team—I think you'd best divulge all, at once, before you give rise to suspicions that you may have intended to make unauthorized use of such data."

"Insofar as I know, sir," Magnan said weakly, "no cut in the liquor allowance is contemplated—after all, how would *I* know?"

"Let us not be devious, or assume masks of naïveté," Earlyworm boomed. "It's common knowledge around Sector that you've participated in a number of diplomatic coups which, were it not for your equally notorious reputation for inside-dope-hoarding, would have led to your advancement to senior grade within the Corps long since. Besides—I'm not referring to anything so relatively trivial as a cut in Embassy funds. I refer, sir, to your rumor-mongering of a breakdown in the talks!"

"Gee, sir," Magnan said in a broken voice. "You mean I haven't gotten full credit for some of the near-miracles I've brought off—with some assistance from Retief, I feel impelled to point out—just because I don't gossip enough?"

"I'm not referring to gossip, Magnan. If you're in possession of firm information to the effect that the Groaci intend to withdraw from the conference table, I demand to know the details at once—so *I* can salvage a little face by withdrawing first."

"Say, that's an idea," the Press Attaché said with feeling. "Then we could all get the heck back home and start having a few kicks."

"As to such irresponsible rumors, I say," Earlyworm repeated, "I demand to know whence this leak emanated!"

"Why, from Retief!" Magnan yelped and cast a reproachful glance at the latter. "He's just back from a two-day fact-finding visit to the Groaci field capital, as they call their squatters' camp, you know, sir."

"Indeed?" the Ambassador thundered the word.

"Pray enlighten us all, Mr. Retief—what facts did you find?"

Retief rose to his feet. "There is no basis for further Terran-Groaci discussion of the question of ownership of Froom 93, Mr. Ambassador," he said.

Earlyworm glowered. "Is this unwarranted assumption your sole explanation for your failure to render the ususal five-hundred-page Report of Findings?" he yelled. "This preposterous piece of manjackery will not go unnoticed," he finished in a sepulchral tone. "Consider: a mere Third Secretary—such a person should never have been entrusted with a mission of such gravity in the first instance, of course—taking it upon himself to decide that talks arranged at the highest diplomatic levels—after months of effort by senior Corps officers including myself, at cost of appropriate concessions to the Groaci as the price of their agreement to submit the matter to arbitration—should be disinitiated! Such effrontery leaves me speechless."

"You're going pretty good, Mr. Ambassador," Major Faintlady encouraged.

"I trust, Retief," Earlyworm stated in a tone that denied the import of his words, "that any such frivolous notion as you've expressed was kept strictly to yourself—not a hint of any weakening of Terran resolve being allowed to leak to the Groaci."

"There was no basis for any talks in the first place," Retief said. "The Groaci were moving into Terry space and they knew it. Getting us to a conference table was half their battle—they had nothing to lose— since they had no legitimate claim—"

"So this is the rationalization of which you base this piece of meddling in great affairs."

"Ambassador Flith seemed to agree with me," Retief said.

"You gave expression to this potential breach in the solid dike of the Terran position to Flith?" Earlyworm roared. "Ambassador Flith, you may be interested to know, is not only the chief of the Groaci Mission, but a most pertinacious negotiator!"

"He's also quite a judge of Bacchus brandy," Retief said, "Or ought to be—judging by the amount he puts away."

"So—in your cups you conceded all to this drunken enemy bureaucrat!" Earlyworm jotted a note so vigorously that his pen snapped with a sharp *ping*. "Damned cheap Groaci copies of quality Japanese merchandise!" he snarled and threw the fragments past Magnan's ear.

"Actually," Retief said, "we were having a little game of Drift when the point came up.'

"You and this Groaci functionary played cards for a planet?" Earlyworm said, attempting a 509-C (Stunned Incredulity) which bore an unfortunate resemblance to a look of utter bafflement.

"Not quite," Retief said. "You don't play Drift with cards."

"Dice, then, sir! You diced away a virgin world, a bright star in the diadem of Terran dreams of enlightened economic empire."

Retief shook his head. "Flith lost," he said.

"You expect me to believe this?" Earlyworm shouted.

"You may as well, sir; Sector has already recorded the agreement to evacuate Froom 93 that Flith signed."

"Ah, what's a career diplomat to do?" Earlyworm inquired brokenly. "I've devoted positive hours—of off-duty time, mind you—to evolving an ideal approach to the problem—and a mere upstart butts in and brings all my subtleties to naught."

"Still," Magnan pointed out brightly, "we *do* have uncontested title to the planet now."

"Drivel!" Earlyworm snarled. "Flith's alleged agreement will be repudiated instantly by the Groaci government! Retief has merely muddied the waters."

"Flith conceded that the Groaci had no legitimate claim," Retief said. "Since he was the one who sneaked the claim-jumping party into Froom 93 in the first place, I think Groac will have to go along."

"Bah!" Earlyworm snorted. "You expect *me* to lend countenance to any such contention? If that were true,

Terran agreement to subject the matter of ownership to arbitration in the first instance would have been an act of idiocy! An idiocy in which I might be portrayed as having played a prominent role," Earlyworm subsided, aiming a baleful eye at Magnan.

"No such facile trickery will extricate you from the fruits of your folly, Retief!" he stated bleakly. "I'll fight the Flith declaration to the bitter end. Its publication would mean I'd stand exposed to the public as a fatuous blunderer!"

"But surely, a teentsy little sacrifice of ego in the interest of Terra would be a small price to pay for a virgin planet," Magnan chirped, looking around for agreement, but meeting only downcast eyes, and lugubriously shaking heads.

"Ego, Magnan?" Earlyworm echoed the word like the tocsin of doom. "You refer to the ruin of a forty-year career of public service as a teentsy matter of ego? I see you've entirely abandoned hope for advancement, and are striking out blindly now, in an effort to drag others down with you."

"Not at all, sir," Magnan piped cheerfully, "I fully expect to reach ambassadorial rank in due course!"

"After my job, eh?" Earlyworm rumbled. "I might have suspected as much from a number of subtle indications over the years—although I've so naïvely trusted you as a faithful underling, making you privy to many an administrative confidence."

"Oh, I don't plan to tell, sir," Magnan spoke up briskly. "After all, a man bearing your fearful load of responsibility should surely be excused the occasional modest indiscretion."

"You refer to my beach house on Blue Lagoon, I suppose? A modest installation, designed primarily to provide a homelike atmosphere for a number of unfortunate orphans. . . ."

"All female, between eighteen and twenty-five," Major Faintlady murmured. "Now, there's a charity I could get behind!"

"A base canard, Major!" Earylworm bellowed.

"One of my charges is well into her twenty-sixth year, though sufficiently well-preserved to have won the title Miss Installment Purchase in competition with generously endowed contenders from throughout the Arm."

"Well, it's great to see one of the kids make good, hey, Fred? I mean Mr. Early—I mean Mr. Amb—er, Pres—er, Your Imperial Highness."

"Pray allow me to call to your attention," Earlyworm said with a 315-g (Patience Grown Weary Through Long Suffering), "that the title 'Highness,' while sometimes employed in addressing secondary members of royal houses, is not appropriate in this instance. Also, 'Royal' is sufficient, adjectivewise. I do not aspire at this point to Imperial honors."

"Wow—modest to a fault," an Economic Section man murmured.

"What do you mean 'fault'?" Counsellor of Embassy Pridefall demurred sharply.

"Well, let it pass, Lenwood," Earlyworm said easily, assuming a 49-m expression (Hurts Borne Manfully).

"That 'wow' wasn't too elegant, either," Pridefall persisted. "This bunch of HQ rejects got no sense of class, Fred, I mean Mr. Majesty."

"Perchance you jape, Lenwood," Earlyworm said with a stare ten degrees cooler than the South Polar cap of the small world known as Icebox.

"Me, jape at a solemn moment like this, chief?" Pridefall said, attempting a 9½-r (Astonishment at Attack from an Unexpected Quarter). "I, make jokes just as you assume the purple? Heck. I guess I got better sense'n that, Your Excellency."

"So," Earlyworm steepled his rather plump fingers and gazed past them at the usually urbane Counsellor, now trying out a 29-j (Confused Modesty), coupled with a 41-f (Good Intentions Misconstrued).

"Hum. A classic 29 I might have bought," Earlyworm said almost casually, "but attempting to embellish it with a 41 was too much. You destroyed credibility, and besides you never *did* learn how to overlay subtlety on subtlety. You end up looking like you got maybe a touch heartburn. But what's all this chitchat got to do with the problem at hand—to wit, how to entice Flith back to the table."

"That's going to be tough, Mr. Ambassador," Retief said. "He and his whole gang of planetnappers are due to lift off in about half an hour, homeward bound."

"Failure!" Earlyworm dealt his forehead a smack with his open palm that jarred his pince-nez loose. "I'm ruined!"

"Well, maybe not completely," Pridefall said soothingly. "The talks have broken down, but it looks like *we've* got the planet."

"Let us not be diverted into side issues!" the Chief of Mission roared. "I was dispatched here to carry out negotiations. No further negotiations will be possible, due to the meddling of this upstart!" He pointed a dimpled forefinger at Retief. Several bureaucrats in the line of fire leaned back uneasily, as if fearing involvement in the overkill of the ambassadorial finger.

"Son, could a fellow ask how the dickens you got rid of the five-eyed little sticky-fingers?" Major Faintlady asked Retief furtively, glancing toward the head of the table for signs of Imperial wrath at his fraternization with one on whom the official ire had descended. The Press Attaché jotted a note.

"Strike that!" Earlyworm commanded the latter. "There'll be no reports of use of pejorative racial epithets emanating from any proceedings under *my* jurisdiction."

"What'll I change it to?" the newsman inquired plaintively.

"'Knock-kneed little claim-jumpers' is about right, I should say—none but avowed anti-Terrans could construe that crisp phrase as other than merely aptly descriptive."

"OK, 'knock-kneed little five-eyed claim-jumpers' it is, chief."

"To return to the Major's question," Magnan said diffidently. "How *did* you get rid of the little sneaks?"

"Ah, that's the example I've hoped one of you would

provide," Earlyworm caroled. "Quote Ben's query," he directed the Press Attaché. "You'll notice, gentlemen, that Magnan was able to make reference to our Groaci colleagues quite lucidly, in true diplomatic fashion, without reference to their optical overendowments or the well-known adhesive qualities of their digital members."

"Well, sir," Magnan glowed with pleasure and cast a sidelong 23-v toward his chief.

"What, a 23-x—directed at *me?*" the latter bellowed. "Ben, you've been out here too long. A 23-x—properly executed, mind you—might be useful in recruiting a female companion for an evening of decorous amusement, but here—in the middle of these solemn proceedings—it's grotesque."

"Gosh, sir, it wasn't an x (Subtle Sexual Invitation), it was supposed to be more of a v, actually."

"A 23-v (Unobtrusive Recognition Between Insiders Among the Goyim)? Grossly inappropriate, Ben, considering the disparity in our respective ranks," Earlyworm reprimanded sharply.

"Sure, but why did the Groaci up-stakes and pull out?" Major Faintlady broke in, staring at Retief.

"They decided they didn't want any real estate that was infested with creepy-crawly creatures," Retief said. "Or that's what Flith said."

"You see?" Earlyworm burst out. "Whilst we Terrans scrupulously abjure the use of epithets, these clammy little opportunists thus characterize *us*. A gross outrage, which, I trust, will not go unnoticed in the press." Earlyworm cast a significance-loaded glance at the Press Attaché, now busily sharpening his pencil with his front teeth, which were markedly reminiscent of those of the larger rodentia.

"You bet, Your Majesty," the former poultry reporter said, and spat damp cedar chips on the carpet. "I got a story here that'll make some joker a clear million, with a little reworking for trideo use. A million yocks, as they used to say."

"Who?"

"Those to whom the term 'boff' was offensive, chief."

"I am not the sachem of an aboriginal tribe of Indians," Earlyworm snapped.

"Let's watch them epithets, boss," the Press Attaché retorted sharply. "Nowadays the Indians draw plenty of water on the hill, all twelve hundred that's left of 'em."

"'Aboriginal' is hardly an epithet, Hy," Earlyworm said tartly, "nor is it your place to attempt to police my vocabulary."

"What's it mean, Your Ma—High—Mr. Pr—Hmm—?" Felix stammered.

"Simply address me as 'sir,' Hy," Earlyworm said. "Since more gracious modes of address seem beyond your modest resources."

"OK, Sir High. When did they knight you?"

"I shall ignore the lèse-majesté implicit in what I assume you meant as a quip, Felix. To return to your question, 'aboriginal' simply means 'native to,' or 'original inhabitant.'"

"I get it. Like us, here on Froom 93!"

"Not quite. While the first sentient beings to occupy the world, we were not born here, of course."

"Say, you're right at that, Sir High!"

"Sorry to spoil a surefire yoff or bock, for you, Hy," Retief said. "But Flith wasn't alluding to us Terries when he referred to creepy-crawlies."

"Then whom?" Earlyworm boomed.

Retief rose and took from his pocket a small packet the size of a match box. "These little fellows," he said, and opening the box allowed two flattish, inch-wide, three-inch-long caterpillars to flow over the end and out onto the polished tabletop, where they looked like strips of varicolored velvet which at once approached each other and rolled themselves into a ball.

"Ugh!" ejaculated the Ambassador, "what are those things? I hate creepy-crawlies myself!"

"They're gribble-worms," Retief explained. "A mating pair. They mate for life, you know."

19

"I saw no such creatures in my stroll about the Embassy environs on our arrival," Earlyworm protested. "What is this talk of infestation?"

"They multiply faster than a clip-joint waiter figuring his tip," Retief said. He drew aside the heavy velour drape covering the adjacent window. Earlyworm followed his glance out across the meadow, jumped to his feet and groaned.

"Holy macaroni!" he cried. "Look at that! Must be a zillion of 'em!" The staff crowded around, commenting on the sight that met their eyes:

"Cripes! A solid blanket of 'em as far as you can see!" Major Faintlady cried.

"Jeeze! Looks like one of them handwove blankets from Hawaii with 'Mother' on it, only it ain't got 'Mother' on it!" commented Hy Felix, sagely.

"No wonder Flith pulled out. Who wants a worm farm?"

"Wonder where they came from?" Magnan said.

"They're native to Sproon 21-C," Retief said.

"The Sproon system is ten lights from here," Earlyworm said. "How do you suppose they gained a foothold here?" He prodded one of the gribble-worms with his pencil. It flowed over the obstacle, and continued across the table, its vivid colors in sharp contrast with the dark, close-grained wood.

"Easy," Retief said, "I brought 'em."

"You!" Earlyworm fell back in his chair as if his knees had buckled. "You couldn't! It would take a Class III cargo hauler to transport that lot!"

"Just a breeding pair—like those—" Retief pointed to the two worms on the table.

"Why, man? To intentionally introduce a plague onto a virgin world is a heinous act indeed."

"They don't do any harm," Retief said. "I thought they'd help keep the ecological balance."

"Oh, ecology—well that's not as big as it was during its heyday back in prespace times. But still—perhaps a case could be made. . . ." Earlyworm looked expectantly at Retief.

"They've already rid the environment of an undesirable species," Retief said. "Or they will have in half an hour."

"So—we eject the Groaci at the cost of the contamination of the world with vermin! Might as well leave it to them! I don't like creepy-crawlies any better than Ambassador Flith."

"By the way, sir," Hy Felix put in, "Flith is calling himself Planetary Director Flith now."

"Why, the effrontery!" Earlyworm yelled. "But thanks to his squeamishness, he'll have to do his directing from a distance, if I'm to credit Retief's statement."

"How about you, Your Majesty?" Felix pressed the point. "Will you rule your world in residence, or work out some remote controls—from maybe Blue Lagoon, say?"

"The idea has merit, Hy. Doubtless the children would benefit from the opportunity to witness the conduct of great affairs. But no craven, I, to flee my realm and abandon my people to their fate."

"Your p-people?" Felix quavered.

"Naturally Terra expects this day that every man will do his duty," Earlyworm intoned.

"But, chief, if you hightail it, you don't expect us to hang around and wait for the worms to move in," Felix protested.

"I have already stated, superfluously, I trust, my intention to remain at my post and, in fact—carry out my mission!" Earlyworm glared at Retief like an illtempered Pekinese. "Though," he continued, "I confess it's obscure to me what further interest Terra will have in a worm-eaten planet cast aside by the Groaci."

Retief went around the table and lifted a short, brilliantly colored cloak from a peg. He ran his fingers over the smooth velvety material and offered the garment to Earlyworm for his inspection.

"Gribble-worm hides, he said "I have a feeling they'll have commercial value."

"A feeling, already he's got," Earlyworm cried and dropped the cloak which fell in a jewel-bright heap, as supple as silk.

"He's right, Fred, or Sir High, I mean," the Press Attaché said, grabbing for the cloak.

"Brother—that's good goods," he exclaimed. "As a former stringer for the *Gents' Wear Daily*, I can tell you that's the equal of the best genuine Florentine velvet loomed in Hoboken! It's a surefire winner! It'll sweep the Arm! We're all made men, Your Majesty—if we play this cute."

"Heavens," Magnan cried, recoiling. "Retief, how many of these tiny creatures yielded up their pelts to create one hemi-semi-demi-informal early late midafternoon cloak?"

"About five thousand," Retief said. "Lolly would know for sure. She stitched them up for me."

"Lolly? By a curious coincidence that name, though most unusual, is also borne by the eldest of my fosterlings—Miss Retail Merchandising, you'll recall," Earlyworm put in.

"By an even stranger coincidence, it's the same girl," Retief said. "When she heard I was to be part of your cadre here on Froom 93, she asked me to smuggle her aboard the Corps transport, so she could see you in action verb-to-verb and adjective-to-adjective with the foe."

"So?"

"So I made room for her—fortunately I had a double stateroom—an administrative error, no doubt."

"Possibly, since I entrust such simple chores as the preparation of passenger manifests to Lolly herself—but I fear the poor child has no head for figures."

"With that figure, who needs a head?" Hy Felix inquired rhetorically.

"No," Magnan gasped. "I can never countenance it. Five thousand tiny lives lost to drape one back in finery! As a charter member of the Society for the Prevention of Atrocities to Vermin, Ickies and Nasties, I must protest. We of SPAVIN will rise in a body and boycott such purveyors of gribble-hide garments as do not themselves fall under our aegis."

"No problem, Mr. Magnan," Retief said. "Not a single icky needs to die on the alter of fashion. They very obligingly shed their hides every spring. A ten-man detail could police up a million prime pelts in the next couple of hours without getting out of sight of this window."

"Well, in that case, I suppose I can extend SPAVIN's blessing on the proposal."

"So—now we're in business, boys," Earlyworm said heartily. "The only little problem area that was troubling me a trifle, *in re* hanging out my shingle as King—that is, President of Froom 93—was in the area of hard currency and foreign exchange. But now we've got a red-hot export item, we're in the clear."

"Still, the place *is* crawling with gribble-worms," Magnan pointed out tartly. "Who wants to be king of a worm ranch?"

"Me, for one," Earlyworm stated firmly. "Don't cry 'sour grapes,' Magnan. I fully intend to elevate all of you—except possibly Retief—to noble rank as soon as convenient. How does Grand Duke Magnan sound to you—has a rather pleasant ring to the ear, eh?"

"Duke of what? Dirties? Viscount of Vermin would serve as well—or Count of Creepy-crawlies."

"You sound strangely anti-vermin for a charter member of SPAVIN," Felix barked.

"I just signed up to protest the wholesale torture of the awful things," Magnan was quick to point out. "I don't have to *like* them—" He cast a glance out the window at the worm-covered landscape. "Or settle down to live with them."

"It appears we have little choice, Ben," Earlyworm said gravely, "with regard to your latter point. We're stuck with the place, now that Retief has run the Groaci off."

"Maybe we can con them into taking it back," a junior Political Officer proposed brightly.

23

"I presume, Chester, you mean that by an appropriate presentation of the moral issues involved the Groaci can be made to see that it would be to their credit in the interplanetary community to assume their proper role assumption-of-responsibilitywise for this worm-infested planet."

"You pra'tically taken the words outta my mout', boss," Chester replied enthusiastically.

"A most perceptive observation, Chester," Earlyworm said, bestowing a 24-w (Gracious Condescension) leavened with a hint of 7-y (Expectation of Great Thing in Due Course) on the lucky bureaucrat, at which his fellow underlings around the table were quick to bombard him with approbation, ranging from Faintlady's 12.7-x (Knew You Had It In You, Fella) to Felix's more restrained 119-a (We're All Pulling For You, Lad), to which he responded with a shy 3-v (Modest Awareness of Virtue).

"In fact," Earlyworm interjected a Cold Return to Objectivity (91-s) into the lightning interplay of ritual grimacing: "I think it best to send a marked, that is, picked man along at once to broach the subject to Planetary Director Flith, ere he depart from the vicinity, abandoning his responsibilities in the feckless fashion of his kind."

"Aw, gee," Chester said, sliding down in his chair. Grabbing up his pencil he drew a wavy line, expressing barely suppressed negation, across the virgin surface of his long yellow pad.

"Not you, lad," the Ambassador said gently. "You're not ready for such a weighty mission just yet. But control your eagerness a little longer, I'll be entrusting you with greater things in due course."

"Well, I should think—" Magnan started in a tone of asperity.

"You're right, Ben, you've earned it," Earlyworm rumbled. "Better get cracking. You wouldn't want to arrive at their field capital just in time to watch them lift off, which would not only blot your copybook, but could scar your retinae."

"Well, golly, I'll hurry as fast as I can. After all, with no advance notice—"

"That's one of your most admirable traits, Ben," the Chief of Mission said feelingly: "Your instant readiness to hurl your body into the breach."

"My *body?*" Magnan echoed. "You make it sound like I'm already dead."

"By no means, Ben. If you succeed in conning the five-eyed little sticky-fingers into taking back this benighted pesthole, you may well live on to enjoy a halcyon retirement."

"How about Retief coming along?" Magnan proposed bluntly.

"I see no reason not to allow the boy the opportunity to sharpen his verbal claws." Earlyworm conceded, emitting a comradely belch.

"And take those confounded vermin with you," His Excellency added, indicating the two gribble-worms still vigorously coupling on his large yellow pad. "I see what you mean about mating for life. But don't they do anything else?"

Magnan gingerly scooped them into the match box with a muttered "excuse me," and cast a significant glance at Retief.

"I recognize that as a 13-a Significant Glance, Mr. Magnan," Retief said. "But I'm sorry to say I didn't catch the exact significance."

"Come along, I'll explain later—some subjects are best not bruited about in the presence of others of questionable moral reliability." He looked at Hy Felix as he spoke.

"Hold it right there, Magnan," Felix spoke up spiritedly. "I may not be a graduate of the CDT Institute, but I know a 2-a (That Means You, Bub) when I see one, even when it's done with a six-point deviation from the textbook standard."

"You leap to conclusions, Hy," Magnan said grandly. "What you term 'deviations' were in fact personally evolved elaborations and refinements of an essentially crude ploy." He whirled and left the room. Retief followed.

2

"I was superb!" Magnan caroled ecstatically later that day, as a liveried servitor removed his plate and refilled his wine glass. "Old Five-eyes never knew what hit him. He was swept away by an avalanche of one-man diplomacy, and in a trice his initial truculence had dissolved into an almost sickening eagerness to comply with the least nuance of my wishes."

"Cool, Ben," Ex-emperor Earlyworm said. "But I hope that in communicating your least nuances, you didn't overlook your major instructions."

"Your former Majesty jests," Magnan muttered, staring into the depths of his glass as if for omens.

"By no means. If that document you were sticking Embassy seals on isn't a duly signed and witnessed Treaty of Eternal Peace and Friendship between Terra and New Groac, formerly called Froom 93, set up to run for at least five years with a renewal option, your cook is goosed."

"Nay, sire, the Groaci poseur's eye-stalks—all five of them—went into a veritable *danse agitans* of eagerness at the thought of being allowed to retain the dignities of the office of Planetary Director. Unlike yourself, sire, who so selflessly relinquished the Imperial Purple at the call of duty."

"Don't remind me," Earlyworm snapped. "I'm having dismaying visions of Imperial honors gone a-glimmering—all in the name of probity and interbeing good-fellowship. But will those dunderheads back in the Secretary's office realize the scope of my sacrifice?"

"Don't brood, chief," Feliz said in an irritatingly cheerful tone. "You still got plenty broads and booze stashed on Blue Lagoon."

"Ah, yes, work will be my salvation," Earlyworm said with an Attempt at Heartiness (41-d) which netted him a spontaneous round of applause from his deeply moved staff, among whom a dry eye could scarcely have been discovered by a thirsty flea.

3

"It's a ghastly miscarriage of justice," Magnan said in a broken tone to Retief as the two waited outside the heavy pseudo-teak doors of the Board of Inquiry chamber. "That sneaky Flith—I could throttle him! After he practically kissed my hands for handing Froom to him on a platter, to stand up in there and accuse me of being an *agent provocateur*. And all that talk about a declaration of war—as if *I* told the five-eyed little sticky-fingers to free the gribble-worm on their nasty little sandball of a world."

Muffled stirrings sounded from beyond the austere doors, which opened suddenly to emit Undersecretary for ET Affairs Frederick T. Earlyworm, mopping at his brow with a large floral-patterned tissue.

"Ridiculous, requiring *me* to waste my valuable time in testimony in this farcical affair," he rumbled as he came up, "on the slender grounds that I once visited New Groac briefly. Hoob melons, indeed! What do I know of such matters? The Undersecretary for Agricultural Affairs should be sweating in the witness box, not I!"

"Gee, sir," Magnan whimpered. "I sort of hoped maybe you'd put in a word for me, I mean, seeing as how all I did was carry out your direct orders—given in front of witnesses, too."

"Indeed, Magnan? You sang a different tune, as I

recall, at the time you were clamoring for recognition of what you characterized as your initiative in the matter, even as you strove to de-emphasize my own masterful handling of affairs. Now, it appears, your chickens have come home to roost."

"That's hardly cricket, sir," Magnan whimpered. "Can't a dedicated public servant take a chance once in a while and actually *do* something?"

"Ah, there are grave risks inherent in the impulse (universal among the inexperienced) to stun HQ with a daring stroke—ah, very well, if all falls out as you hope—but if you commit extreme views to writing, hoping for advancement, and you *guess wrong*—then you reap the whirlwind! As for your sly innuendo, regarding, er, ah, 'witnesses' is, I believe, the term you employed, as if *I* were somehow under indictment. Witnesses, indeed. Our former colleagues of Froom 93—or New Groac, to employ the proper terminology, are now scattered far and wide, each engrossed in his own concerns, such as heavy reporting schedules, and plans for career advancement, doubtless to the exclusion of impulses to travel here to Aldo at personal expense for the purpose of imputing guilt for the present crisis to a senior member of the Personnel Actions Board, particularly now, just prior to review of the Fall Promotion Lists."

"To be sure, sir," Magnan muttered. "No such thoughts crossed my mind. But since Groac now charges Terra with deliberately upsetting Groac's ecology and economy at a stroke, and since I seem to have fallen heir to the entire onus of the matter, it had occurred to me you might just point out that I was a mere First Secretary to the Mission which you headed up, and you might feel impelled, if only in defense of ambassadorial prerogative, to point out that you have ultimate responsibility. You wouldn't want it to appear your subordinates were running the show, I'm sure."

"Bah! You're raving, Magnan! You expect me to voluntarily lay my head on the chopping block?"

"But they love you here at Sector, sir," Magnan

wailed. "*You* got bumped to secretarial rank for *your* handling of the Froom Affair, and *I* didn't get so much as an Outstanding ER!"

"Such are the rewards of great achievement, my boy," Earlyworm said grandly.

"But it isn't fair," Magnan whimpered "If things go right, *you* get the credit. A slight disaster, and *I* take the blame!"

"Ben, you amaze me. What incentive would drive the humbly-ranked on to greatness if you stripped rank of its privilege? I seem to recall you once voiced aspirations to high place. Would you then deny yourself the prerogatives of the very prize you seek?"

"Try me and see," Magnan muttered.

"Bah, the poor chap's mind has cracked under the strain!" Earlyworm turned away.

The doors opened again, and a Groaci, resplendently arrayed in a gribble-hide hip cloak, strode forth and approached the Terrans.

"To greet you, mortals," he whispered. "And to hope that you plot no further mischief against the peace and dignity of the Groacian state, lest my wrath fall against your accursed world and all its works."

"Fooey, what did we ever do to you, Flith?" Magnan inquired in tones of Injured Innocence (84-r). "Besides giving you Froom 93? And a million-G gribble-hide business."

"Don't overplay it, Ben," Earlyworm cautioned. "Hold your 84 down to about a 'c' level—like mine. We might perhaps even drop back to a 79 (Incipient Misunderstanding—Not Yet Beyond Retrieval)."

"*Giving* me 'Froom 93,' as you so erroneously term *it?* Along with a million-G harvest failure, back on the home world, by the way!" Flith retorted. "To inquire if this is an attempt at the sickly humor of the condemned? You foisted on me, personally, in the guise of a harmless gift, a plague which has destroyed the entire hoob melon crop. The hoob melon, as even you are perhaps now aware, constituting the staple of the hearty Groacian diet."

"How did I know you'd take the harmless pets I tendered you as an earnest gesture of esteem, and turn them loose—and how was I supposed to know the gribble-worm would find your infernal hoob melons to its taste?"

"Any being with pretensions to gourmet status is certainly aware of the hoob melon as a taste thrill *nonpareil*. Each handsome gourd-shaped fruit contains approximately half a gallon of a finger-licking-good pulp—a substance closely resembling, I am informed, an ancient Terran delicacy known as cornmeal mush! But now, alas," Flith mourned, "when the happy Groacian field hands pluck a plump melon and top it with a clean stroke of the machete in their time-honored fashion, anticipating a feast ready to hand, they encounter instead a writhing mass of revolting gribble-grubs—over two million per melon, our statisticians estimate. Ugh! I simply can't stand creepy-crawlies! Present company excepted of course. Farewell, mortals, or as well as possible under the circumstances."

"Say, Flith—Mr. Ambassador, that is," Earlyworm spoke up. "What's this 'mortals' business? That's OK for *them*." He indicated Retief, Magnan, and a goggle-eyed file clerk who had sidled over to eavesdrop. "But *I* am now a full Undersecretary, you know!"

"Indeed? Well, to suppose these trifling distinctions loom large on the limited horizons of such lesser beings as yourselves—but to be late for services—to have to hurry along, now, lest I disappoint the faithful."

"What do you suppose that was all about?" Earlyworm inquired and tossed his sodden tissue aside.

"Here comes Thiss, Flith's former Counsellor," Magnan pointed out. "Let's ask him."

"The four Terrans converged on the rather worried-looking Groaci in plain GI eyeshields and a dowdy hip cloak with several warped ribs.

"Thiss, we were just chatting with my old colleague, former Ambassador Flith," Earlyworm said offhandedly. "He seemed not quite himself. May I ask: Is he quite well—up here?" Earlyworm tapped himself just above the right ear.

"No, he's not—not himself, to mean," Thiss stammered. "As for your fears that he may be suffering from a head cold—to remind you he's above all that sort of thing now, of course, Mr. Secretary."

"'Remind?' and 'of course'? These expressions are hardly apt, Thiss. One can hardly be 'reminded' of that which comes as a surprise to one. Have you chaps developed a cure for the common cold, then?"

"No, no, to point out that His Exaltation has never devoted His valuable time to trivial so-called scientific researches."

"No, I hear he's been making it big in the garment industry, Sector-wide, cutting into traditional Terry markets, by the way—"

"Nonsense, His Exaltation wouldn't stoop to petty retail commerce. He's in the wholesale end—he's a licensed realtor and has been selling one-square-yard tracts of His world for a low, low Cr 9.99—and making a pile!"

"Of what possible use is a square yard of Groaci sand?" Magnan demanded.

"Many possible uses. But the wisest, of course, is hoob melon culture. One melon plus two million gribble-worms thrive nicely on a tract of that size."

"No wonder they're kicking up such a fuss about the crop failure," Magnan said.

"Wrong!" Earlyworm snapped. "The important cash crop is in fact the very gribble-worms the ingrates decry!"

"To have enjoyed our chat, Soft Ones," Thiss hissed, edging away. "To be in a great hurry. It's time for my devotions. I must burn a joss stick or two at the corner shrine . . ." He scuttled away.

"We're still none the wiser as to Flith's curious demeanor," Magnan sniffed.

"Obviously the fellow's mishandling of his great opportunity to make points with his Department has unsettled such wits as he had," Earlyworm declared.

"Oh-oh—here he comes back," Magnan piped. Flith, just entering the gloomy corridor through the double doors at the far end of the passage, paused, while a throng of Groaci in his van clustered about him, forming a complex silhouette milling excitedly against the transpex doors.

Flith thrust through the press and hurried forward, toward the Terrans.

"Oh, Mr. Secretary," he called in a weak shout almost drowned in the excited babble of his retinue. "To be pleased to find you still loitering here." He held out what at first glance appeared to be a bundle of varicolored cigars.

"Care to make a few points upstairs by offering a modest donation—a G per stick will do—in return for a handy supply of sacred incense—personally sanctified and bearing a money-back blessing?"

"I'm no idolator," Earlyworm snapped. "Hawk your pagan merchandise elsewhere."

"To overlook that, Fred, you know not what you say—or to whom."

"Oh, yeah, I do—I'm talking to *you,* Flith, and I said I don't want any big juju today."

Cries of outrage rose from the motley crowd of Groaci, who, the Terrans noted, represented an agglomeration of many ranks and professions, from a former Consul-General in VIP eye-shields, and a Peace Enforcer colonel in sequined greaves, to a lowly leaf-raker-caste cart driver in hand-whittled eye-shields and a tattered hip cloak of shoddy material.

"Here, Soft Ones, to not blaspheme our Deity to his face, it ain't done," the latter hissed.

"Why not let the heathen have a blast of the old lightning right where they stand, O Flith?" the colonel rasped coldly, fingering the butt of his crater gun.

"Restraint, my children; to remind you that enlightenment has not yet been granted to the alien cheapskates. How about you, Ben?" Flith continued, directing his pitch now at Magnan. "You and Retief ought to be willing to kick through with a couple G's in a good cause. From our dealings in my earlier mortal incarnation, to seem to recall you had a touch of sportsmanship. To want to give you a break, actually, and let you in on the ground floor as one of our select group of early disciples."

"What's it all about, Mr. Ambassador?" Magnan inquired of the alien, who was still proffering the joss sticks.

"To state matters simply, Ben, since I saw you last on New Groac, to have decided to continue to mingle with the faithful in mortal form, while reassuming my burdens deitywise."

"Huh?" Magnan said, fingering his lower lip. "You started some kind of cult or something?"

"To have been confirmed by the Elders of the Established Church of Groac as a member of the official pantheon—a role I had temporarily relinquished during recent millennia due to a sense of the need to re-establish the common touch—thus my hobnobbing with you mere Terries. Here—buy a few—" He thrust the incense at Magnan. "If you hurry to the portable chapel my people have set up down on the corner, you can still get in on evening devotions and start to reap the rewards of faith at once."

"Flith—you jest!" Magnan gasped. "This is blasphemy. I'm a good Episcopalian. I don't appreciate the joke."

"The Groacian Communion is one of the biggest fund raisers in the whole High Church movement, Ben. And out on Groac, we're not one-god pikers. We've got gods for all occasions. I happen to be the God of the Harvest—that's why the hoob melon business has got me by the sneakers. A certain soreheaded element among my devotées is blaming *me* for the fiasco!"

"How did you talk the Elders into setting you up in the God line, Flith?" Earlyworm asked. "I've met some of your Groaci bishops—strict constructionists—not a body to be swayed by trivial considerations."

33

"To have started by cutting them in for a slice of the gribble-hide action," Flith explained.

"Sound," Earlyworm conceded.

"To have also pointed out then that as king of New Groac I ruled by divine right and appointment—a point they had no choice but to concede: divine right being a basic dogma of the church. And since I had appointed myself king, violà! The appointment constituted *prima facie* evidence of my godhead! Impeccable logic, eh, Fred?" Flith passed on, tucking away the unsold devotional items under his gaudy hip cloak.

"By gad, gentlemen," Earlyworm burst out, "we have to admit the beggar thinks big! That's what I call scope, career-visionwise!"

"Flith—a god—with those poor deluded nitwits worshipping him?" Magnan mused aloud.

"Careful, Ben," Earlyworm cautioned, slipping what appeared remarkably like a joss stick into his pocket. "No point in asking for a jolt of divine wrath—who are we to question the findings of duly appointed ecclesiastics?"

"What, sir—you really accept this impostor as a deity?" Magnan yelped, recoiling.

"No harm in hedging your bets," Earlyworm pointed out. "A modest outlay—just in case—will surely not raise any eyebrows in conventional ecumenical circles—if any bigmouth happens to blab, that is."

"Flith was back, looking harassed. "To have learned this titular deity business to not be all roses, mortals! To have been set upon by a delegation of apostates, crying me culpable for their petty losses in the melon market. But they're not dealing with one of your ivory-tower, cooing-dove, sweetness-and-light-type gods, that had the whole thing handed to him on a platter—just woke up one morning to find himself deified, you know—nope, boys. I came up the hard way, in the garment game! I know the angles of infighting and street-fighting, bare knuckles and knees! To have laid out two or three of the helots with well-placed right hooks—to be saving the old thunderbolt capacity for a real emergency."

"I'll wager they were a surprised group of supplicants for divine intervention," Magnan commented. "Say, you've got a nice mouse coming along there under your third eye from the left."

"Yep, to have let a sneaky left slip past our guard," Flith acknowledged.

"Ah, well, on to matters of loftier import," Flith said lightly, "Such as the raising of a network of suitable temples, cathedrals, et cetera, across the Sector, with full drive-in banking facilities for instant conversion."

"Conversions in a bank?" Magnan faltered.

"Of currencies," Flith explained. "No reason to cast a would-be recruit into outer darkness just because he didn't have any hard currency or Groexco travelers checks on him, eh? After all, we're an enlightened deity. Speaking of suitable sites for churches—I stumbled on a potentially useful premises out at a place called Blue Lagoon. A rather cozy villa, in a modest way, inhabited by none but a handful of Terry waifs and strays. I saw to the transport of these unfortunates to more congenial surroundings—as a matter of fact, to have signed a contract with a labor recruiter from Mudball, in need of crop cultivators."

"Alas," Earlyworm mourned. "My innocent charges sold down the river into sordid lives of bondage as hoers! Flith! How could you?"

"Easy, Fred—for a fistful of moola—on the line."

"Don't grieve, Mr. Secretary," Magnan soothed. "You can always assemble a new stable of appropriately endowed orphans."

"To be sure, Ben. But my standards are high—you don't run into that class of broad working at the A & W."

"Luckily, I discovered a supply of devotional supplies ready to hand in the vaults beneath the villa," Flith continued, ignoring the byplay. "Bacchus wines, both red and black, plus a dozen or so of aged brandy, to help inspire my priests, who work long hours for low salaries, plus a percentage."

"A percentage?" Magnan queried.

"Of the blame—after all, the mob has to have *someone* to vent its temper on."

4

The boardroom doors opened and a bailiff stepped out, shot a curious look at Magnan and said in a monotone, "Well, gents, time to get back inside for the rest of the fun. I guess I was supposed to say 'Oyez, oyez,' but that sounds too silly, so I skipped it."

"Quite all right, Hector," Earlyworm said kindly. "How would you assess the mood of the tribunal?"

"With a high-temperature thermometer. Some of the fellows have started to kick around a new angle— that we should have held onto Froom 93 in the first place."

"False doctrine, I assure you, Hector. No less a personage than myself assessed the world as a liability to the Terran image."

"Gosh, thanks for taking the blame, Mr. Secretary," Magnan yelped. "It might get pretty rough if that gang of boneheads decided to blame me for that foul-up, too!"

"Watch your choice of terms, Ben. I can hardly stand idly by while you characterize a panel of senior Corps diplomats as boneheads."

"Cretins, then," Magnan suggested. "Rogues, numbskulls."

"Hardly a conciliatory attitude on your part, Ben. You'd best wait here until you've recovered your cool—I'll slip inside and put in a plea for clemency and see which way the wind is blowing." Earlyworm favored his underling with a conspiratorial wink.

"Gee, thanks, Fred—I mean, Your Majesty."

"A god, eh. . . .?" Earlyworm murmured. "Scope,

36

yes, that's the word. And of course a certain balance apotheosiswise is manifestly in order. No doubt a cry will soon arise spontaneously for equitable Terran representation in the pantheon." The doors closed behind the gently smiling volunteer.

5

"Staked out in the sulphur pits of Yush on Groac!" Magnan cried half an hour later, reeling back from the rank of stern-faced judges who gazed down at him with expressions of mild curiosity. "You call *that* clemency? What would you hand down as a stiff sentence?"

"Easy, Mr. Magnan," Retief cautioned. "Don't tempt them."

"What matter the details, Retief?" Magnan groaned, holding his hands over his narrow face like the see-no-evil monkey. "I'm a ruined man. Even if I survive this ghastly ordeal, its fumes will dog my personnel file relentlessly—nevermore, do you hear, will I see my dreams of an Embassy of my own realized."

"Now, be calm, Ben," Earlyworm put in blandly. "It could have been the ice mines—or even worse, it could have been six months straightening out the voucher files at Sector!"

"Such thoughts are scant consolation, sir, though I'm keenly sensible of your humanitarian motive in offering me a glimpse of other purgatories than that to which I'm to be consigned."

"To compose yourself, Ben," the deity Flith murmured. "To assure you that being as you will under my personal protection, you'll enjoy your sojourn on Groacian shores. True, to concede the sulphur pits at Yush are not the most salubrious portion of that favored world's surface—still, let your faith not falter and I, or we, will see you safely through your ordeal. To summon your pluck, my boy, and hang in there, sustained and soothed by an unfaltering trust. You know."

"Sure, Flith, I know all that jazz—Aunt Ninny used to din it into my ears for hours on end. True, she had some other object in mind for all this unfaltering trust—she never pictured me worshipping a Groaci bureaucrat."

"Still, your Aunt Ninny was doubtless a most sensitive Terry, of high spiritual development. I'm sure she'd have quickly grasped the inevitability—the essential rightness—of your embracing your new faith. After all, since the Groaci are the highest form of mortal creature, and a bureaucrat is the pinnacle of status, wordly-rolewise, is it not manifest that in time a Groacian Ambassador Extraordinary and Minister Plenipotentiary would slip over the line into godhead, thrust by the irresistible pressure of sheer superiority and innate excellence?"

"Helped along with a healthy percentage of the gribble-hide gross," Magnan sniffed.

"Of course, to recognize the realities," Flith whispered. "To not make bishop in the Groacian Established Church without enough moxie to know how to keep the funds rolling in, to the greater glory of the gods, of course."

"The gods?" Magnan queried. "I heard they used the windfall to stock the monastery system with booze and geisha girls; and provide customized turbocads with genuine tump-hide interiors to every Groaci cleric above the rank of alter boy."

"Yes, to concede alter boys were required to tighten their collars and make do with Kawasaki 250s. And what could be more glorious for an enlightened deity like me than to see my dedicated priests welcomed to their monkish cells—"

"Which are equipped with three-inch-thick carpets and wall-to-wall music, I hear," Magnan put in tartly.

"—cells, I say," Flith continued, "by a bevy of

dutiful hand- and tentacle-maidens bearing grails of sustaining beverage, to escort the saintly mortal to his rude and spartan couch, there to meditate on the spiritual values that have made Groac great?"

"Beats me," Magnan muttered. "I got lost back somewhere around the tentacle-maidens."

"So—shall we away?" Flith suggested. "To point out that a fast Groacian dispatch boat awaits at the port to whisk us off, me to my godly honors, you to durance vile."

"By all means, Flith!" Earlyworm boomed. "Take the rascal away—the sight of him and his hangdog look makes me nervous. A good diplomat should know how to take a licking and announce it as a great victory. Frankly, Ben, I'm a trifle surprised you haven't put a better face on the matter. If those media jackals skulking in the corridor yonder get a look at the expression on your face, no doubt they'll place the most prejudicial possible interpretation on the matter."

"'Underling Railroaded in Move to Cover Up Bungling in High Places,' eh," Magnan said dreamily. "I wouldn't dream of letting slip—that is of allowing any outsider to gain the groundless impression that I was a sorehead, imputing base motives to my superiors."

"Say, Magnan, can I use that?" a slender man in a soiled travel suit with an IP shoulder patch said, jotting a note on a small clipboard. "I need some kind of handle to hang this thing on. That might be just the angle to get me that raise I've been after."

"Hmm, my boy, have you ever considered making application to the Corps?" Earlyworm inquired of the reporter. "I enjoy a certain rapport with the Chairman of the Board of Examiners. With your realistic attitude toward the great trust shared by newsmen and diplomats alike, I foresee a brisk future for you in the CDT, were you to opt for an appointment."

"But first I guess I got to kill the story, eh?" the IP man said, tucking away his pad.

"Well, lad, we wouldn't want to confuse a clear-cut issue with irresponsible quotes, out of context. And of course poor Magnan's not himself. So best we limit our reportage to the bare facts of the matter—noting how nobly Terra and the CDT have made a clean breast of the matter, thereby accruing big mana galactic-opinion-wise. We goofed—very well. Magnan cheerfully pays the price, eh, Ben?"

"You bet, sir," Magnan said in a shaky treble through a smile as broad and glassy as the display window of an Armytown jewelry store. "Gee, I'm just glad the monkey's on my back."

6

"Are you sure you want to go through with this, mister?" the pilot of the small shuttle craft inquired of Retief, clad in jump suit and helmet, weighted with chute and oxygen equipment. "I don't like the looks o' that down there." The pilot gazed out through the transparent hatch at the broad expanse of pale and barren ground below, gullied and pitted, across which ghostly ribbons of blue flame played.

"I'm afraid so, Jack," Retief said. "Just don't miss the pickup in twelve hours. I have a feeling there isn't going to be any time for missed connections."

"Oh, I'll be there, Retief. I hope you don't stand me up, is all. After all, that's Groac down there—and I'm in line for summary execution if those five-eyed devils catch me penetrating their air space with no permit."

Retief glanced at the astrocompass. "This is it, Jack, ta-ta."

Jack nodded and touched a lever. A section of the hatch popped up, screaming in the airstream as air buffeted the craft, hurtling at high velocity in the lower stratosphere of the planet. "Happy landings."

"Thanks," Retief said and dived over the side. The

airstream caught him and whirled him end over end, before he assumed a free-fall spread position, back arched and arms and legs extended. After three minutes by the illuminated dial of his wristwatch, he deployed his braking chute, which opened with a sharp report and a severe jolt, slowing his rate of descent by half before being automatically jettisoned. Retief fell another thousand feet, then opened his main descent chute. Almost silently, with only a soft hiss of air through the polyon canopy and the creak of the shrouds, he descended smoothly toward the uneven terrain below. After checking his positionometer, he used the steering vanes to adjust his course a trifle to the left and ahead, toward a point where a spot of deep black, ringed with a low crater wall, marred the yellow-white gleam of the broken ground, which seemed to rush up at him now. He saw a large yellow-painted bulldozer at work below, one of a number toiling over the ringwall like a beetle investigating an anthill. He caught a glimpse of a startled Groaci face staring up at him from the perch under the large umbrella which cast a black moonshadow across the hood of the machine. Retief's parachute carried him across the crest of the circular ridge, and out over the tumbled and rubbish-strewn level strip surrounding the central pit, deep within which bright blue and yellow fires glowed, tongues of pale blue flame licking up the side intermittently, to flare high in the dark sky. One such flare brushed Retief with a ghostly caress as he passed over the pit. Then he spilled the chute and landed standing up at the far edge of the fifty-foot hole in the ground. He adjusted his visor for optimum visibility, glanced around and saw a small platform which had been erected at the side of the pit a dozen feet distant from where he stood. On it, a man lay on his back, arms and legs extended, secured, Retief noted, by stout shackles. As he advanced, the soot-stained prisoner uttered a feeble cry:

"Murderers! O mighty Flith, I call on you in this, my

hour of affliction, to get me out of this one, and I'll never ask for anything again!"

"To make no rash promises regarding the future, Ben," a breathy voice sounded near at hand.

"Relax, Mr. Magnan, it's just me," Retief said. "I thought you might be wanting a short snort about now." He extracted a flask from his belt and handed it over. Magnan flopped helplessly.

"Ye gods, it actually worked! Maybe there's something in it—" Magnan broke off, then resumed: "Retief, unlock these infernal cuffs, they've abraded my wrists and ankles most painfully."

"Stop struggling, Ben," the soft Groaci voice spoke again, "and you came pretty close to outright blasphemy that time. What do you mean 'maybe'?"

Retief stopped to cut the gyves from Magnan with four quick passes with a bolt cutter laser. Magnan grabbed the flask and drank deep.

"Thank you, Flith!" he cried, choking a bit on the last swallow.

"How does Flith enter the picture?" Retief asked.

"Simple, two-way closed circuit trideo hookup for dependable round-the-clock prayer and thanksgiving service in full glorious color—what other faith can offer such up-to-the-minute service?" Magnan's breath wheezed, Retief noted. He detached a spare breathing mask from his belt and handed it over.

"Thanks, Flith—and you, too, Retief," Magnan gasped. "As the agent of divine providence—those sulphur fumes were beginning to get to me."

There was a sudden rumble and clank, and with a rushing sound, an avalanche of football-sized objects came bounding down the slope across the pit and cascaded down into the smoking interior from which rose an odor reminiscent of roasted peanuts.

"What's all this?" Retief asked.

"The hoob melon crop—gribble-grub infested, you know; they're getting rid of the spoiled fruit by dumping it into the sacred fires."

"What's sacred about burnt sulphur?" Retief asked.

"Ask the bishops. I just work here," Magnan snapped.

"Work? You seemed to be taking it pretty easy when I arrived."

"But you *did* arrive! That's just the point. My job is to nonstop pray to the gracious Flith to accept this offering of a million-G melon crop as evidence of the reverence and piety of us, his humble worshippers. I was just putting in a plug for a little personal relief, and there you were! Gads—and I was on the verge of becoming a backslider. I thought Flith had abandoned me to my fate."

"Don't backslide now: you'll go over the edge and end up among the sacrificial melons," Retief cautioned. "Do the Elders really think Flith is dumb enough to consider a zillion tons of garbage as a suitable offering?"

"Garbage? Retief, you jest! Those melons were all grade A fancy number one—right up until the gribble-worms hit them. And anyway, each one is full of grubs, each of which, on maturity, would yield three square inches of prime hide. But, sad to say, they'll never grow up now. As a charter member of SPAVIN I feel, or think I ought to feel, a sharp sense of outrage at that. But what the heck, it's all in a noble cause: to the greater glory of Flith."

"No more gribble-hide trade, then?" Retief asked. "The Groaci are wiping them out?"

"By no means. For every grub dumped in the flaming sulphur pits, there are a million more, happily destroying what's left of the melons. We're all relying on Flith to pull a nifty out of his hat, to save the melons, and the hide trade, too"

"He'd better get busy—and so had we. Let's go, Mr. Magnan. Our pickup will be waiting at the north edge of the sulphur fields, in two and a half hours."

"What? Abandon my post?" Magnan cried, recoiling. "What will happen to my big ER in the sky then?"

"Rather depressing, to contemplate carreer considerations pursuing us beyond the grave," Retief said.

"It's not just that," Magnan said sulkily. "Think how lonely poor Flith would get if his regular parishioners stopped reporting in."

"Last I heard, he'd collected a bevy of Groacian orphans around him over at Blue Lagoon, carrying on in the same spirit of charity established by Secretary Earlyworm," Retief pointed out.

"Indeed, mine is a beneficent deity," Magnan agreed. "But now, if you'll excuse me, Retief, I must return to my devotions."

"You're sure you wouldn't rather be whisked back to Sector for a bath and some balm for your wrists and ankles, and a good dinner and a clean bed?"

"Pah, Retief, such material considerations have dwindled to insignificance in light of the vast new spiritual insights granted me in recent days."

Retief snorted the odors of sulphur fumes, charred hoob melon, and roasted gribble-grub from his nostrils. "Kind of a penetrating stench," he observed. "Why not try the breathing mask?"

"Actually, I've rather come to like it," Magnan objected. "As an effluvium emanating from the sacrificial material duly blessed by the GEC, it of course enjoys special status, accumulation-of-meritwise."

Above, the bulldozers snorting at the brink of the rise thrust forward new cascades of condemned melons, which rolled and bounded downslope, some bursting to distribute handfuls of small, blind, limbless, dead-white grubs, which almost at once assumed an ochreous tinge as the sulphur flames licked across them.

"Delicious," Magnan declared, drawing a deep lungful through his nostrils. "You may keep your tenderloins and breasts of peacock!" he cried. "I'll take some more of these marvelously tasty and deliciously crunchy toasted nid-nuts!" He picked up a well-done grub and popped it in his mouth, chewed, smiled blissfully, and swallowed. "Try a few, Retief, you'll soon be addicted."

Retief declined. "I think I'll just hang grimly on and make do with a three-inch tenderloin, rare, and a bottle of 'sixty-nine Beaujolais," he said. Magnan scooped up more toasted grubs and gobbled them hungrily. "As you will, Retief, but don't neglect to gather a few sample bushels of these delicacies to bring along." At that moment, starting to rise, he slipped, dropped over the edge of his platform, and hung by one clutching hand, suspended about the fiery abyss.

Retief caught Magnan's wrist and hauled him to his feet. "We'll have to figure out a method of shelling them," he said and spat a gribble-grub husk over the side. "Strangely enough, you're right: they taste like almonds and pecans mixed."

"Thanks to you, Flith, for not allowing me to perish in the fires," Magnan cried fervently.

"That wasn't Flith that pulled you up, Mr. Magnan, it was me," Retief pointed out.

"Flith chose to employ you as his agent," Magnan said, "Mysterious are the ways of Flith."

Back at the designated rendezvous spot, twelve hours later, after a fatiguing trek across the smouldering sulphur fields, Magnan and Retief watched a small Corps heli descend from the larger vessel waiting overhead. As soon as it had touched down and the hatch popped open Magnan darted forward, clutching a beret stuffed with well-done grubs he had gathered along the way.

"Why, hi there, Jack!" he greeted the pilot, "Have a tasty snack—something special, I assure you!" He proffered half a dozen peanut-sized smoked gribble-grubs on his open palm. "Just spit out the skins," he said.

"Hmm," Jack said dubiously, accepting the offering. He munched one, then another and another at an increasingly rapid rate, as a smile spread over his wide, homely face.

"Cripes, them are A-OK, Mr. Magnan! Where'd you get real old-time corn parchies way out here? You look in pretty good shape, except for that asthma," he continued. "Tell you the truth, I din't figure you'd make it. Most guys get staked out in the sulphur pits, it's good-bye. No water, no food—"

"Food in abundance, Jack—if you like corn parchies, that is."

Retief came up, bearing a large bag improvised from the opera cape Magnan had been wearing at the time of his dedication to the god Flith. He hoisted it inside the copter, assisted Magnan up, and followed him.

"Say, got any more o' them dandy crunchies?" Jack inquired, looking hopefully over his shoulder.

"About a million G's worth, I'd estimate," Retief said. "Mr. Magnan, I have a feeling Flith may yet turn a profit on the hoob melon crop, thereby recouping his position with his cultists."

"Cult, shmult!" Magnan snapped. "Any spiritually oriented organization with an annual million G's in negotiable holdings is no mere cult!"

"Congratulations, Mr. Magnan," Retief said, "I've just had a prophetic flash. I seem to see you playing your cards just right and parlaying your findings into a three-grade rank jump, while at the same time making points on your celestial ER."

"Eh, curious, I didn't know you had the second sight, Retief."

"I don't, it was the third grub that Jack snuck from my baggage that convinced me."

"Don't worry, I'll cut you in for a slice of the action, Retief," Magnan said graciously. "After all, Flith *did* employ you as the agent of my deliverance—so in a sense, I suppose it could be argued that you stand in well with Him, in spite of a certain attitude of skepticism I fancy I've noted on your part from time to time.

"From now on, count me among the believers," Retief said, selecting a particularly succulent toasted gribble-grub. "Any outfit that can turn a million-G

46

crop failure into a million-G snack production has got to have something going for it."

"Ah, how gratifying, Retief," Magnan sighed. "I do believe at last you're developing the faculty for noting which side of your bread-substitute has the icky-wax on it—a skill indispensable to true high-level diplomacy!"

THE GARBAGE INVASION

1

"I think it's an outrage," said Anne Taylor, who was tall and beautiful and held the title Field Curator of Flora and Fauna, assigned to the unpopulated world, Delicia; she stamped a riding-booted foot soundlessly on the carpet covering the floor of the office of Vice Consul Jame Retief of the Corps Diplomatique Terrestrienne, on detached duty to the Galactic Regional Organization for the Protection of Environments, temporarily also assigned to Delicia as Acting Wildlife Officer.

"It's an outrage," Anne repeated, "that those sticky-fingered little Groaci should have the temerity to even make application to GROPE to have Delicia declared an authorized disposal area."

Retief and Miss Taylor were standing by the wide French doors, which were open to the spring breeze. Below them a sweep of tree-dotted emerald sward stretched away over low hills until it was lost in the deep purple shadows of the forest clothing the slopes of the mountain range rising in the middle distance. Scattered herds of sleek, deerlike ruminants grazed peacefully across the plain; tall, rose-colored birds waded in the shallow lakes that mirrored the morning sun. Here and there, patches of vivid wildflowers added chromatic variety to the scene.

"GROPE hasn't yet OK'd the Groaci request," Retief replied mildly, "so things could be worse."

"Why, when I was first assigned here," Anne Taylor said, "I didn't know a thing in the world about Delicia.

But it's all so perfectly lovely and unspoiled, it's absolutely captivated my heart. I'd almost go so far as to say it's even prettier than back home on Plantation II. It would be perfectly horrid to spoil it all by turning it into a garbage dump. And you can never tell what those ninnies back at GROPE might do. There are two Groaci on the Interspecies Council, you know. They may get their way yet."

"Still, while the air remains unsullied we may as well breathe a little of it," Retief said. He led the way out onto the small railed balcony outside the third-floor office. They drew a deep breath of the untainted air, scented delicately of magnolia blossoms.

"Don't give up hope, Anne," Retief said. "The Terran proposal that Delicia be declared a galactic park is still pending. It may win through in spite of Groaci opposition. Mr. Magnan will no doubt bring news on that point when he arrives this afternoon."

"Now just why is this Mr. Magnan coming here?" Anne inquired. "I know he's another diplomat like you, only higher-ranking, but why is he interested in an out-of-the-way place like Delicia? I thought I was doing a pretty good job here all by myself with just my half-dozen rangers to do the heavy work. And now all a sudden I've got CDT types dropping in to take over. Not that *you* aren't welcome, Jame. Of course, you're a perfectly charming gentleman. But I don't know about this Mr. Magnan. What kind of fellow is he?"

"Mr. Magnan is a seasoned diplomat," Retief said. "He tends to be a bit jumpy at times—but his instincts are basically sound."

"Why is he coming here?" Anne asked. "Nobody's visited me since that bunch of GROPE busybodies, last year."

"Just a routine observational visit, I suppose," Retief said. "I think you'll find that Mr. Magnan will be happy to just sightsee and leave the responsibility to you. As for myself, I have no intention of taking over."

"Well, that's a relief," Anne said. "After two years

49

on Delicia, I've almost come to feel as though it's my private property, and I hate to think of anyone changing things." Miss Taylor extended her arms in a stretch. She was a slender girl, with a trim yet curvaceous figure, an aristocratically pretty face and luxuriant auburn hair. She was dressed in gray whipcord jodhpurs, a starched white blouse, and a fringed suede vest of Lincoln green. Her hair was tied back with a red ribbon. The silence of the sunny morning was broken by a distant dull rumble.

"Oh, dear," Anne said, "I hope it isn't going to rain. I've been thinking we might take a stroll before lunch."

"That's not thunder," Retief said. "It sounds like a shuttlecraft cutting atmosphere. I suspect that it's Mr. Magnan arriving right on schedule."

"Well, I hope he has the good taste to land in the parking area and doesn't just drop in here on the grounds of Admin House and tear up the lawn and mash my flower beds," Anne said.

A moment later it was apparent that her wish was to be fulfilled, as a small, squat, bottle-shaped landing craft appeared over the foothills, descending slowly, supported by the glowing purple column of a gravitic drive. The grazing herds of wild animals scattered as the craft descended amid a muted rumbling and a shrill whine. It came to rest squarely in the center of the triangular landing pad and the glare of its drive faded to a dull pink and winked out.

Retief and Anne left the office and rode the escalator down to the lobby, a spacious room bright with sunlight tinged green by the broad fronds of the potted plants arrayed before the wide windows. Outside, Retief pressed the button of his pocket signaler, which caused an automated two-man carrier to back from the garage behind the tall jade-green building, and scoot smoothly around the circular drive to brake to a halt beside them, open its hatch, and wait, balanced on its two soft-tired wheels, its turbine-driven gyros humming softly.

Retief assisted the girl into the forward of the two

contoured seats, and climbed in after her. The interior of the vehicle smelled faintly of new paint and tumpleather. He turned the gnarled knob which reduced the scale of the map displayed on the location screen, so that it showed in detail an area of roughly one square mile, centered on the Admin complex. The newly arrived vessel was indicated by a point of green light approximately a quarter mile distant. Retief noted the coordinates and punched them into the guidance console, then pressed the ACTIVATE button. The hatch closed silently; the air blowers started up with a rhythmic *whirr*. The vehicle rolled forward a few feet on the paved drive, then executed a neat turn to the left, hopped a foot into the air, and scooted smoothly forward on a direct course for the gray vessel squatting incongruously beyond the row of heo trees that lined the landing pad. Anne activated the car's tape system and a Puccini aria emanated from the quad speakers. The car shot through an opening between two trees, circled the base of the newly arrived shuttlecraft, came to a halt, and sank down onto its wheels with a soft *whoosh!* of released air cushion. Retief poked a button and the transparent clamshell hatch opened. A moment later a ladder deployed from the side of the spacecraft looming above. A rectangular port opened at its upper end and a thin, narrow-shouldered man in an impeccably cut gray executive coverall with a CDT pocket patch appeared. He waved jauntily, turned and started down the ladder.

"Gracious, Retief," he called over his shoulder, "I do hope my visit hasn't interrupted any important undertaking here on the local scene."

"I'm afraid not," Retief said. "Miss Taylor and I are still at the formal stage." He smiled at the girl. She grinned cheerfully at him in return.

Retief climbed down out of the car.

"Miss Taylor," he said formally, "may I present Career Minister Magnan of the CDT. Mr. Magnan," he addressed the senior diplomat, "you'll see many beauti-

51

ful sights here on Delicia, none more delightful than the person of Miss Anne Taylor, who is Field Curator of Flora and Fauna, the sole and highest-ranking official on the entire planet, a position, I'm sure you realize, of considerable responsibility and one which Miss Taylor has fulfilled with commendable efficiency for the past year."

"I'm enchanted to make your acquaintance, Miss Taylor," Magnan said, bowing from the waist as elegantly as could be managed while clinging to a ladder. "Goodness me, haven't you found it desperately lonely being the only rational creature on an entire world?"

"I have a half a dozen rangers," Anne said, "several of whom are quite rational when they haven't had too much Alpha Pale ale."

"Of course," Magnan said, and managed a faint blush. "I meant to cast no aspersions on your colleagues, no matter how humble their station. I merely had reference to the curious fact that Delicia, while ideally suited for organic life as we know it, supports no indigenous form more highly evolved than a grazing ruminant."

"Don't worry, Mr. Magnan," Retief said, "the combined heights of those six rangers is thirty-nine feet, but I won't tell them what you said."

"Retief, I'm here with news of some importance, and quite frankly, I wish your advice. I trust you're not going to be difficult," Magnan said with some asperity.

"That depends on what you want me to do," Retief said. "If you'd like me to stay here for another six months on full per diem allowance, I'll go along with the idea with no complaints." He turned to the girl: "Why don't you take the car back, Anne? I'll escort Mr. Magnan over and we'll meet you at the office. It will give you time to mix us a couple of tall cool ones, and to punch in a nice dinner to celebrate Mr. Magnan's visit."

"How does *fried chicken Sanders* sound?" she asked.

"Oh, nothing overly exotic, please," Magnan protested. "Simple hearty fare suits me very well. In fact I've been known to spend an entire afternoon munching contentedly on a Hebrew National salami-on-rye, while a state banquet proceeded in an adjoining room."

"Sorry, my culinator's not programmed for any of those unchristian vittles," Anne demurred. "I had a team of inspectors in here from someplace called Pakistan a few months back. Up till then I always thought curry was something you did to horses."

"Please, no apologies, my dear," Magnan said, and almost slipped off his rung, attempting a curtsy. "Come, Retief," he said, casting a regretful glance after the girl as the car moved off. "It's a perfect morning for a stroll. Quite an attractive, though undeveloped world," he said, looking around at the parklike lawn scattered with wildflowers. "Rather a pity, actually, that it will not long remain so."

"You mentioned some important news, Mr. Magnan," Retief said.

"Ah, of course. You'll recall that I have for some months been acting as CDT liaison officer to GROPE. We're faced with a deeply perplexing problem at the moment. It's necessary that I find a solution to the Basuran question at once or forever disappoint Mother's hopes for a great career for me."

"Is that the news that you hurried out to Delicia to pass along to me?"

"Don't make light of the problem, Retief. We're discussing the imminent prospect of the utter extinction of an entire intelligent species, due to the fact that they've overfed their range to such an extreme degree that, although their metabolisms are such that they can sustain themselves on a diet of raw metals and silicon if necessary—there remains not an assimilable molecule on their entire planet, which as you know, lies only a parsec distant from Delicia."

"And you still consider them an intelligent species?" Retief commented.

"Such situations are not uncommon," Magnan reminded Retief. "Think for a moment of the fate of the Mainland Chinese, back on Terra, six centuries ago. By the way, I've often wondered why they were called Mainland Chinese—also Red Chinese? The few persons of Chinese ancestry I've met have had rather sallow, yellowish complexions, not red at all."

"Surely there's more news to come," Retief said.

"By all means," Magnan replied. "Unhappily, at the time of my departure, the GROPE docket was crammed with over one hundred urgent appeals from member worlds facing ecological breakdown due to the accretion of waste products both biological and industrial. For some curious reason Chief Ecological Coordinator Crodfoller allocated seventy-nine of these applications to me for solution, a task approximately equivalent in complexity to rescoring an equal number of Groaci nose-flute cadenzas for a steel band, Jew's harp and comb. When I sought counsel of Director of Ecological Affairs Straphanger, far from interceding to effect a more equitable distribution of workload, or even commiserating, he assigned me additional duty as project officer for facilitation of the Terran resolution anent designation of Delicia as a galactic park."

"What are the prospects for GROPE adoption of the resolution?" Retief asked.

"Dim, I should say," Magnan replied. "Shortly before my departure, I conferred with Ambassador Fiss, head of the Groaci delegation to GROPE, and he was quite adamant. He insisted it was his government's unalterable position that the provision of suitable offworld dumping grounds was a matter of far greater import than the perpetuation of primitive natural conditions on Delicia as a recreational habitat pleasing to the unformed esthetic instincts of lesser species. Alas," Magnan sighed eyeing the unspoiled landscape, "I fear that unless Fiss can be placated, all this is doomed. Fiss, as you know, is a formidable negotiator, and I fear that he has secured the support of a number of the other worlds faced with similar disposal problems. But let us not dwell on such depressing prospects. I intend to carry on with my planning on the off-chance that the park scheme should win through. Gracious, I'm all abubble with plans," he went on, rubbing his hands together. "Two hundred million square miles of unsullied meadows, uplands, hills, valleys, lakes, seas, islands—all waiting the creative hand of the landscape architects."

"What's wrong with leaving it as it is?" Retief suggested.

"Mmm. It has a certain bucolic charm, of course," Magnan conceded. "But I can hardly accrue mana ER-wise by resting on my oars. No, I picture a planetwide complex of miniature golf courses, roadside zoos, artificial rock gardens, and chlorinated swimming pools, all linked by a network of ten-lane superhighways, with adequate paved parking, of course; plus the necessary motels, service stations, beauty emporia and souvenir shops to convert the wilderness into a true, unspoiled garden spot. Why, the concessions alone will net enough income to finance a planetwide system of forty-foot billboards advertising the beauty of the place!"

"A prospect to set the heart of any conservationist to beating, if not into fibrillation," Retief commented.

"Here, what's *that?*" Magnan pointed a well-manicured finger at a scrap of paper blowing across the lawn on the spring breeze.

"Litterbugs?" he exclaimed in an anguished tone.

"Maybe one of the rangers tossed it down, doubtless in defiance of Miss Taylor's instructions," Retief suggested.

"If so, I'll have him transferred to the Icebox System and assigned to snow-worm tally!" Magnan retorted. "Come along, Retief!" Magnan pounced, came up with the offending object, a plastine bag lettered KRISPY KRUNCHY KORN-KURLS.

Retief stooped, caught up a second paper as it

tumbled past. "Sulf-R Smoked Gribble-Grubs," he read.

"Gribble-grubs?" Magnan queried. "That's a Groaci export item."

More papers came sailing across the grass: candy wrappers, dope-stick sleeves, a large pink newspaper printed in unfamiliar characters. Magnan darted after them, uttering sharp cries of indignation as more and more waxed sandwich bags and crumpled paper napkins whirled toward them from upwind, driven by the rising breeze.

"Let us investigate the source," Magnan suggested, planting a foot on a gallon-sized potato-chip bag. "They're gaining on us."

"It's coming from over that line of hills," Retief said.

"Let's hurry; I want to catch the vandals in the act!" Magnan said.

"I suggest we check with Miss Taylor first," Retief demurred. "She may know what's going on."

2

Retief and Magnan entered the Admin building, rode the escalator to the third floor, and went along the corridor to Retief's office. Anne Taylor stood by the window staring out in the direction of the landing pad. A flurry of white paper scraps came drifting across the grass, accompanied by a straggle of small objects that rolled, wind-driven, scattering out to mar the smooth-mowed turf.

"What in the world is that?" she cried, and whirled to face the two diplomats. "Did y'all see that bunch of garbage blowing around the lawn?"

"We saw it," Retief said, "and thought perhaps it was something you had authorized."

"Never! I don't allow my rangers to so much as spit on the grass, if y'all will pardon the expression."

At that moment, the large Navy issue communicator panel set amid the bookshelves on the right wall of the office crackled and lit up, displaying a round Terran face of a mottled mauve hue that wore an expression suggesting an acute dyspeptic attack.

"Why, it's Director Straphanger," Magnan cried, in a tone of patently artificial delight. "Why, hi, there, Mr. Director! I'm here on Delicia as you see, and I have matters well under control."

"Have you indeed?" Straphanger inquired in a voice suggesting the premonitory rumblings of a volcano on the brink of eruption. "That's gratifying news, I'm sure, inasmuch as everything here at Sector has been deteriorating toward full disaster status with a speed which would be incredible to one unfamiliar with bureaucratic life."

Magnan cleared his throat delicately. "If you'll recall, Mr. Director," he said, "I predicted that my departure at this time would have unfortunate repercussions efficiencywise in the progress of our programs."

"No man is indispensable, Magnan, least of all you," Straphanger bellowed. "The dire straits in which I find myself are, luckily for your future, only peripherally related to your singular lack of effectiveness in developing a solution to the disposal problem. The immediate cause for my call is an untoward development *in re* the Basuran question. As you know, an emergency program was initiated by GROPE last year, and large shipments of foodstuffs were transported to Basur. But even with this dietary supplement, they continued heedlessly with the destruction of their habitat, and since they find both igneous and sedimentary rocks quite palatable, they have now consumed the northern half of their main continent, including a number of their largest cities, thus compounding their problem. Driven to desperation and energized, perhaps, by this remarkable piece of gluttony, they have now burst forth from their system with a gigantic fleet of surplus war vessels which were donated by Boge as emergency rations, and have unabashedly announced their intention to invade whatever hapless worlds lie in their path, in quest of food. It appears that unless firm steps are taken at once, they will come sweeping up through the Eastern Arm, like a horde of all-devouring locusts, stripping every world in their path bare to the magma. Even now these voracious gluttons are approaching Delicia."

3

"In spite of the heavy pressure of my duties," Straphanger pointed out, "I have taken time to notify you of their impending arrival, although making this call has cut seriously into my lunch hour, thus affording you an opportunity to make good your escape."

Magnan bobbed his head at the fading image on the screen. "Most thoughtful of you, Mr. Director," he said fervently. "There, Retief," he continued, turning to the younger man, "you've just overheard a most heartwarming example of the esprit which informs the Corps from the highest echelons to the lowest."

"The man's all heart," Retief agreed. "But there's still garbage blowing across the garden."

"Quite," Magnan said briskly. "You may as well step along now and put an end to the nuisance."

"You don't have a gun, do you, Anne?" Retief inquired of the girl.

"I surely do," she replied. "No real lady would allow herself to be found alone on a planet with six big old rangers with no means of defending her honor." With a deft motion, she extracted a slim-barreled 2mm needler from her *décolletage* and handed it over.

"Amazing," Retief said. "I wouldn't have thought

there was room in there for anything else." He tucked the gun into his belt.

"Retief! Whatever are you thinking of?" Magnan squeaked.

"I'm thinking of how surprised those picnickers or whatever will be when I don't simply appeal to their better natures."

"Heavens, Retief, every situation can be dealt with by use of appropriate words," Magnan reproved. "That's the basic tenet of diplomacy as we know it."

"Maybe that's what's wrong with diplomacy as we know it," Retief said.

4

Outside, Retief noted that the quantity of scrap paper and plastic blowing over the grass had, if anything, increased in the last five minutes. He stooped to pick up one of the solid objects included in the drift of rubbish invading the lawn. There were hundreds of identical six-inch cylinders, of a porous texture, a dull gray-and-tan color. They rolled easily, pushed by the breeze. The object in Retief's hand was feather-light, with the feel of foam plastic. On close scrutiny he recognized it as a compacted cylinder of shredded gribble-grub husk, a by-product of the Groaci snack industry. More and more of the cylinders rolled down the slope, spreading out across the close-cropped verdant sward. Retief walked toward the point of origin, a saddle-shaped notch in the grassy ridge a few hundred yards west of Admin House. More and more debris came swirling downwind. Retief reached the crest of the rise, looked down at the long narrow valley which extended southward, rimmed on both sides by wooded slopes. The floor of the valley was a level grassland dotted with crimson-foliaged trees. A sparkling stream wound along the center of the valley, fed by a picturesque waterfall tumbling down over the rocks at Retief's right and feeding into a lake at the far end of the valley, which reflected the blue sky and bits of whipped-cream cloud. Halfway down the length of the valley, a mile and a half from Retief's vantage point, a space-scarred space-yacht of unmistakable Groaci design rested on its side beside the stream. Around it, half a dozen Groaci stood, apparently admiring the view. Immediately beyond the spacecraft lay the first of a string of a dozen immense gray sausagelike barges, each with an identical symbol blazoned on its prow: a group of alien characters which appeared to spell out *eggnog*. Each of the big gray cylinders had opened a set of doors which ran nearly the length of its hull and was busily discharging raw garbage in giant windrows, from which the breeze was snatching away papers and bits of other light debris, sending them rolling up the slope, through the notch, and down across the Admin House grounds.

As Retief started down the slope, he heard a sharp cry from behind him and turned to see Magnan struggling over the hilltop clutching his beret against the wind's efforts to send it skittering after the waste paper.

"Here," Magnan shouted, the word almost inaudible over the fluting of the wind and the splashing of the waterfall. "Never mind bothering about these bits of paper and waste. A crisis of far greater magnitude is at hand." He half slid down the steep slope and clutched at Retief's arm just in time to retain his balance.

"They're here," he yelped. "Just as Director Straphanger said! The Basuran fleet has taken up orbit a few thousand miles out, and their leader, a ferocious fellow named All Conqueror of Foes Cheese, threatens drastic action if we don't surrender our fleet on the instant."

"What drastic action?" Retief asked.

"AC of F Cheese didn't specify," Magnan said in a choked tone. "But judging from the bellicosity of his attitude, he's ready to stop at nothing."

"Good," Retief said. "That's about all we've got to stop him with."

"Retief, if we hurry along briskly, we can reach my shuttlecraft before Cheese has landed," Magnan blurted.

"And then what?" Retief inquired.

"Why then we can whisk ourselves off under his very nose and leave him none the wiser."

"What about Miss Taylor?" Retief asked.

"I'm afraid she's in no position to help us, having no transportation at her disposal."

"So you intend to desert her and leave her to her fate?"

"I suppose it does sound just the teensiest bit unchivalrous when you put it that way," Magnan conceded. "However Miss Taylor seems a resourceful young person. I'm sure she'll understand. Besides, no one will know."

"*She* will," Retief said. "And what about those thirty-nine feet of ranger?"

"Unfortunate, but there's no help for it. They'll simply have to hope for an attitude of clemency on the part of Cheese."

"And just what does this Cheese expect from us?" Retief asked.

"He demands the immediate surrender of our fleet. I told him quite candidly that we had no fleet here, but he openly accused me of perjury, and insisted that he had seen the fleet maneuvering offworld a few hours ago. It was that which attracted his attention. He demands its immediate surrender on pain of drastic reprisals. Goodness me, Retief, whatever shall we do?"

"We'd better surrender the fleet," Retief said.

"Either you haven't been paying attention or that remark is intended as another of your ill-timed japes," Magnan snapped. "I'm going to return to the office and brew a nice pot of sassafras tea. You may join me if you wish."

"Thank you," Retief said. "First I'd like to speak to the gribble-grub lovers."

Magnan glanced past Retief, saw the grounded garbage scows. "Oh, I see. It's a party of picnickers camped by the stream. I authorize you to speak sharply to them, Retief. It's atrocious the way they're littering their waste about."

"Armed with such instructions, how can I fail?" Retief inquired rhetorically, and turned to continue his descent, as Magnan scrambled back up the path.

"On second thought," Retief called after Magnan, "I haven't had a cup of sassafras tea since the Fustian Ambassador's reception for the Admirable F'Kau-Kau-Kau of Yill, and on that occasion Colonel Underknuckle spiked it with half a gill of Bacchus Black."

"I recall the incident," Magnan said sharply. "Disgraceful. Ambassador Longspoon, suspecting nothing, downed three cups while having a cozy chat with the Groaci military attaché. Alas, far from pumping General Shish of the details of the Groaci maneuvers in the Goober cluster, the colonel divulged the details of all Terrestrial peace operations in the Arm for a five»year period, resulting not only in a number of embarrassments for Secretary Barnshingle, when nosy parkers poking about in our goodwill convoys uncovered what they claimed to be offensive weapons, but also in Secretary Barnshingle's relegation to the Jaq desk in the department over which he had once towered as chief. Not only that, Retief, but you'll recall I was assigned as catering officer for the affair, and during Colonel Underknuckle's or should I say Corporal Underknuckle's court-martial, certain small-minded individuals went so far as to suggest that a share of the blame should be laid at my door. Thus sassafras tea, while a warmly sustaining beverage, far more suited to the dignity and responsibility of one's role as an officer of the CDT than harsh spiritous distillates of the kind favored by certain rowdies, is not without its melancholy associations."

"I don't want to precipitate a traumatic emotional

experience for you, Mr. Magnan," Retief said, "so perhaps we'd better just crack a magnum of Lovenbroy autumn wine."

"As it happens," Magnan called over his shoulder, "I have a dozen of Lovenbroy aboard the lighter, a gift to you from a Mr. Arapoulous, who visited my office at Sector yesterday with an outrageous proposal for CDT sponsorship of some barbaric festival at which he specifically requested your attendance in the capacity of Inspector of Prizes."

"You accepted on my behalf, I hope," Retief said.

"By no means," Magnan said in a tone of sharp rebuke. "I have reason to believe that the prizes to which he alluded are nubile young women selected for pulchritude and but scantily attired. Imagine! Handing out girls to champion grape pickers as if they were hand-knitted tea cosies."

"It's fantastic, isn't it?" Retief said. "With that going on only a few light years away, we're sitting out here planning a sassafras tea party."

"Never mind, Retief. Such depravity does prey on one's mind, but there are reasons to hope that in time these excesses will be halted."

"Let's hope so," Retief said. "In the meantime we can make a start by pouring the sassafras tea into Miss Taylor's potted froom-froom plants."

5

As the two diplomats entered Retief's office, the communicator screen set in the ornamental bookcase crackled softly. "Ah, there you are, Magnan," a metallic voice said.

Only one familiar with the Basuran physiognomy would have recognized the composition displayed on the picture tube as the face of a living creature. It resembled a geometric approximation of a giant clamshell executed in flat planes of bluish metal.

"Oh, sorry to have kept you waiting, All Conqueror Cheese," Magnan called. "I've just been discussing your proposal with my colleague."

"Perhaps," the Basuran said in a voice like an eight-pound hammer hitting an anvil, "you misunderstood me, Terran. The terms I outlined do not constitute a proposal, but an ultimatum."

"Goodness me, I understand perfectly," Magnan reassured the alien. "Your insistence on my surrender of the Delician war fleet is quite understandable, and I'm doing my best to make the arrangements, so I trust you'll withhold the saturation bombing for a little while."

"I'll give you a few moments longer," Cheese said graciously. "I don't wish it to be said that I was overly harsh in my dealings even with mere Terrans."

"What's that about the Delician war fleet?" Retief asked.

"We have to surrender it at once," Magnan said, "or Cheese will bomb the planet to a cinder."

"That being the case," Retief said, "we'd better get busy."

"I couldn't agree more heartily," Magnan sighed, "but just how does one go about surrendering one's fleet when one doesn't have a fleet?"

"One does the best one can with what one has," Retief said.

6

Magnan deftly scaled his beret across the room, scoring a bull's eye on a plaster bust of the long-defunct first Terrestrial Ambassador to an alien species: Fenwick T. Overdog, who, according to a brass plate on his chest, was sent out from Terra as Ambassador Extraordinary and Minister Plenipotentiary to the then newly discovered world Yalc in the year 450 A.E. (A.D. 2899), the bright-colored headgear lending an uncharacteristic air of jauntiness to the old diplomat's grim visage. Moments later a bland odor of licorice filled the air. Magnan fussed busily over the dainty cups and saucers he had unpacked from his CDT field kit and soon poured out the steaming pink fluid.

"Oh, I almost forgot," he said. "Your present from that bucolic person I told you of." From his briefcase he extracted a foot-long, tapered bundle of dusty tissue paper and handed it over. Retief stripped away the wrappings to expose an age-blackened hand-blown bottle of deep green glass through which the sunlight glowed, eliciting glints of ruby red from the wine the flask contained.

"You said something about a dozen," Retief said. "You haven't got eleven more bottles in that briefcase, have you?"

"Never mind," Magnan said, "I won't trouble you with the rest. You may leave them aboard the lighter. I'll dispose of them somehow. They're all dusty and dirty anyway, as though they'd been cleaned out of some old cellar somewhere. Hardly a tasteful offering even to a mere Third Secretary."

"I'll make room for them somehow," Retief said. He stripped the wire from the bottle, eased the cork out with his thumbs. It popped up with a sharp report, and a rich and fruity aroma at once permeated the room.

"Well, I'll declare!" a feminine voice said from the door. Anne Taylor stood there looking fresh and charming in buckskin skirt and beaded blouse. She sniffed the air.

"What a perfectly heavenly smell," she exclaimed. "It reminds me of the time Uncle Harry, the senator, christened our yacht. Funny thing," she went on "a minute ago, I thought I smelled paregoric or some nasty old machine."

"Tea, Miss Taylor?" Magnan said, proffering a cup.

Retief picked up a Yalcan wine goblet of violet glass from the table at the side of the office, poured it half full of the deep red wine, and offered it to the girl. "Will you join me?" he said, and filled a second goblet, this one of paper-thin crystal-clear glass.

"No thank you, Mr. Magnan," she said with a smile refusing his cup, and took the purple glass from Retief.

Her eyes strayed across the room to the communicator screen on which AC of F Cheese was still gnashing his mandibular plates with a sound like a dishwasher demolishing a platter.

"Well, what in the world is *that?*" she cried.

"That, my dear," Magnan replied coolly, "is the commanding admiral of a vast fleet of hostile warships which are even now orbiting the planet with the intention of demolishing it utterly unless I perform an act of incredible cleverness at once."

"It looks more like the front end of my li'l ol' turbocad—the one with the bad brakes. But you talk as if it was a somebody instead of a something."

"AC of F Cheese is, I fear, legally classified as a somebody—rather an important somebody—and quite capable of carrying out his threat."

"What is this simply incredibly clever thing you're supposed to do, Mr. Magnan? Anything special, or will just any old incredibly clever thing do? I'm dying to hear about it."

"All Conqueror Cheese insists that I surrender the Delician war fleet at once."

"How can you do that?" Anne demanded. "There's no such thing."

"That's what requires the cleverness," Magnan replied tartly.

"So what are you going to *do?* You've just got to save this sweet li'l ol' planet!"

"I intend," Magnan said grandly, "to deal with the matter in my usual decisive fashion."

"But *how?*" Anne wailed.

"Retief, kindly advise All Conqueror Cheese of our intentions."

Retief turned to the screen. "Where would you like the fleet delivered?" he asked.

"Oh, never mind about that," Cheese said in a tone as genial as the crunch of a fender. "I'll just swoop down and gather it in where it lies at its cleverly camouflaged base."

"If it's so cleverly camouflaged, how come you know it's there?" Magnan cried.

"My chief intelligence officer, Intimidator of Mobs Blunge, shrewdly ferreted out its location from a study of various documents of a highly cryptic nature which fell into his hands. For a time, I confess, it appeared we'd be unable to crack your code. Symbol groups such as 'Sulf-R Smoked Gribble-Grubs' were rejected by our computers as utterly devoid of intelligence. Then it occurred to me that it was not necessary to decode the documents; the mere presence of encrypted material was sufficient evidence of military activity. I merely traced them to their source. But enough of these civilities: I must personally inspect my warheads now. Infinite attention to detail is the secret of success in great enterprise."

"But gribble-grubs are a Groaci delicacy," Magnan protested to Retief. "They're not bad, actually; a bit like Quoppina sourballs. But why would the Groaci be carrying out military maneuvers *here*?"

"Y'all gentlemen better get busy being incredibly clever," Miss Taylor pointed out. "Time's awasting."

"Before we break the news to All Conqueror Cheese that there's no fleet here to conquer," Magnan said, "why don't you just nip over and say a word to those picnickers, Retief? I'd like to turn over the planet in tidy condition."

"An excellent notion, Mr. Magnan," Retief said. He left the office and took the path across the lawn to the vantage point from which he had studied the Groaci garbage barges discharging cargo. The process had continued apace during his half-hour absence. A great dike of refuse ran the length of the valley, paralleling the now-empty scows. As Retief descended the hill, a spindle-legged Groaci in a magenta hip cloak of extreme cut emerged from the yacht and came bustling up the slope to meet him, trailed by a pair of Peace Keepers with slung crater guns.

"To recognize one unhappily familiar to me from past encounters," the leading Groaci cried in his breathy voice. "None other than the notorious Retief, I'll hazard, or I am the littermate of nest-fouling drones!"

"To feel like going for a little ride, Shluh?" Retief inquired genially in Groaci.

"To have completed my task here in exemplary fashion, and to be about to enjoy a well-earned siesta," Shluh replied with a contemptuous clack of his nether mandibles. With a wave he dismissed his escort, who hurried back to the nearest scow.

"To request a look at your authorizing order from GROPE permitting you to dump your gribble-grub skins here," Retief said.

"To point out reluctantly that your jokes are as atrocious as your accent, Soft One," Shluh hissed. He turned away.

"To wonder how long it will take you and your boys to load that stuff back aboard the barges," Retief remarked, eying the quarter-mile-long, twenty-foot-high heap of refuse now fouling the stream.

"To point out that the tub of hot sand readied for my slumbers is cooling rapidly whilst we natter of these trivia," Shluh whispered. "To hurry away now and leave you to ponder your own inscrutable riddle."

"To suggest a method of discovering the answer empirically," Retief said. "To distribute shovels and tell them to start in."

"Not to be so easily duped, Retief. To realize that so soon as my lads batten down the last hatch your interest in research would stand revealed as ephemeral—a mere ploy to accomplish your true aim of negating my achievement. To insure that by your Terran glibness you do not hoax some unfortunate underling of mine into falling in with your scheme, I am lifting my command at once, to return for a second load."

"To offer a suggestion," Retief said gently. "If GROPE hasn't authorized this visit, to consider the possibility that a flock of Peace Enforcers might be here any minute to interfere with your siesta."

"An unlikely eventuality," Shluh breathed airily. "To be as aware as yourself of the fecklessness of that irresolute body known as GROPE, the very name of which is an acronym in the Groaci tongue equivalent in blandness to an unsulphurated gribble-grub."

"To burrow into your hot sand and heap it up over your auditory membranes, while events proceed without you," Retief urged.

"To have no fear, Retief; the nubile Groacian lady who awaits me will doubtless have hollowed out a burrow capacious enough to accommodate us both in cozy juxtaposition. To anticipate no event more exciting than the discovery of an overlooked gribble-grub in a castoff package whilst I take my well-earned ease."

Retief and the Groaci looked up as a shrill sound like a distant siren echoed across the hills, followed by a deep rumble.

"Retief," Shluh said, "a less sophisticated person than myself might take alarm at that sound, imagining hordes of vengeful Terry Peace Enforcers to be swooping down, bent on interfering with my peaceful and legitimate errand. But seasoned veteran of the interplanetary conference table that I am, I'm fully aware that GROPE's function is a purely conversational one, for all their brave talk of attacking the time-honored institution of environmental pollution and of unnatural interference with inscrutable nature's weeding out of the unfit via ecological pressure, the history of galactic diplomacy assures us that no act so direct and effective as the use of force would be contemplated for a moment by that huddle of aging bureaucrats. Accordingly, I remain my usual suave and poised self. To pay no attention to the *petite* tremor of my lower throat sac which you may observe; it's but symptomatic of a touch of *Vrug* which is no worse than a bad cold and will clear up spontaneously in a few days. Nonetheless, to be best if my personnel not wander too far afield." Shluh took a small brass whistle from a loop in his belt and blew a piercing blast. A moment later Groaci navvies in baggy ochre coveralls, spotted and stained by their labors in unloading their unsavory cargo, began emerging singly and in twos and threes from shady spots beneath the trees near the river, and hurrying toward their assigned vessels.

Shluh gave a violent start, dislodging two of his plain silver eye shields, as a sonic boom rolled across the valley, followed by a diminishing roar. A scarred and space-burned ship appeared above the hills, rushing straight toward the spot where Retief and Shluh stood. Its lumpy and asymmetrical hull, tumorous with gun emplacements, was obviously that of an elderly Bogan-designed warship, Retief saw at once. Half a dozen others followed in line astern. Their trajectory brought them in a low pass over the grounded garbage fleet. The air blast of their passage sent a shower of papers and plastic and light metal containers tumbling from the crest of the gigantic garbage heap, to be caught by the wind and swept up over the hilltop and out of sight.

"Mere sightseers, joyriding, doubtless in defiance of regulations," Shluh commented. "But youth must have its fling. These are perhaps a group of cadets from the Groaci Space Institute trying their figurative wings. Mere high spirits; there's no harm in them." As the Groaci bent over to recover his fallen eye shields from the grass, there was a sharp report and a gout of yellow fire erupted from the stern emplacement of the last vessel in line. Shluh straightened and whirled in time to see a twenty-foot crater appear adjacent to the prow of the converted yacht which served as his flagship, attended by a geyser of mud and garbage which clattered down, with a long, drawn-out drumming sound, along the dorsal keel of the ornate vessel. Rich purple-black mud, not unmixed with fruit rinds, glimp eggshells and chicory grounds flowed down over the highly polished bright-plating and colored porcelain inlay work.

"Poor, dear, fragile Lady Tish!" Shluh groaned. "To have been terrified by the blast, poor innocent, having no way of recognizing it as a boyish prank."

"To better duck before this next prank takes your head off," Retief said. He threw himself flat, pulling the Groaci down with him. Accompanied by a long drawn-out screeching sound, an arrow of fire was arcing toward them from the direction in which the six warships had disappeared.

"A toy rocket!" Shluh cried, springing up. "No doubt an RC scale model of a *Dumbo*-class luxury liner of early Concordiat times. To capture it in midflight before it sustains damage on striking the ground! My nephew, young Pilf, will be delighted with the trophy! Zounds!" he continued, grabbing at his remaining eye shields as a violent involuntary twitch of his eyestalks dislodged them, "there's another." He pointed. "And another!"

"And four more," Retief put in. "Are you sure they're just scale models of antique ships? If they were late-model Bogan warheads, they'd have us nicely bracketed."

"To be beyond a doubt, " Shluh said. "Drat! To have tarried too long. The Dumbo model is about to strike!"

The slim, yard-long missile slammed into the turf and detonated with a deafening report, sending clayey soil fountaining to patter down around Retief and the Groaci official. In swift succession six more explosions racketed across the valley. Retief got to his feet to see seven fresh craters neatly ringing his position.

"To look into this matter," Shluh shrilled, and dashed away downslope toward his mud-splattered yacht.

"I have a sudden craving for sassafras tea," Retief commented aloud. "The party's getting rough."

"Alas!" Shluh keened, slowing to a mock-casual saunter. "To sense, somehow, that all is not as it should be. Doubtless a mere touch of nervousness on my part, arising from the well-known Groacian sensitivity to subtleties of mood."

"To not ignore your hunch," Retief advised. "That stick of bombs was enough to make a Fustian elder start tearing a hanky to shreds."

"To ignore the sly intimation implicit in your choice of terms, Retief," Shluh whispered. "To have safely brought my command through parsecs of hostile space, safe to the designated destination, and to have discharged my cargo with exemplary promptitude, not intimidated by your hints of impending bureaucratic vengeance. Not to panic now."

"To admire your *savoir-faire*," Retief called after the Groaci. "Most people would think seven near-misses to be a sufficient hint that the hinting was over."

"At what do you hint now, unspeakable Soft One?" Shluh paused to hiss.

"To look for yourself," Retief said and pointed. Shluh hesitated, then whirled so quickly that all his eye shields once more fell to the grass. The blunt prow of one of the black-hulled warships was just nosing back into view over the rim of the hills, supported silently on beams of mauve light. It advanced, flattening the tall grass in a wide swathe as it glided downslope toward the river, followed by its six sister ships. The guns bristling from the vessels' turrets traversed restlessly, but did not open fire.

"To not believe a word of it," Shluh whispered a bit hoarsely over his shoulder. "GROPE wouldn't dare!"

"To point out that you're up against hardware, not conversation," Retief said. "A battle cruiser speaks for itself."

With a sudden growl of atmospheric engines, the menacing ships deployed to ring in the grounded Groaci barges in a semicircle, and came gently to rest.

"You there!" a harsh PA-amplified voice boomed from the lead ship and echoed across the valley.

"There—there! Stand fast—ast! One move and I clear the dust out of every gun in my fleet!"

"To protest!" Shluh wailed in a halfhearted tone. "To consider this an outright act of war!"

"By your own Cadet Corps?" Retief asked.

"To possibly have mistaken the identity of the culprits," Shluh said faintly.

"Then who are we going to blame?" Retief inquired.

"Who else but the perfidious warmongers and provacateurs of GROPE?" Shluh wailed.

"To have agreed GROPE is all talk and no action," Retief reminded the Groaci.

"To now reconsider my earlier position." Shluh groaned. "In light of late developments."

"To mean you agree to load up now and haul your garbage elsewhere?" Retief persisted.

"To see no other choice in the face of such brutality," Shluh whispered. "And now to hurry back to Lady Tish and my waiting bath." He scuttled off toward the yacht.

Retief retrieved the Groaci's forgotten eye shields from the grass. As he dropped them in his pocket, a single sharp report rang out and a gout of turf exploded from the hillside a few yards behind Shluh, who accelerated his pace to a knock-kneed sprint. A second shot scored the ground directly in his path. He nimbly leapt the furrow thus created, and dashed madly for the shelter of the yacht.

"The shots had come from the leading ship. It did not fire again, but ascended abruptly to treetop level and cruised slowly along the length of the garbage heap, turned, and came back. A hundred yards from Retief it settled to the ground.

"Make no further move to escape!" the metallic voice boomed out from the ship. "You and all your minions are my prisoners! I observed your crews hurrying to man their guns, and but now observed your second-in-command rushing for his post, doubtless to convey your 'open fire' order. I suggest you repair at once to your flagship and countermand any such rash instructions. Your fleet, though of formidable bulk, lies under my guns, and exists at my sufferance! Be warned, small creature!"

Retief drew his pistol and assumed a firing-range stance, left fist on hip, right arm, with gun, extended, and took careful aim at the point of the grounded ship's hull which, he knew, indicated the location of the periscope lens. At his shot, a loudly amplified yelp erupted from the ship. At once, gun muzzles depressed until Retief could see several meters into their polished bores. He took out his pocket signaler and punched in the call-code for the ground-car. Moments later, its arrival was signaled by a sudden jump in the direction of aim of the guns. Retief looked behind him. The small, highly polished official vehicle, poised daintily on its fore-and-aft wheels, sat on the ridge, silhouetted against the sky, now turning a soft violet with the onset of twilight. A split second later, gunfire roared out from the valley, and the car seemed to leap straight up, disintegrating at the top of its trajectory. Pieces rained down. A pneumatic wheel fell to the ground at Retief's feet. Landing flat, it rebounded a few inches, and fell back.

"A pity you forced me to destroy your accomplices," the PA voice announced. "But you should not have fired at my ship—though of course your toy weapon caused me no damage. Now, throw it aside and advance, slowly. I will meet you."

As Retief ostentatiously tucked the gun back in his pocket, a second wheel from the car came rolling past him, continued downslope, bounding high as it encountered obstacles in its path. White fire lanced from a secondary turret of the grounded warship, scoring a gouge in the soil a foot to the right of the rolling wheel, which spun on, straight toward the vessel. A second shot missed by a wide margin.

"So—you attempt to take advantage of my good

nature by dispatching missiles at me!" the voice roared out. A third shot blasted rock harmlessly, wide of the mark.

"Wait there!" the PA commanded.

Retief halted, watched as a small personnel hatch opened just aft of the ship's blunt prow. A large and ungainly three-legged creature clambered out, resembling an assemblage of old plumber's pipe and battered sheet metal. Faint clanging sounds came to Retief's ears as the creature descended the curved side of the ship via a series of rungs. It dropped the last few feet, turned, shied as the runaway wheel hurtled past, then started determinedly up toward Retief.

At a distance of ten feet the newcomer still resembled a hasty construction of scrap metal, but Retief recognized the arrangement of plates at the upper end as the visage of All Conqueror of Foes Cheese.

"That's close enough, Cheese," the Terran said.

The Basuran halted, his facial plates meshing restlessly.

"I see your spies have been busy," he said. "Ferreting out my identity."

"Your Excellency is too modest," Retief said. "Everyone on this planet knows by now of All Conqueror of Foes Cheese."

"Remarkable!" Cheese snorted. "But you presume too far, fellow, attempting to order me to halt, as if I were some common Maker of Threatening Gestures, First Class. I shall approach as closely as I desire." He took another step. Retief took the gun from his pocket, fired a blast into the dirt at Cheese's feet, sending a shower of gravel to rattle against the armored shins of the alien, who uttered a raucous cry and backed away.

"That is as close as I desire to come," he stated rather primly, turned and marched back downhill toward his ship. He had gone only a few steps when he stopped, turned, and made a sweeping gesture with a pipelike arm.

"By the way, Admiral, I hereby notify you, just as a

professional courtesy, that you may now consider your fleet and personnel captives of war. Also, this continent is now under Basuran occupation and rule. You may return to your king, or Principal Facemaker, or whatever, and inform him of the new status of affairs."

"Wrong," Retief said. "It's you and your collection of junkers that are prisoners of war."

"What war?" Cheese demanded indignantly. "Insofar as I know, no war has been declared."

"Well, I'll declare," Retief said. "An oversight, no doubt. But ever since you violated Delician space, a state of war has existed between us."

"My, who'd have thought you'd be so touchy? And anyway, this planet was listed as 'uninhabited' in my handbook. But that's the way the egg cracks, eh?" Cheese whirled suddenly and set off at a run toward his ship.

"If you want to claim capture of an AC of F," he called over his shoulder, "you'll have to catch me first."

Retief fired a shot which exploded a small boulder to the right of the fleeing Basuran's line of retreat. The latter shied violently and skidded to a halt.

"Anybody can shoot an AC of F in the back," he said in a shrill voice. "But only a live captive will win you a million green stamps toward a Grand Cordon of the *Légion de Cosme*." He turned and resumed his descent at a more moderate pace.

"I should warn you, I took the precaution of aligning and locking a battery of antipersonnel rifles on you before leaving my ship," Cheese called out. "I have in my hand the remote control unit which will activate them."

Retief took several steps sideways. As he did, a cluster of slim gun barrels projecting from a blister at the prow of the Basuran ship traversed smoothly to follow him. Cheese gave a triumphant cry and pointed, then turned and continued on his way.

A wheel from the destroyed ground-car lay at

Retief's feet. He picked it up, took aim, and sent it rolling downhill after the Basuran, who paused for a moment, with his head cocked as if listening, then proceeded on his way.

"I am not so callow as to be distracted by your ruse," he called. "You make furtive sounds, suggesting that you are creeping up on me from behind, in the hope that I will abort the firing of my armaments, lest I myself be caught in their withering blasts."

"A good point," Retief responded. "All I have to do is stay close to you and your automatics are neutralized." At that moment, fire spouted from the guns, accompanied by a sharp, multiple report which racketed back and forth across the valley. Retief felt the airblast as the covey of projectiles rushed past him to smack the slope behind him and erupt thunderously, sending high a shower of dirt and stones. Cheese turned quickly to observe the effects of his attack. His facial plates slid over each other and came to rest slackly, expressing astonishment as clearly as a dropped jaw and raised eyebrows. "Impossible!" he gasped. "My aim was true, my guns accurate to the millimeter!"

"Right," Retief nodded agreement. "But there's no rule that says I can't duck."

"Perhaps I underestimated the speed of your reflexes, Terran," Cheese concluded. "It seems my intelligence reports, if not my guns, were inaccurate."

"Those, and a few other things," Retief agreed.

The Basuran turned aside to catch up one of the tin-can-sized pellets of compressed grub-husk that littered the meadow. He studied it carefully, turning it over and over; then suddenly he thrust it into an orifice at the base of his short, thick neck. There was a crunching sound, like a pebble being pulverized between heavy gears. Cheese tossed aside the husk of the pellet, from which a large bite was now missing. "Not at all bad," he commented. "I must concede your rations are superior to those issued in the Basuran

Navy." He glanced around at the hundreds of similar cylinders strewn around him. "But I must say your chaps are careless in their handling of such precious cargo."

7

"I've already spoken sharply to them about that," Retief said. The Basuran jumped suddenly aside as the wheel which had been rolling steadily toward him whizzed past, narrowly missing his shins.

"Missed me," Cheese cried, and scooped up a second garbage pellet. As he munched contentedly, the wheel rolled down across the last few yards of open ground and struck the side of his ship with a dull impact. Cheese whirled alertly. "A dud," he exulted, and turned back to face Retief. The wheel, rebounding in a high arc, struck the ground behind Cheese and came rolling swiftly upslope. The Basuran leapt aside— too late. The wheel caught him squarely, full in the back, and sent him sprawling, face-down among the wildflowers and litter.

"Cleverly done," came a faint cry from the background. The spindle-legged figure of Shluh emerged from the shadows in the lee of his mud-splattered yacht. He paused, turned to speak to someone out of sight behind him. "All is well, my dear," he whispered. "It's as I said; the situation is well in hand." A slight figure, even more spindle-legged than Shluh, and otherwise very similar, except for its garb, which consisted of a short, ribless hip cloak, came forth to stand beside him. Fine silver-gray sand was trickling down from the folds in their garments, Retief saw as they came forward.

"My dear Lady Tish," Shluh piped. "To allow me to present a longtime associate, Mr. Retief, of the Corps Diplomatique Terrestrienne, of whom you have doubtless heard me speak, if not flatteringly, at least with feeling." Shluh turned to Retief. "Have I exaggerated the charms of my fair companion?" he inquired rhetorically.

"Confidentially," Retief said quietly, I'll have to admit she's stacked up like a sheet-metal toolshed."

"We sophisticated cosmopolitan beings-of-the-galaxy have much in common, eh, Retief?" Shluh whispered. "In spite of our occasional differences arising from our naturally divergent viewpoints as representatives of competing species."

"Lady Tish," Retief addressed the female Groaci, "to have the honor to present All Conqueror of Foes Cheese, who's here on a little job of fleet-capturing."

"To feel a trifle faint," Lady Tish said, graciously offering a grasping member to the Basuran.

"Charmed," the latter grated, in heavily accented Terran. "What's a nice-looking kid like you doing in the company of this pair of sharpers?"

"See here, Retief," Shluh broke in. "So much for the social amenities. But we have important business outstanding. Now, what about this foolishness of GROPE allegedly trying to throw its weight around by interfering in legitimate Groacian operations?"

"You're surrounded," Retief pointed out. "Better give up."

"Eh?" Shluh barked, eyeing Cheese. "Who is this fellow Cheese, anyway? He, or it, looks to me like one of those feckless Basurans who've eaten themselves out of burrow and home. At my last briefing, they were reported begging us at GROPE for relief. Now it seems this was a mere ruse, to allow you unprincipled Terries to enslave yet another hapless breed and set them to doing your dirty work—in this case manning your illegal vigilante force."

"Wrong, you five-eyed pipsqueak," Cheese cut in harshly. "In the first place we Basurans don't beg, we *take*, and in the second we don't stooge for any bunch of Terries. We operate our own vigilante service. That's how come I caught you and your raiders flatfooted on the ground."

79

"Raiders, indeed!" Shluh hissed. "The vessels of my command with which you have so rashly interfered, to your eventual sorrow, are units of the Groacian Merchant Navy, bound on a peaceful errand."

"Oh, yeah?" Cheese responded airily. "I'll just take a look. Care to go along, cutie?" He offered an arm to Lady Tish, to whom he had addressed the invitation. She took it shyly, and they strolled off toward the nearest barge, stepping over the drifts of overspill from the garbage heap.

"The miscreant comports himself with an arrogance incompatible with his role as supplicant for GROPE alms," Shluh snorted. "And I suggest that now, whilst he's out of earshot, it would be as well if we concluded some agreement between ourselves in consonance with the dignity and integrity of the Groacian state."

"Agreement as to what?" Retief asked.

"As to the precise status of my little convoy of utility vessels, *vis-à-vis* your rather abrupt proposals of few minutes since."

"To make a suggestion," Retief said. "If an alternative dumping-ground was made available to you . . ."

"In that case to willingly make use of it in future," Shluh breathed. "To assume, of course, adequate capacity for the volumes of debris generated by the vigorous Groacian way of life. Hark! to note the approach of the fellow Cheese."

The Basuran, with Lady Tish on his arm, was sauntering toward them from the direction of Shluh's yacht.

"It seems," he called, "my G-2 chaps made a slight error in their identification of the precise nature of your convoy. Instead of war-hulls bristling with armaments, I find empty shells, unequipped even with individual guidance systems—mere stripped hulks. This is rather awkward for me, since I've already alerted High Command of my feat in neutralizing a major enemy force."

"To point out, initially," Shluh said, "that no state of official war has existed between our respective governments, prior, that is, to your audacious meddling here. Secondly, by intruding unbidden within the sacrosanct precincts of units of the Grocian Navy, you offer irremediable provocation."

"Looks like point number two takes care of technicality number one," Cheese responded cheerfully. "So now we're at war, OK, pal?" He paused to pat the hand of Lady Tish. "But that doesn't include you, doll, just these feckless fellows here."

Shluh seized Tish's hand and stalked away.

"If you hurry, maybe you can amend that report before it gets to the top," Retief suggested to the Basuran. "If I know my bureaucrats, this would be a good time for you to do a little emergency career salvage."

"Not to worry," Cheese said airily. "In light of the present logistical situation at home, my capture of a provision convoy and a major supply dump will go far to console High Command for the absence of a captive task force."

"You can make it better than that," Retief said. "Suppose you reported no need to launch and provision an invasion fleet, because you've arranged for delivery to your door of enough imported delicacies to keep Basur eating gourmet style for at least a Galactic year?"

"Ah, the vistas such a coup would open up are bright indeed, Terran. Kindly fill in the details of your capitulation offer. You know how headquarters types love statistics."

"What about a firm commitment of immediate shipments from seventy-nine worlds," Retief proposed.

"Sounds good—but quality has to be up to the standard of this sample." Cheese took another bite from the half-consumed cylinder of compressed gribble-grub husk in his hand and chewed noisily.

"Certainly," Retief assured him.

"But just a minute," Cheese said suspiciously. "What are you asking in return? I seem to recall that you had, by treachery, momentarily gotten the drop on me when your collegue appeared. That means dictating the settlement is your prerogative."

"Just load up your captured goodies and haul keel out of here," Retief said. "Tell your bosses the invasion plans are off—one sneaky move and the relief shipments are cancelled."

"You surprise me, Terry. I didn't anticipate such generosity."

"Just be sure your boys police the area thoroughly before you seal hatches," Retief admonished the Basuran. "And you can call on Admiral Shluh's crews for help loading up."

"Exceptional," Cheese commented. "I see this moment as the beginning of a cordial *entente* between Basur and Terra. A splendid footnote to Galactic history, showing how beings of good will can iron out differences to their mutual benefit—though I confess I feel a bit abashed at having conceded so little in return for your unexampled magnanimity. Are you quite sure your government will sustain you in this *beau geste?*"

"Oh, I think they'll be satisfied," Retief said. "Mr. Magnan might even make Career Ambassador out of it."

8

Back at the office, Retief found Magnan slumped in a chair beside the windows commanding the view across the west lawn.

"Ah, there you are, Retief," the Career Minister sighed. "I've been at sixes and sevens as to just how to extricate myself from this miserable contretemps. As you know, I'm no whiner, but it seems to me Sector has heaped more on my plate than any mere mortal can deal with. Doubtless Director Straphanger will be back on to me at any moment, demanding impossible results. Why, I've no idea what to say to placate him for the moment. And while I wrestled alone here with the Herculean labors assigned me by heedless Sector taskmasters, you absented yourself, doubtless enjoying a halcyon stroll in some sylvan dell.''

"Didn't you notice the invasion?" Retief asked.

Magnan made choking sounds. Miss Taylor, seated across the room, sprang to her feet, an expression of alarm on her pert features.

"Whatever do you *mean?*" she cried. "Invasion?"

"The seven ships must have come directly over this building," Retief said. "Didn't you hear the shooting?"

"Shooting? Heavens!" Magnan yelped. "At whom? And by whom are we invaded?"

"This is no time for grammar," Miss Taylor said sharply. "Who in hell's butting in now to spoil Delicia?"

"All Conqueror of Foes Cheese," Retief said. "You'll recall he gave us fair warning."

"True enough," Magnan sighed. "I suppose we may as well accept the inevitable."

"Certainly," Miss Taylor sighed, "just so all those nasty creatures go away."

"Alas, I see they're already taking an owner's pride in their new acquisition," Magnan remarked, glancing out of the window. Below, a loosely organized line of Basurans and Groaci were moving steadily across the lawn, stooping to pick up each offending scrap of paper or rubbish.

"O-ho!" Magnan cried. "Unless my vision fails me, those are Groaci, working cheek by jowl with the Basurans. I might have known that upstart AC of F Cheese wouldn't have dared such insolence unless with powerful backing." He whirled on Retief. "It's as I suspected from the beginning: Groaci participation in GROPE was a mere gambit to infiltrate the organization and subvert its noble purpose."

At that moment the screen went *ping!* and lit up. The face of Director Straphanger appeared, wearing an expression of grim disapproval.

"Ah, well," Magnan sighed, his narrow shoulders drooping despondently. "As well to put a good face on the matter . . ." He approached the screen, adjusting a look of pleased surprise on his face.

"Why, Mr. Director, how flattering to recive another call so soon," he gushed. "I have matters well in hand, of course, and expect to report a complete solution to the Delician problem very soon. Over-and-out."

"Gracious, Mr. Magnan," Miss Taylor cried. "I'm just positively busting with curiosity. Just how are you going to clear up all our problems here so quick, when Mr. Retief just said now we've got an invasion on top of all that trash out there?"

"Quite simply, my dear," Magnan said. "The Corps rids itself of the Delician problem by ridding itself of the source: Delicia. I intend to recommend that the planet be declared outside the Terran sphere of interest. Let the Basurans have it and welcome!"

"Why, you awful little man!" Anne cried, and swung the heavy leather purse she was holding by its foot-long straps. The bag, bulging with tight-packed contents, caught the slightly built diplomat on the side of the head and sent him reeling back against the desk, at which he grabbed ineffectually before sliding down to sprawl across it.

Retief stepped in and relieved the girl of the bag. Hefting it, he estimated its weight at ten pounds. He thumbed back Magnan's eyelid.

"Slight concussion, maybe," he said. "I don't think I need to return your gun, Anne. You don't need it."

Once again the screen emitted its tone and glowed into life. Barnshingle glared out at Retief.

"Mr. Director," Retief said, "Mr. Magnan hadn't quite finished his status report when he signed off last time. You'll be interested to know . . ." Retief briefly outlined the agreements with Shluh and Cheese.

"Bully for Magnan," Straphanger declared. "I think that clears his docket nicely, and clarifies a number of other matters which had been troubling us here at Sector as well. I think the way is cleared now for the immediate passage of the resolution declaring Delicia a Galactic park." His eyes cut to Magnan's limp form.

"Poor Ben," he rumbled. "Savaged by the Basurans, I assume?"

"Not quite, Mr. Director," Retief said. "You might say he was struck by the wild beauty of the place."

THE TROUBLESHOOTER

"This time, gentlemen, it's full-scale disaster!" Undersecretary Crankhandle pushed back his VIP-model Hip-U-matic conference chair with built-in recording and scrambling equipment, refreshment bar and full-comfort attachment, rose to his full sixty-four inches of well-fleshed height, and directed a complicated glance along the row of tense bureaucratic faces waiting expectantly for details of the rumored disaster which had cast an uneasy pall over CDT Sector HQ all morning.

"Heavens, Retief," Magnan, the Chief of the Groaci Desk, muttered, leaning toward the larger, younger diplomat seated to his left. "It appears matters are more serious even than my usually reliable source had indicated; as you doubtless noted yourself, His Excellency's expression, after beginning as 458-b (Mild Reproof, With Full Cognizance of Extenuating Circumstances), with which he favored Colonel Underknuckle, at the head of the table, modified through a 65-c (Exhausted Patience) to a full 99-x (Incipient Loss of Self-control) by the time the glance reached us, or me, I should say, inasmuch as you were shielded from the full force of the reproof by the interposition of myself."

"I thought his features were writhing a bit, Mr. Magnan," Retief replied. "But I assumed he was merely having an attack of some kind."

"And now," the great man said in a tone like a falling guillotine, while directing what Retief correctly assessed as a 97-d (Justified Fury Held In Check By Sheer

Force of Character) on the luckless Magnan, "if you and Retief are quite finished with your chat, Ben, perhaps I'll be permitted to continue now with this conference."

"Gosh, yes, sir, pray continue, Mr. Secretary," Magnan said in a tone of Eager Congratulation (12-b). "Mr. Retief and I were merely comparing notes on matters relevant to Your Excellency's remarks."

"So far, the only remark I've been able to squeeze in is the simple statement that disaster has struck. Inasmuch as I have not yet specified the precise nature of the disaster, I'm frankly puzzled as to how you're able to speak so glibly of relevance."

"Why, ah, sir, a usually reliable source . . ." Magnan began.

"Bah! No offense to the custodial staff intended, of course, but rumors passed along by the janitor hardly qualify as adequate basis for staff planning!"

"To be sure, sir, but George assured me he got his dope direct from Miss Lynchpin's wastebasket."

"Impressive documentation, indeed," Crankhandle conceded. "Still, inasmuch as I am waiting to announce, officially, the precise information on the ferreting out of which you're expending your ingenuity, why not permit me to get on with it? Unless, of course, this is your method of dramatizing your intention to terminate your career?"

"Why, nothing like that, sir!" Magnan exclaimed. "In fact, I'd imagined my zeal might well produce results of such startling effectiveness that my advancement profile might well be enhanced sufficiently to suggest to the board the propriety of a spot on the upcoming promo list."

"Hey, if it's not too much trouble, Mr. Secretary," a plump-faced man in military uniform interjected hesitantly, "would somebody let us peasants in on what it's all about? A disaster, you say; maybe we ought to be doing something, instead of sitting here jawing."

"Easy, now Fred," the Undersecretary soothed the colonel. "I should have thought that after Ben's disclosure of a shocking security lapse, in the matter of Drusilla Lynchpin's wastebasket, you'd have felt it politic to maintain a low profile for the nonce, security being your personal responsibility."

"Sure, I know all that jazz. But the point is, we got a disaster on our hands; Old Druzies's sloppy disposal habits are old stuff. She'd have been canned long ago if she wouldn't of been so big in the Women's Re-enslavement Movement."

"But to return to the matter of the current disaster," Magnan put in in an ingratiating tone, "if we're faced with the imminent massacre of some unspecified number of Poor Terry Trash out on some frontier world, the name of which escapes me for the moment . . ."

"The threatened planet is none other than Furtheron itself, Magnan," a thin, white-haired, youngish man on the other side of the table said severely. "I'm surprised you could forget a world so important in the annals of peaceful Terran colonization. Furtheron is virtually a showcase example of enlightened Terry colonial practice, being, as it was, a completely uninhabited world to begin with, though of nine-point similarity with Terrestrial standards, thus requiring an absolute minimum of Terraforming, as well as necessitating no thinning out of indigenes, and thus inviting unfortunate commentary by second-generation hindsight."

"Of course, Perry; you've no need to deliver a first-grade lecture on the history of extra-solar colonization," Crankhandle said severely. "Even Ben knows that Furtheron represents all that is dear to the heart of all red blooded Terrans of whatever political stripe; Com-cap and Libreac alike will rise up in righteous wrath when word of this dastardly attack leaks out." Crankhandle fixed a cold secretarial eye on the Information Agency man fidgeting in his hard chair.

"Well, golly," Magnan burst out. "Naturally I know all about the grand story of Furtheron—about the cherry tree and all, and all about the 'one if by rocket and two if by transmitter'; George just didn't happen to mention that part. All he said was about some Poor Terry Trash, like I said."

"Look, fellows," Colonel Underknuckle said in a somewhat forced tone of heartiness as he rose, gathering up pencils and pad. "I got a hot security meeting to chair, so I guess I better shove off."

"You will 'shove off,' as you phrase it, when I so direct, Colonel, and not before," the Undersecretary said in a glacial voice. "And I'm sure you had no conscious intent of sequestering CDT property to Navy use." He stared pointedly at the pencils in the colonel's hand.

"Right, chief," the latter said crisply and resumed his chair, replacing the pencils. "But how would it be if you came right out and said what's cooking out on Further-on?"

"Unlike you military people," Crankhandle said solemnly, "we of the diplomatic service have learned to consider well before committing ourselves to actual speech, a lesson which might go far in enhancing your own growth-potential curve. The locution, 'Your Excellency,' for example, or at least, 'Mr. Secretary,' might have suggested itself for use in direct address to myself in place of 'chief,' a nominative more appropriate to Sitting Bull than to a senior career diplomat, and one, moreover, who will soon be preparing your ER."

"Right on the button, Your Excellency!" Underknuckle said fervently. "By golly, I guess that puts the monkey on *my* back." His expression reflected strain, possibly at the burden of the figurative pithecine. He squirmed in his chair. "Well, seeing as Ben, over on the Groaci desk, seems to be in on this, it's not so hard to deduce the Groaci are at it again," he hazarded. "Trying to grab off our best planet, eh? Why, the lousy sticky-fingered little five-eyed thieves. What say I lay an interdictory strike right on Groac City? Nothing heavy enough to disrupt the planetary crust, of course, just a few old-time nukes to remind 'em where the power is."

"Hot dog!"

"Just what I was going to say!"

"Right on!"

The congratulatory chorus was cut off abruptly by the Undersecretary: "Typical military thinking—not totally inappropriate, perhaps, except for the circumstance that the Groaci, for once, are in no way involved in the Furtheronian crisis."

"Too bad."

"Let 'em have it anyway, just on general principles."

"A megation of prevention . . ."

"Now gentlemen, cool heads must prevail," Crankhandle chided gently. "Though I can understand a certain zeal for chastisement of the Groaci, we must take no action which might lay us open to later charges of immoderation."

"Why not?" Colonel Underknuckle spoke up sharply. "What do we care what some do-gooder muckraking historian says a hundred years from now? A good Groaci is a vaporized Groaci."

"Just so, Fred," Crankhandle conceded soothingly. "Still, we mustn't impair other CDT programs such as galaxywide image-building, in the enthusiasm of the moment."

"Sure—but if it's not the Groaci in the woodpile, who is it?" Underknuckle scratched at his head; the harsh rasping of brittle fingernail against dry scalp made for a show of deep perplexity.

"A group of Basurans, Fred, an element not unknown in the annals of galactic malfeasance."

"Sure—they're the greedyguts that practically ate their home world down to the magma," a tired-looking political officer volunteered.

"Tried to take over a nice piece of ground called Delicia, too," an econ man put in.

They posed a pretty problem for the Galactic Regional Office for Preservation of Ecologies," a round-faced fellow spoke up. "For a time, in fact, we at GROPE were well-nigh at our wits ends, but of course an equitable solution was found; I believe you were instrumental, Magnan." He nodded his congratulations to the latter.

"Of course. But what are they doing now? George didn't mention—"

"Possibly George failed to examine Miss Lynchpin's rubbish so closely as might be desirable if he is to serve as an official channel of staff information," Crankhandle pointed out.

"Ah . . . perhaps. But knowing the Basurans as I do," Magnan hastened to state, "I suspect their voracious appetites are at the bottom of the problem."

"To be sure. They have established a foothold on Continent One, a few miles from the capital, and are openly attacking the inoffensive Terran farmers in the boondocks, while carrying out a massive envelopment of the city itself. They make no bones about the matter; they intend to take the world by force—and to lay it waste as only Basurans can do, ingesting all known forms of matter as nourishment as easily as you and I munch gribble-grubs."

"Urp! Please don't mention gribble-grubs, Your Excellency!" Magnan cried. "Forgive me, but even the thought of them sets my stomach to groaning."

"Forgive me, Ben, we're all aware of the difficult time you had on Groac due to your part in the failure of the Groacian hoob melon crop. Thoughtless of me to remind you."

"All's well that ends," Magnan commented airily.

"You said these Basurans plan to lay Furtheron waste," a narrow-faced chap with an undernourished moustache said uncertainly. "Now, just how do you mean, sir? Do they openly avow an intention to despoil the crops, that sort of thing?" He shuddered.

"Basur now stands, or rather, orbits its sun, as an object lesson in Basuran techniques, Elmer," Crankhandle said gravely. "The planet has been stripped to bedrock, and, in places, deeper. They now propose to apply the same technique to Furtheron."

"Gracious, that's awful!" said a fellow who looked as if his name should be Melvin.

"We've got to stop them!" another bureaucrat asserted.

"What are we waiting for?" a youthful diplomat inquired. "Heavens, they'll strip the entire harvest!"

"Harvest, shmarvest!" a plump man cried. "They'll take the crops, then the topsoil and outbuildings and livestock, and finally, the farmhouses with the farmers' families inside! The planet will be decimated!"

"Not if I get the word to stop them in their tracks!" Colonel Underknuckle stated, rising. He gathered in a fistful of pencils, including Magnan's, but under the stern undersecretarial eye, replaced them and wiped the offending hand on his gold-striped trousers. "Just gimme the word is all," he muttered and gazed at the far corner of the room.

"Go get 'em, Tiger," someone said in the pregnant silence.

"Sure, it's time for a little action," another voice confirmed.

"Those Basurans are asking for it—"

"They can't push Terries around!"

"Gentlemen!" Crankhandle called the group to order. "Let us not lose sight of the fact that this is a diplomatic conference, not a war council!"

"Yeah, but . . ."

"That will be quite enough, Clarence!" the Undersecretary said sharply to the small man who had begun the protest. "My goodness gracious me, we mustn't fall into the error of precipitate action where deliberate conversation is called for."

"Suppose we sum up," a veteran political officer said crisply. "On the one hand we have the Basurans penetrating Terran space, seizing Terran property, and harassing, if not murdering, Terran nationals. On the other hand we have Terra, or the Corps Diplomatique to be specific . . . ah . . . how shall I phrase it . . .?"

"Watching," some suggested.

"Sitting around with its finger up its nose," came another offering.

"'Doing nothing' covers it nicely, I think," Underknuckle said tartly.

"Nothing, Fred?" Crankhandle echoed in tones of Stern, Yet Kindly Reproof (41-c). "We're discussing the matter. I'd hardly call that 'nothing'!"

"Mmmm," the Information Agency man said, steepling his fingers and leaning forward. "Still, it's hardly a technique likely to influence the course of Basuran aggression, Mr. Secretary."

"Best you inhibit your tendency toward truculence, Wally; some hint of immoderation might inadvertently creep into your press releases."

"Truculence, sir? I merely reminded you that the Basurans are not likely to cease their depredations merely on hearing a rumor that we're talking over the problem."

"You think not? Have you no faith in the hallowed axioms of enlightened diplomacy?"

"Nope, not a bit," Wally said flatly.

In the shocked silence, throats were cleared nervously. Wally extracted a toothpick from his shirt pocket and plied it energetically to his rabbity front teeth, surveying the results critically before tucking it away again.

"Well, gentlemen, the floor is open for constructive suggestions," Crankhandle said in tones of Stoic Martyrdom (29-f). "No hot-headed proposals, now, gentlemen. Nothing which you will not be proud to hear discussed by the personnel actions board next promotion season."

"Let's toss it back to the department on Terra," someone proposed brightly.

"How about if we refer the whole file to SCROUNGE?" Clarence put in quickly.

"Indeed, Clarence? You propose this seriously?" Crankhandle said in a tone of Deep Interest, Juniors, for the Encouragement of (238-x), or possibly Ominous Sarcasm (1104-b), Magnan was not sure which. "And in what way, pray, does an alien invasion fall under the aegis of the Special Council for the Rehabilitation and Overhaul of Underdeveloped Nations' General Economies?" Now Magnan was sure it was an 1104, possibly a w (With Hint of Impending Reprimand, Written).

"Well," Clarence said, clearly unaware of the drastic nature of the reproof he had suffered, "we could take the position that we see it as basically a problem arising from an economic crisis back on Basur, see, so if they'd just get the lead out and overhaul the system, the Basurans would stay home and we'd all be pals, right?"

"Wrong," Crankhandle said flatly. "Our error was in failing to establish a being-to-being rapport with these creatures on first contact, some decades ago."

"Sure, you mean when they ambushed one of our survey convoys and wiped 'em out to the last man," the Information Agency man said. "Kind of hard to build a big rapport on a deal like that."

"Hard, yes, but not impossible, Wally," Crankhandle chided gently. "A capable negotiator might have offered official apologies at once, hinting at largesse in the offing."

"You mean a Basuran negotiator?"

"Certainly not! Far be it from me to meddle, even theoretically, in a sovereign state's conduct of its affairs."

"Yeah, but, gosh, what did we have to apologize for? They jumped *us*!"

"To be sure," Crankhandle acknowledged vaguely. "But it might have been a nice gesture to express hope that the survey teams were not unpalatable."

"Retief," Magnan whispered, "we're privileged to hear a master at work. The man has certain irritating mannerisms, perhaps, but what a thinker! Where you, or even I, might have reacted in terms of pique, with a sharp rejoinder, he creates a classic enunciation of the basic diplomatic finesse of oblique sincerity."

"I never understood how oblique sincerity differs from hypocrisy, Mr. Magnan," Retief said.

"Ah, therein lies the subtlety of the technique, Retief. While the opposition is recovering its cool, trying to decide whether we're trying to pull a swifty, as Fred would say, we hit them with massive foreign aid and cultural exchange proposals left and right, and zowie! Before you can say 'Jack Dools,' we're staging a good old-fashioned trade fair in their capital. When the downtrodden peasants get a look at those genuine Japanese cameras, and Hoboken Navajo blankets—we're in!"

"I quite understand, Ben," Crankhandle said gently, "that your apparent contempt for the etiquette of staff meeting is no more than a bid for attention, which in turn suggests that you and Retief have a proposal worthy of our time."

"Why, who, *me?* I mean, Retief? Heck, Mr. Secretary, we were just commenting on your inspiring leadership, and perhaps I got a trifle carried away."

As the assembled diplomats squirmed in empathy with the luckless Magnan, vague thumping sounds were audible in the middle distance, accompanied by a thin screeching, suggestive of sheet metal failing in shear.

"What now?" Crankhandle inquired rhetorically. "Are our august proceedings to be disturbed by tots at play in the hallowed corridors of Sector HQ?"

"Sir, if I might make a suggestion . . ." Magnan said in a frail voice, as all heads turned toward the door beyond which the sounds of a scuffle were audible.

"Indeed, you'd better—" Crankhandle replied.

"I understand, uh, that is, George mentioned that the Basuran Ambassador is visiting HQ just now. Would it not be well to invite His Excellency to participate in our deliberations?"

"I was on the point of designating one of you to hasten to the Basuran legation and extend just such an invitation."

"Gee, sir, sure you were, I just . . . I mean . . ."

"That will do, Ben."

"Uh . . ."

"Sit down," Retief suggested; Magnan sat.

At once, half a dozen eager functionaries were on their feet vying for the honor of running the errand.

"Say, chief, I was just going to the john; on the way I could . . ." a junior vice-consul proposed.

"I need the exercise, boss," Clarence offered.

"On the other hand," the Undersecretary said, his voice cutting through the chatter like an edged weapon, "it had occurred to me that to invite a representative of the invading forces to join a Galactic Utter Top Secret conference regarding measures to be employed to deal with the invasion might be interpreted by the uninitiated as in some way a breach of security, or something. In any event, I have given strict instructions that our deliberations are to be interrupted by no one on whatever pretext. We'll have meals sent in."

"Gosh, boss, how could anybody . . . I mean, I'll go get him on the QT, OK?" This from Perry, a middle-aged, middle-rank bureaucrat still dreaming of top-echelon favor.

"I think, Perry, I made it *quite* clear that whatever comes to pass, no Basuran will be permitted ingress to *my* GUTS priority meeting!"

Crankhandle directed a stern look at the unfortunate, who subsided, mumbling.

"Yeah, but you said . . . and then you said . . ."

"Kindly spare the group any out-of-context quotations, Perry. I am, of course, well aware of my own recent remarks."

"Sure you are, chief. I only meant . . ."

"Sit down," Magnan suggested. Perry subsided.

"And, in case I neglected to point it out, I wish to emphasize that I intensely dislike the appellations 'boss' and 'chief.' You may address me simply as 'Mr. Secretary' or 'Your Excellency'"

"Sure, chief. Whatever you say. I mean, Mr. Secretary."

There was a faint scratching at the door.

"Magnan, kindly attend to that," the Undersecretary said curtly. Magnan hurried to the door and opened it.

"Say, sir, about that Basuran ambassador," a small man with narrow shoulders and a small paunch said brightly. "Maybe I could just scout around the building and round him up."

"It's difficult, Hector, to see just how you could do that without committing an act of gross insubordination, in view of my instructions to the contrary," Crankhandle pronounced.

"Not me, sir, I'd never dream of being insubordinate. Forget it. It was just an idea."

"And a poor one, Hector. However, when the tapes of this meeting are reviewed, I shall attempt to convince Personnel that no actual mutiny was contemplated."

"Gee, that's big of you, sir."

"Is he really here, Mr. Undersecretary?" Magnan inquired.

"'Mr. Secretary' will do, Ben," Crankhandle rebuked gently. "No need to emphasize the prefix 'Under' in that fashion, which you no doubt regard as subtle."

"I only meant . . . I mean I didn't mean . . . I mean . . ."

"Of course, Ben. We all understand." Crankhandle smiled a smile such as a crocodile might have smiled if it had buck teeth, a receding chin, and rimless glasses.

"Maybe I better just go line up this Basuran ambassador, after all," Hector said, edging toward the door. "Hi, George," he said to man lurking there. "Whereat's the Basuran AE and MP?"

"I don't know. Wait'll I check Miss Lynchpin's wastebasket." George hurried away.

"Now, gentlemen, let us assume an appropriate posture, pending the arrival of this upstart Basuran," the Undersecretary proposed in a tone of Benign Command (4-g). "Our unassailable position is that if we have in any way given offense to Basur, or if any action or policy of Terra or of individual Terrans appears in any way in conflict with her legitimate aspirations—"

"How would you define 'legitimate aspirations'?" Perry inquired in his mild tenor.

"Why, traditionally, of course—in dealing with inferiors, anything whatsoever they may choose to do—particularly at our expense—is a legitimate aspiration."

"I get it," the Information Agency man said, smirking. "It's a joke. He's pulling our leg."

"By no means," Crankhandle put in coldly. "If you had any awareness of history, gentlemen, you would recognize this hallowed principle."

"Then . . ." Perry faltered, "whose side are we on?" He frowned at his ashtray, then jabbed his dope-stick out in it.

"Our own," Crankhandle intoned. "The bureaucrat, like the lawyer, is above petty allegiances. But to return to the germane, let us be quite clear in our minds that we have no intention of adopting a reactionary attitude, or indeed, any position which would lay us open to criticism. We shall be above reproach."

"Who are you afraid will criticize us?" asked a youngish fellow recently integrated into CDT from the Terran Civil Service.

"You're new, Harlowe," Crankhandle diagnosed sadly. "Who, indeed? It's traditional with us of the Corps that our posture in all delicate matters must be unassailably correct, punctiliousnesswise."

"Sure, I know all that stuff," the young fellow said. "I was just kind of wondering who in his right mind would criticize us for looking out for ourselves—and why we'd give a hoot if they did. 'Sticks and stones . . .'"

"I appreciate the classic allusion, Harlowe, my lad, but *words*—now, they're a different matter than mere missiles."

"OK, sir, I get it."

"Splendid. But to return to the point at hand: our position is clear, gentlemen. We will not be stampeded into hasty action by Basur, no matter how provocative her attitude might appear to amateurs."

"You mean they've got a clear ticket to do as they

like and we do nothing, eh, chief?" Wally asked rhetorically.

"Succinctly phrased, Wally."

"Gosh, in that case I guess we can all go home," commented a plump Budget-and-Fiscal type.

"Not until we've provided Wally with substantive material for an appropriate despatch to the Agency," Crankhandle corrected. "We mustn't lay ourselves open to charges of inactivity, after all."

"Yeah, chief, but we *are* inactive. You just said . . ."

"Please, Bob, let us avoid elementary semantic errors. I said nothing against carefully thought-out inactivity. It is the *reputation* for inactivity which poses a threat to time-honored diplomatic processes—*and* to the careers of those identified therewith."

"Sure, boss, my boner. Won't happen again." Bob slumped in his chair.

"But we must *do* something!" Colonel Underknuckle said faintly, baring his teeth in what he perhaps thought was a fierce expression. "Even if it's wrong, as it probably will be."

There was a thump at the door.

"What's that?" Crankhandle said sharply, staring at the offending portal.

"That's a thump at the door," Magnan volunteered.

"A thump? I recall hearing of no such species having representation here at Sector, Ben."

"You got X-ray vision or something?" Clarence inquired. He went to the door, opened it a few inches.

"Heck, it ain't no thump, it's George," he said.

"Yes, do come in, George," Crankhandle said, using, as Magnan noted, a full 87-b (Effusive Condescending Cordiality).

"Uh, say, Mr. Crankhandle—I mean, Mr. Undersecretary—" George began, as if embarrassed.

"See, George says it, too," Magnan commented *sotto voce*.

"I mean, well, sir, what I mean is, I got this here Eety wants to see you boys." George stepped back and the door was thrust wide by a creature who gave the appearance of a caricature of a broad-shouldered midget assembled from fragments of smashed ground-cars. He thrust past George into the room with a metallic clanking and squeaking that heightened the illusion.

"Well," Crankhandle gasped, recoiling. He rose to his feet. "Whom, or *what* have we here?"

"I'm I of IU Honk," the intruder announced insouciantly in heavily accented Terran. He took out and lit up an eighteen-inch cylinder of dark-brown vegetable matter, drew on it, and emitted a cloud of dense yellowish smoke that smelled very like a metropolitan rubbish incinerator.

"You're a *what?*" Crankhandle yelped. "What do you mean, fellow, intruding on a top-level diplomatic conference?"

"Modify your tone, fellow. I stated quite clearly, in your own barbarous tongue, that I enjoy the rank of I of IU. Have you no awareness of protocol at all?"

"Enlighten me, Fred," Crankhandle hissed at Colonel Underknuckle. "You're an old hand at equivalent rank and all that. What in the world is an I of IU?"

"That's a Basuran military title," Fred replied. "It means an Intimidator of Insolent Upstarts. Outranks a Maker of Ritual Grimaces, as I recall."

"Well, how does it compare with Space Arm ranks?"

"Oh, somewhere between a lance corporal and a buck general, I'd say, sir."

"Splendid. In that case I outrank him forty ways from Sunday. Heck, I outrank a fleet Admiral, even if I don't get to wear as many medals."

"I suggest, Terries, that you avoid an unfortunate diplomatic incident," Honk said harshly, "by at once according me the honors due my exalted position."

"How about it, Glen?" Crankhandle inquired of his Chief of Protocol. "What are the honors due an Intimidator of Insolent Upstarts?"

"Twenty-three guns would be about right, I should imagine," Glen replied. He had a round well-tanned face with a small moustache, like an antique tailor's dummy, and was never seen without a battered yachting cap placed askew on his boyish hairpiece.

"Eh, guns?" Honk exclaimed. "But I was given to understand—"

"Purely ceremonial, I assure, you my dear Intimidator," Crankhandle hastened to reassure the alien. "By the way, what is it you want?"

"Want? I am here, Terrans, as the personal representative of the Ultimate Ego of Basur. I am fully accredited to the Terran CDT as Ambassador Extraordinary and Minister Plenipotentiary. And whom have I the dubious pleasure of addressing?"

"Why, Mr. Ambassador, you may present your credentials to me. I, as it happens, am Undersecretary for Troublesome Affairs, and surely Terran-Basuran relations fall in that category."

"So. Well, perhaps you'd better show me your ID first. After all, as Basuran Chief of Mission, I don't present credentials to just *any*body. Technically, I should insist on a *tête-à-tête* with your top dog, emperor, chief or whatever. But I'll not bother with that. I'm a most liberal being, especially considering I'm an I of IU and all."

"Most gracious of Your Excellency. By the way, how did you know where to find me?"

"Quite elementary, my dear Terry. A usually reliable source . . ."

"Oh, George," Crankhandle called to the custodial type still hovering just beyond the half-open door, "you wouldn't by any chance be working both sides of the street?"

"Who, me, chief? Heck, maybe this junk-piece slips me a little tip now 'n' again and maybe he don't—after all, I deserve it, just for breathing, you know; like taxi drivers. So if I can maybe give him a little help sometimes, it's no more'n fair."

"To be sure," Crankhandle conceded, "but the question of divided loyalties might arise among the coarseminded."

"Loyalties—not me, sir. I been working around HQ long enough to know which side of my bread substitute's got the icky-wax on it. I look out for Mrs. Smother's boy George; that's a full-time job."

"We'll make a diplomat of you yet, George. I see my confidence in you was not misplaced."

"Sure, that's cool, but how's about a little bump in the old pay envelope, sport. I can't eat compliments."

"It's indeed heartwarming," Crankhandle commented to the staff as he resumed his seat, "to have this opportunity to practice old-fashioned eyeball-to-eyeball diplomacy. I trust all you junior officers will observe closely."

"Skip all that jazz," Honk commanded, pulling out a chair for himself, and motioning its previous occupant aside. "I'm not here to conduct elementary classes for green Terry diplomats. What I want to know is—" he hit the table with a horny fist, causing ashtrays to jump, "what are you planning to do about the outrage out on Furtheron?"

"Why, what a coincidence," Crankhandle twittered. "We were just talking about that—weren't we, fellows?" The great man glanced at his underlings for ritual corroboration.

"Right, sir!"

"You betcha, chief!"

"Sure, but—" this comment from young Harlowe, "I mean," he floundered on, "what we decided— that is *you* decided Mr. Secretary— is, uh, we'd do nothing—just like we're doing now."

"*Au contraire*, my boy," Crankhandle chided gently. "We agreed that talk would handle the matter—"

"One moment!" Honk cut in. "Am I to understand you propose to employ brute conversation to attempt to bludgeon a deserving emergent race into submission?"

"Perish the thought, my dear Intimidator. I merely meant—"

"Have a care, fellow! Have you considered the impact upon Galactic Public Opinion of cavalier treatment of an underprivileged people such as mine? Besides, you can't get away with trying to brush aside proud Basur."

"Talk about working both sides of the street," George commented. "One second he comes on like a poor little fella that's being picked on—next he's the big tough guy that nobody better step on his shadow."

"Umm, agile," a fat bureaucrat murmured admiringly. "But just watch Cranky. He's known for her verbal footwork, you know."

"Calmly, please, my dear Intimidator," Crankhandle urged. "Let us not leap to unfortunate conclusions prematurely."

"You imply," Honk said, "that later on, unfortunate conclusions will be in order."

"Surely; later. Much later."

"Time, sir, is of the essence!" Honk yelled. "At this moment, Basuran nationals are suffering hardship, danger and privation! This is an intolerable situation! I demand prompt and effective action on your part to relieve this terrible injustice!"

"Why—ah, I'm not sure . . ." Crankhandle stammered. "Just what situation is it to which you refer? And in what way am I obligated to take action?"

"What situation? Surely you jest! Over five hundred thousand Basuran nationals are at present suffering grievous hardships on a raw frontier world. And you, representative of bloated Terra, are by your own arrogant admissions, doing nothing whatever to relieve them!"

"Yes, but . . ." Crankhandle stammered, "after all, they're *your* troops; nobody asked them to come trampling down the crops of the noble Terran pioneers on Furtheron! They could all go home!"

"What is this talk of troops? These deserving Basurans are tourists, innocent, fun-loving bird- and wildlife-watchers, seekers after scenes of natural grandeur such as ripe crops, gold mines and shops stuffed with consumer goods. We Basurans are consumers of unparalleled virtuosity. As for returning home prematurely, as you so callously propose, what would they eat, pray tell? We are at present undergoing a severe famine on Basur. It's time, sir, that you faced up to realities. These personnel are suffering! Something must be done! At once!"

"Well, uh, this is just an observation, mind you, but after all, you weren't actually invited to come to Furtheron. And it's actually rather cheeky of you to hint that you Basurans are in fact not troops. They've already overrun half the planet."

"But, my dear Terry, they are unarmed, defenseless. To describe them as troops, surely it will be necessary for you to establish that they bear arms—which, as I said, they do not."

"A fine point, Mr. Ambassador; one over which our Deep Think teams can mull for weeks, I suppose. But troops or tourists, their presence on Furtheron surely constitutes trespass on Terran-owned soil. Certainly you'll not dispute this point?"

"As is obvious to any unbiased observer, the world Bliff, which you perversely refer to as Furtheron, comes well within the sphere of Basuran manifest destiny, lying as it does inside the natural sphere of Basuran aspiration."

"Indeed, sir? How so? The Furtheronian sun is well over five lights distant from your own."

"Statistics! Bah! The planet's very name bespeaks its ancient place in the Basuran mythos, 'Bliff' being a contraction of 'Bomourlerfoof,' which in the mellifluous Basuran tongue means 'admirable member of the horny one.' Even in ancient times, as primitive Basuran rock-gatherers lay around while the foreman wasn't looking, and studied the lights in the sky, they gazed in awe and envy on this stellar superstud, dreaming of future conquests."

"Aha! You let it slip then! Conquests, precisely," Crankhandle exclaimed happily.

"They were thinking of another sort of conquest, entirely."

"Then they'd best stick to skirt-chasing and leave Terran-owned worlds alone."

"Is this your reply to a cry of need? I suspect that the galactic press will give this outrage wide coverage. Coverage that will reveal you Terries as the heartless exploiters you actually are!"

"Exploiters? That is hardly the appropriate word, Mr. Ambassador. Terra has in no way exploited you Basurans. *Au contraire,* you have invaded and laid waste a world long and peacefully settled by honest Terran pioneers."

"Bah! Over one hundred thousand persons are now marooned on a hostile planet without adequate food, supplies, or equipment, and you have the audacity to openly state that you intend to give them no assistance whatever. Incredible!"

"What's incredible is that you seem to actually expect us to maintain your invading armies as though they were a group of harmless picnickers in distress!"

"Mere semantics, sir!" the Basuran stated hotly. "People are suffering while you prolong this discussion! I demand immediate action!"

"Look here," Crankhandle said, "since you Basurans are able to subsist on raw minerals, how is it your people are suffering from hunger? Eh?"

"As to that, while it is true that the superior Basuran metabolism can make do with elemental substances in emergency, we far prefer correctly prepared meats and vegetables—which you willfully withhold from us."

"So. We're not only expected to support your invading armies, but to support them in luxury, eh? Remarkable!"

Honk got to his feet. "Your cynicism does you no credit, sir! I came here in all sincerity to plead for help for my deserving countrymen. But instead of the assistance which you could so easily have granted from your vast resources—instead of help, I say, you offer nothing but harsh rejection! It's apparent that the fate of some thousands of Basuran citizens is nothing to you. Good day, sir! You may be assured I shall report this matter to the press in full!"

"One moment, sir!" Crankhandle called heartily. "Pray leap to no hasty conclusion! My staff and I are even now planning appropriate action!"

"Planning, indeed!" Honk snorted. "As if the correct measures to relieve this disgraceful situation constituted a great technical mystery! The proper course is quite obvious! And I shall expect prompt and effective action. And now, good day to you sir!" The Basuran turned and strode from the room, slamming the door behind him.

"Uncouth," Magnan commented.

"Heavens," a slender econ man murmured. "If he speaks to the press . . .'

"We must take the initiative!" Crankhandle stated firmly. "Ben!" He fixed his gaze at Magnan. "Go after him; make sure he leaves. If you can't manage it, keep the media chaps away from him, and later on this evening bring him around to my apartment. I'll regale him with hearty anecdotes, feed him some bonded spirits, give him the feeling he's moving in high circles. I'll dazzle him with true Terran hospitality: he'll be so overwhelmed that all thought of mischief-making will be forgotten."

"Good thinking, sir!"

"Right on, chief!"

"It can't miss!"

Crankhandle waved away the chorus of congratulations. Magnan, blushing slightly at the honor thrust upon him, hurried in pursuit of Honk.

"I'm just dreadfully sorry, Mr. Secretary," Magnan stammered some hours later, standing at the half-open door of the Crankhandle apartment, from which the sounds of bibulous merriment came. "I invited him, I *urged* him to come, but no—he was off to the port, where, he insisted, a fast scouting vessel waited to whisk him back to Furtheron."

106

"What was so urgent about getting back there?" Crankhandle demanded, taking a sip of the tall drink in his hand. "I'd invite you in for a drink and a bite, in spite of your modest rank, Ben," he said, "except that I'm sure a career man of your dedication wouldn't dream of drinking while an important assigned mission remained uncompleted."

"You mean—" Magnan cried. "You mean I don't get to take a snort until that Basuran barbarian shows up for your shindig?"

"You ignore my question, Ben. Why did His Excellency find it vital to return to the bleak outpost world, Furtheron, with such precipitate haste?" The Undersecretary sipped again. "And the scene of warfare, at that," he added. "Seems the sort of place an experienced diplomat would avoid as a plague . . ."

"Oh, didn't you know, sir?" Magnan shuffled his feet awkwardly, eyeing the tall glass in Crankhandle's hand. "Intimidator Honk is in supreme military command at Furtheron. The whole invasion was his idea, actually; his military career is at stake. And in view of what he termed the regrettable absence of Terran cooperation in the realization of Basuran destiny, it's essential that he be at hand to personally direct operations."

"Oh, quite understandable; had I known, I'd of course have placed suitable transportation at His Excellency's disposal. I shouldn't like to be instrumental in the destruction of a promising career."

"Sure not, sir. But it's OK. He's got his own scoutboat that we refueled and supplied while he was at HQ to negotiate a victory."

"Ah, yes; as to that, much as I regret the necessity for being instrumental in denying a fellow diplomat the laurels of a successful negotiation, I was unwilling to give Honk that triumph at the expense, not only of my own professional reputation, but of Terran interests in general. I hope you understand, Ben. It was not because of any lack of consideration for a colleague that I did not join with Ambassador Honk in condemning Terran policy on Furtheron. Here, hold this; but don't drink any." Crankhandle thrust his glass at Magnan, and turned back into the crowded room.

"Why, sir, I wouldn't think of it . . ." Magnan sniffed the glass cautiously and peered after the Undersecretary as the latter circulated among his guests. While the great man's back was turned, Magnan slipped quickly into the room, put the glass on the bar, and spiked it with several ounces of gin; then he selected a prepared cocktail for himself, took it down in one gulp and turned toward the door, ditching his empty glass on a messy end table.

"Ah there, Ben," Crankhandle's unctuous voice caught him in mid-escape. "How nice of you to drop by. By the way I don't suppose you've seen anything of that Basuran upstart?"

"Who, me, sir? I mean, I? That is, ah, as a matter of fact I saw him at the port."

"At the port? I suppose the rascal is attempting to steal away with our, that is, my rightful demands unanswered; you didn't let him slip away, by chance?"

"Actually . . ."

Crankhandle held up a hand. "Too bad. No telling what sort of mischief he might get into now that he's at large again. But at least we've kept his visit here secret."

"Hey, Cranky!" A plump man with bleary eyes and his tie askew called cheerfully from across the room. "Where's that Basuran warlord-cum-peacemaker we've been looking forward to meeting?"

"Alas, His Excellency couldn't make it," the Undersecretary said sadly. He turned to Magnan. "Get me a drink, Ben," he commanded, frowning. Magnan handed him the spiked drink.

"Look here," said a small lean woman with a tight hairdo and a thin, pointed nose, thrusting her way through the throng surrounding the Undersecretary. "We, that is to say, I'm president of the Aroused Citizenry for Halting Expansionism. Now, what we at ACHE demand is that an end be put at once to this

disgraceful planet-grabbing, like out of Furtheron."
She placed her knobby fists on her lean hips and stared
challengingly at Undersecretary Crankhandle.

"A commendable program, madam," he said
smoothly. "Unhappily, the planet-grabbing is being
done by another species, not by us; thus we find it
difficult to terminate the outrage as briskly as desirable."

"I ain't no madam, you!" the lady interjected
sharply. "You just keep a civil tongue in your head!"

"Now, Clementia," a small, timid-looking man said
behind her. "I'm sure Mr. Crankhandle didn't mean
anything derogatory. He was just talking diplomatese."

"Don't you try to butter me up, Henry!" she replied,
whirling on the little man. "I guess I know when I been
insulted! A madam is a female that runs one of them
sporting goods houses or whatever they call 'em!"

"Be assured, my good woman," Crankhandle
soothed, "that I could never for an instant envision you
in such a context."

"Oh, you couldn't eh?" the lady retorted, shifting
her weight to one foot, and thrusting out a hip. "What
have them hussies got that I ain't got?"

"It isn't what you've got, it's how it's organized," an
anonymous voice volunteered from the crowd of
interested bystanders. "Cool down, Clemmie; let's
hear the excuses this tool of the power structure's trying
to make."

"Yeah, let him hang himself!" another voice proposed.

"OK, what about it?" Clemmie demanded. "Just
what *is* your excuse?"

"For what?" Crankhandle inquired coolly. "And to
whom?"

"To meem. For what's going on out on Furtheron."

"Precisely what, in your view, *is* going on out on
Furtheron?"

"You know. Oppressing the downtrodden, and all
that jazz. Like the Establishment's always doing."

"The downtrodden on Furtheron are the Terran

population, mostly third- or fourth-generation Furtheronians. They are being downtrodden by the Basurans, due, I regret to say, to our failure to allow the latter to die a natural death some years ago when they had destroyed their own habitat.''

"Listen! You all heard that!" Clemmie whirled to confront the company. "Listen how casual he talks about germicide, or whatever they call it when a whole bunch of foreigners gets kilt all at once!" She turned to stare accusingly at the embarrassed bureaucrat, who held up his hands as if warding off a barrage of vegetables.

"Dear me, ma'am. I hardly think you have a correct grasp of the contretemps with which we're faced on our far-flung frontier!"

"Far as I'm concerned, it's been flung too far already. We ought to pull them Terry colonists back outta every place they've went and got inta!"

"That's hardly a practical proposal, ma'am, in view of the fact that a vast armada of immense transport vessels would be required, none of which are in existence, to say nothing of the logistical problems incident to such an enterprise, plus, of course, the circumstance that Terra is already in grave difficulty in attempting to accommodate the indigenous eight billions of population, and has absolutely no space in which to house the refugee inhabitants of half a hundred overcrowded worlds."

"Hah! Alibis! Folks got rights, you know!"

"Just which folks' rights are you now defending, Clemmie?"

"Why, them poor colonists which they went and believed a bunch of government promises and upped stakes and went out there to carve homes outta the wilderness. And now you act like we got no room to welcome 'em back home again. Some gratitude!"

"Hmm; it appears you've inadvertently changed sides, Clemmie. A moment ago you were characterizing these same deserving colonists as exploiters and downtreaders."

"Hah! I guess I know what side I'm on—the side of right and decency is where I stand!"

"To be sure. Isn't it a pity we sometimes have such difficulty in determining just where niceness and goodness are to be found."

"I don't have no difficulty, buster! Maybe you just put your finger on what's wrong with you big government men."

"Perhaps, Clemmie, you'd be kind enough to advise me just how you'd resolve the Furtheronian dilemma?"

"I ain't here to do your dirty work for you! You figger it out yourself!"

"Suppose then, that in order to secure the rights of the colonists whom you so spiritedly defended a moment ago, we should take positive steps of a military nature ensuring their freedom from molestation by any outside group such as the Basurans?"

"There you go! Talking doubletalk about starting up a war like you was planning a tea party!"

"I take it, then, that you feel we should stand by and see these people dispossessed of their wordly goods."

"Listen at him, trying to weasel out of sticking up for our own folks out there on that Furtheron place!"

Crankhandle turned sadly to Magnan. "You see, Ben, what we're up against. Damned if we do and damned if we don't."

"You lay off that there cursing and taking His name in vain in front of a lady!" Clemmie cautioned shrilly.

"Awkward indeed, sir," Magnan acknowledged. "What shall we do?"

"It's time for stern measures. I feel I must act personally now."

"You, sir? Personally?" Magnan gasped.

"Quite right. I'm always ready to take my place in the firing line. So I'm going to personally appoint a legman to go out there and look the situation over."

"Oh, praiseworthy, sir! Ah, whom, may I ask, will be honored with this assignment? I'd volunteer in a second, of course, but my bunions have been acting up lately."

"I wouldn't think of taking you away from your substantive duties, Ben, as liaison man with the Interplanetary Tribunal for Curtailment of Hostilities."

"Oh, good—that is, I mean, whatever is for the good of the cause, sir."

"What about that fellow, tallish chap, I recall you've been associated with him in a number of somewhat unconventional affairs . . . can't place his name . . ."

"You may be thinking of Retief, sir. Excellent choice. As you so perceptively pointed out, his methods, though sometimes outside the realm of the strictly conventional, have at times proven effective."

"Umm. don't see what he can do this time; frankly, I'd say it's hopeless. The planet's been overrun and already largely stripped by the beggars. But at least he can go out and put a good face on it for the invadees, so that we don't find ourselves faced with a delegation of survivors demanding compensation on the flimsy grounds that the Corps should have seen out a flotilla of Peace Enforcers to run the Basurans back home even faster than they arrived."

"Yes, indeed, sir. Shall I tell him?"

"Why not? We can't keep it from him forever."

"Oh, there you are, Retief," Magnan caroled as he caught sight of the junior officer among a crowd emerging from the personnel gate to the port. Retief made his way to Magnan's side.

"Yes, here I am," he confirmed. "What brings you out in the bracing morning smog, Mr. Magnan?"

"Why, I happened to be chatting with the Undersecretary last evening," Magnan replied, "and he mentioned—that is, he empowered me, or ordered me, or requested me, almost politely, actually—but why are you here, Retief?"

"It occurred to me that Cranky might have a sudden attack of common sense and decide to send a working party out to Furtheron to look over the ground at close range. So it seemed like a good idea to slip five to the maintenance chief for a quick look at Honk's little one-man dreadnought."

"Ah, indeed? And did you, in fact, inspect the vessel? And why?"

"I thought it would be advisable for our inspection team to get there before the enemy commander-in-chief arrives to muddy the waters; and if we're going to be chasing him, it will help to know what kind of drive and firepower he's sitting on."

"My idea exactly," Magnan said, nodding. "But, alas, I see the boat's already lifted." He gazed sadly at the spot where Honk's compact craft had been parked, now empty except for a litter of candy-bar wrappers and dope-stick butts.

"It's OK, I got here early," Retief consoled him. "Nice little job, Bogan-built, packs Hellbores fore and aft, and a class Y power plant."

"Heavens! Aren't our medium cruisers powered by class Y units?" Magnan looked shocked.

"Right. If his space-hull doesn't fall apart, he'll set a new record getting out there."

"Then we have no chance of preceding him. Pity." Magnan looked sad.

"We might," Retief said. He took from his pocket a small metal cylinder and tossed it up and caught it. "While I was looking at the emergency boost gear," he said casually, "the auxiliary converter solenoid sort of jumped out and landed in my pocket."

"Gracious!" Magnan said. "Won't that prove awkward for Ambassador Honk when he tries to shift into hyperdrive?"

"Yep. It won't shift; he'll have to limp along at about nine-tenths light."

"How curious," Magnan mused. "I wonder how on earth it happened to fall into your pocket . . ."

"Confidentially, I helped it a little. Not much. Just had to remove a small cover plate and two quarter-inch blivets."

"Retief! You wouldn't—but on reflection, I suppose

you would." Magnan stared out across the acres of concrete as if he expected to see Honk's semi-disabled craft hovering there. "What do you propose to do next?"

"I thought I'd wait around until the delegation for Furtheron makes the scene, and brief 'em on the status."

"Yes; as to that, it happens, Retief, by a curious coincidence, that I hastened here this morning in the hope of seeing you, in order to inform you that after serious consideration, Secretary Crankhandle has decided to entrust you with the very mission about which you speculated."

"It figures," Retief commented. "How did I luck into the job of troubleshooter?"

"Why it was simply fortunate that your name cropped up just as His Excellency was considering the matter."

"In that case, I'd better be getting started."

"Yes, indeed. After all, Honk may be carrying a spare solenoid."

"He had a couple, but unfortunately they fell down the disposal chute."

"Yes, I suppose that was to be expected. Well, good luck, Retief. I can't imagine what you can do to salvage the situation—and Crankhandle's career, to say nothing of your own—but I'm sure you'll do your best."

"I'll try to think of something," Retief said.

Aboard the fast one-man Navy scout-boat which Retief had requisitioned from an astonished clerical type as soon as the latter regained consciousness after demanding nine different notarized forms dated a minimum of two weeks prior to the current date, an alarm bell sounded stridently. Retief laid aside the June 1931 *Astounding* he had been reading, and switched on the PV screen. The sleek form of a standard Bogan number nine hull appeared there on a roughly parallel course. The readout panel indicated that the vessel was

114

at a distance of one hundred twelve miles, and proceeding at a velocity of nine-tenths light. Retief keyed his communicator.

"Ahoy, *The Ripsnark*," he hailed, reading the name from the vessel's prow. "Is I of IU Honk aboard?"

"I'd look pretty dumb if I'd sent it off on auto while I hung around the port until that pest Magnan came back and resumed bugging me about attending some sort of tribal powwow, wouldn't I," the alien's harsh voice responded. "Who are you and why?"

"I'm Third Secretary Retief of the Terran CDT. As for why, I haven't figured that one out yet."

"The CDT. That's the organization mentioned by that objectionable chap, Chief Troublemaker Crankhandle, or something of the sort. *N'est-ce pas?*"

"Correct, Mr. Ambassador. It was the Troublemaker himself who sent me out this way."

"Curious coincidence that you should be here at this remote point at the same moment as myself."

"Not quite. I locked my guidance system to your emission trail."

"Whatever for? If you simply wished to hobnob with the great, you could have done it much more easily back on Terra—if I were granting interviews to nobodies, that is."

"Too late now; I'll just wait and catch you on Bliff."

"Capital notion. I've been casting about for someone from whom to accept articles of capitulation."

"Strange; that sounds almost as if we were at war."

"Of course we are; or we would be if you Terries had the gumption of a sand-bub."

"Didn't you say the Basurans on Bliff are just harmless tourists?"

"Certainly. It's quite natural that I would say anything whatever which might promote Basuran interests at the expense of bloated Terra. The astonishing thing is that those poor Terries seem to accept this nonsense as gospel."

"Not all of them, Honk."

"Well, no matter. In another few planetary cycles the matter will be purely academic, as I expect to wind up this operation at once."

"What will you do when you arrive at Bliff?"

"You expect me to divulge military secrets to a casual passerby? You must think I'm a Terry diplomat."

"Never mind. I have an idea your plans are about to change."

"Impossible! When a Basuran I of IU makes a plan, that plan is carried out!"

"Suppose unforeseen circumstances arise?"

"You imply that a circumstance could exist which my exalted intellect has failed to foresee?"

"No offense intended. By the way, I'll race you to Bliff."

"Rash Terry! But of course you have no way of knowing that my personal vessel is equipped with triple-gain boosters plus full scat gear. It would indeed be a pathetic effort on your part should you actually attempt to pass me."

"In that case, let's keep the stakes modest. How about a case of Bacchus red against a square inch of your hide?"

"As it happens, poor fool, I'm particularly partial to the red Bacchus; accordingly, I'll overlook the insolence of your frivolous personal reference."

"Is it a bet, Honk?"

"Done, Terry. Seals intact, of course; vintage of '61, or any odd-numbered year in the fifties."

"Good choice. Too bad you won't get a chance to sample it."

"Stand clear, Retief! I'm engaging my booster."

"Better check your idiot lights first."

"Whatever for? Are you unaware that a Basuran I of IU is incapable of error, oversight, overconfidence or misjudgment?"

"Is that why you're backing up?" Retief inquired as he engaged his overdrive.

"Hah! Very clever optical illusion, Retief! If I were not a superlative genius, even by lofty Basuran standards, I'd imagine that I had in some way goofed, as your rickety boat appears (quite falsely, of course) to be overhauling me."

"Overhauling is what your tub needs, Honk. It seems to be wallowing along at about .89 light."

"Most curious. And simultaneous malfunctions of my instruments, as well, which appear to be indicating grossly substandard performance."

"So long, Honk, I'll see you at Bliff."

Within moments, the Basuran's vessel had dwindled to a tiny blip astern; then it winked out. Retief poured himself a glass of wine and settled down in an easy chair with his Astounding. Some hours later, the autopilot informed Retief that it was initiating deceleration prior to entering braking orbit around Furtheron. He thanked it and removed a *filet mignon avec pommes frites* from the autochef. By the time he had finished his baked alaska and dry sack, the boat was skimming the planetary atmosphere, which it then entered with only mild buffeting.

"Altering course to enter traffic pattern for landfall," the autopilot said. "ETA plus thirty-one minutes, ten seconds."

Retief took a shower, dressed in an utterly informal black late-afternoon coverall. He took a Mark IV power pistol from a drawer and clipped it into his built-in rib holster. Then he instructed the autopilot to open communications with Traffic Control. A pale, flustered face appeared on the talkie screen, blinking as if dazzled by a sudden light.

"Yes, yes, CDT four-oh-one," it said in a voice that was all ready to get irritable. "I track you five-by-five. I can offer you temporary dockage in area seventy-nine. That's a no-service area, of course. It will just be for a week or two; then I can move you into twenty-five. That's a covered area and includes class-three service. Of course we're quoting an average seven-hour delay in all classes below two for the duration of the emergency. I trust you're familiar with the emergency? Goodness gracious, some people must bury their heads in the sand—I mean, after all, dropping here unannounced and expecting all sorts of special privileges . . . Heavens! It's enough to make one wonder."

"Don't pop a gusset, junior," Retief suggested mildly. "You'll find I filed a flight plan twenty-eight hours ago, and I have the acknowledgement in my hand. And I dock in slot one, area one, and I'll be needing full class-one service, on a no-delay. Better set that up fast; I'm going into communications shadow in a few seconds."

"Well, what nerve! It just so happens, Mister Smarty, that I'm holding slot one-one for an offworld VIP who's already two minutes overdue!"

"Forget it. Your VIP will be along later in the week. You can find a spot for him in area seventy-nine, maybe."

"Well, I'd like to know just who you think you are!"

"If you did your job, buster, you'd know. I'm here on official business, with a double-U priority, not just a tourist hoping to have a chat with you."

"So you say, Mister Smarty. Would you have a name?"

"That reminds me; I'd better have your ID. My name isn't important. You can look it up on the flight plan you should have reviewed when you came to work. But I'll give you an authentication number that will take care of all your problems."

"Why, gracious," the clerk said, and pushed a button before him. A strip of paper chattered from a slot on Retief's panel. On it were printed the clerk's name, and a full set of ID data. "Why didn't you say you were an official of the CDT? Gosh, excuse me, sir. I was just trying—that is, after all, it *is* my job to see that important people get good service, and of course, I can't allow my facilities to become clogged with ordinary run-of-the-mill traffic. Why, just suppose a really big man showed up and I was unable to accommodate him in appropriate fashion?"

"Horrifying idea," Retief agreed. "I'll be in your local pattern in forty-one seconds."

"Certainly, sir. I'll have slot one-one all ready for you. Hawkins is the name, sir, but of course you have my ID."

Retief dropped the strip of paper into the disposal slot. "I'll be needing rapid transport into the city, Hawkins," he said. "Don't bother about the mink upholstery. And gold door handles won't be necessary. And I'll be needing quarters for a couple of days."

"Why, gee whiz, sir, I'll see to it at once." The screen went dark.

"Well, what do you think?" Retief said to the autopilot. "Will Mr. Hawkins hit it off with Intimidator of Insolent Upstarts Honk?"

"If Honk lives up to his title," the mechanical voice replied, "I suspect that Mr. Hawkins is about to be intimidated."

When Retief left his boat and stepped out onto the carpet flooring the VIP arrival bay, a short, stout man in a plain puce executive coverall stepped forward.

"Welcome to Parkiteer City, Mr. Retief," he said breathlessly. "Of course we . . . the Furtheronian government, that is to say . . . I'm Chief Executive Burrsaddle—have been looking forward to some home-world action in this, our time of trial. But frankly, we were hoping for a modest flotilla of Peace Enforcers, rather than a lone bureaucrat. You see, the Basuran Warlord, a ferocious fellow named Honk, seems un-amenable to verbal dissuasion, but is intent on actual conquest and plenty of negotiable loot. Understanda-ble, actually. There's nothing we Furtheronians can do to stop his voracious hordes; our Do-Gooder party was able to outlaw any form of military or defense estab-lishment back when we were getting under way—but of course a single Corps PE could dictate terms to the scoundrels, whip them back to their kennels in short order. Can you offer any hope, sir, that such punitive measures are in fact contemplated by Terra?"

"Sorry, Mr. Chief Executive," Retief said. "All you get is one diplomat; but I'll do the best I can."

"No doubt. And now I suppose you'd like to come

along and take part in the impressive ceremonial welcome I've laid on—"

"I'd prefer to get busy."

"But I've already hired two thousand enthusiastic spectators to line the procession's route of march; and what about all the automatic confetti dispensers I've leased?"

"Save them for the victory parade."

"Hah! You jest. I have no intention of celebrating the Basuran takeover."

"I was thinking of a Furtheronian victory."

"A subtler jest, but still out of place. But as you suggest, we're wasting time. You'll want to see our new Executive Building, the various ministries, and so on. We've still time before tiffin if we hurry along."

"I'm not an institutional-architecture fan," Retief demurred. "I'd like to get a quick look at the occupied areas, and maybe spend some time at the front lines, to see how these Basurans operate."

"They're like army ants, except for more thorough. They begin, of course, with the organic matter, both animal and vegetable. They seem to prefer dense wood. Our forests no longer exist. Pity. We had a mutated variety of bluewood. Useful as a dyewood, as well as for furniture. Very hard, very dense; from pale azure to deep indigo. The striped was most sought after; one of our best export items.

"After clearing all growth, and consuming all animals they're able to trap and kill, including humans, they start in on the topsoil; all produced by bacterial action plus mechanical pulverization and chemical additives, you know. They devoured our soil down to bedrock. The granite discourages them. Then on to infest another ten miles along the front, which is now an arc some fifteen hundred miles in length. Bare rock behind it."

"Sounds pretty drastic. I'd like to see it."

"It's not that interesting, actually. Scoured rock, ending at the working face where the devils are swarming, busy as termites. Understand they've com-

120

pletely stripped their own world. Even attacked the basalt crust."

"I'd like to see it, anyway."

"The nearest point is about twenty miles away now; advances at a rate of ten miles every twenty-one hours."

A fast government ground-car whisked Retief and the presidential party to the city, where Retief saw a typically Terran colonial town, more Terran than Terra. High in a wire-and-glass tower, Chief Executive Burr-saddle showed him a wall map representing the planet's principal, wedge-shaped continent, over half of it blacked out to represent the invaders' depredations.

"Difficult to say how we could recover from such a blow, even if the Basurans were to depart instantly," the official pointed out. "Several thousands of square miles of a desert more featureless than one can well imagine."

"Instead of imagining, how about a fast heli, so I can see for myself?"

"Since you seem so determined, I'll arrange it at once. Though a number of hostesses who've laid on receptions will be disappointed."

"Sorry about that," Retief said. "But I'll be happy to drink a cup of tea after I've done what I can about this." He indicated the map.

Minutes later, he was speeding eastward toward the nearest point of the Basuran line of advance. Below, rolling green hills, forests and tilled farms made a pleasant pattern. Far ahead, clouds of gray dust rolled across the landscape, obscuring the ground.

"We're coming up on it now," the pilot said. "I got to grab me some altitude, 'count of the dust. Them beggars raise dust something fierce, 'bout this same time every morning."

Now, Retief could see below the curved line of demarcation where the green land gave way to smooth gray rock. There was an orderly array of tilled and fenced fields just beneath the heli, ending abruptly where the great curve cut across them. A small river poured glistening water over the edge; it spread out in a wide black puddle. There was a cluster of white-painted buildings near the line.

"Land there, Fred," Retief directed the pilot. The little craft settled gently in a fenced farmyard where chickens wandered aimlessly. There was a large frame farmhouse on one side, a capacious barn on the other. A screen door opened on the back porch and a tall, suntanned man in work clothes stepped out, looking curiously toward the new arrival. Retief stepped down and went to meet him.

"Howdy," the farmer called. "Come on in out of the heat and have a cold beer. I'm Henry Suggs."

Retief shook the man's calloused hand. "I'm Retief of the CDT," he said. "I'd appreciate it if you'd tell me about this situation as it looks from two hundred yards."

"More like a hundred," Suggs said. "And getting closer every day. Took the east forty yesterday, and looks like my woodlot's next. Nice to see the guv'mint taking some notice. So far all I've had is evacuation notices. Not likely! My great granpa seeded bare rock with bacteria on this spot a hundred years ago come next tater-digging time—if we've got any taters to dig then. Granpa built the house and barn—hand-sawed evry board. Pop imported the furniture and fixtures. I don't figger to be the one runs off and lets the rock termites have it."

A plump, ruddy-faced woman came through the door, wiping her hands on a spotted apron.

"Henry! Whereat's your manners?" she said mildly. "Invite this gentleman in for dinner. Just took the roast outen the oven."

"I can smell it," Retief said. "I accept."

Sitting at the table with the Suggs family, consisting of Mr. and Mrs. Suggs and four sturdy children ranging from infancy to adolescence, Retief ate heartily and heard the details of the way in which the rumors of approaching disaster had been followed by the disaster itself.

"No use in getting all riled up when there's nothing much I can do about it," Henry commented. "I'd like to take a shotgun to the varmints, but the word passed down the line is, they don't mind a load of buckshot. Anyways, no point in killing off a bunch of draftees. It's the big shots back home that's responsible."

"A very reasonable attitude, Henry," Retief said.

"I told you the guv'mint wouldn't jest set back there in the city and let us get et alive, Henry," Mrs. Suggs said. "I knew Terra'd send he'p along soon."

"How much firepower you got with you, Retief?" Henry asked. "I reckon the fleet must be waiting in orbit, huh?"

"No, there's just me and my mouth, as I said," Retief replied. "Plus one power gun, if you want to count that."

"Power gun might poke a hole in 'em," Henry allowed. "But it'll take a while, one at a time. 'Bout a hundred years, I guess."

"I wasn't planning anything like that," Retief said.

Everyone at the table looked up as a high-pitched whistling started up outside.

"Sounds like the mail copter," Henry said. "Only louder."

They rose and filed out into the barnyard. A large and ornately decorated copter was settling to a landing in the pasture. The markings indicated that it was a Furtheronian government vehicle.

"Better go inside," Henry said to his family. "I'll handle this."

"Now, don't go hitting nobody, Henry," his wife wailed.

"Don't you worry, Mellie, I ain't aiming to hit nobody don't need hitting." Henry looked apologetically at Retief. "'Course I ain't seen many guv'mint johnnies in my life didn't need a good working-over."

"I was just thinking your restriction wasn't very restrictive, Henry."

"Let's go see what they want," Henry said. He and Retief walked across to the fence nearest the newly landed copter. As they reached it, the machine's hatch popped open and a baroque figure emerged.

"Well, it's I of IU Honk," Retief said. "I wonder what he's doing here."

Honk stepped down and came across to the two Terrans. He halted and stared at Retief.

"I declare, you look like the cheat and trickster Retief," he said in his rusty voice.

"That's me," Retief said. "You look like that slow-poke, Honk."

"That's me," Honk said dismally. "Tell me, how did you trick me?"

"Easily," Retief said. "No mirrors."

"Drat! I trust you'll not bruit it about. I still find it difficult to imagine how I, being perfect, could have been bested at my own game. My boat is a special job, you know. I shall have the hide off that Bogan sharpie who sold it to my government."

"Don't bother," Retief suggested. "Just do a little preflight inspection next time."

"Uncanny! I completed a post-debacle inspection just an hour ago. Found a solenoid had been carelessly left off. Probably by those lackadaisical maintenance chaps back on Terra. And how I shall find a replacement here on this benighted planet, I'm sure I can't guess."

Retief took the solenoid from his pocket and showed it to Honk. "Would this fit?" he asked.

"Of course not! One doesn't find obscure parts for custom-built installations lying about in the pockets of alien upstarts, you know."

"I should have thought of that," Retief said, and tossed the cylinder into a nearby hog trough.

"But I have no time to chat," Honk said briskly. "I'm here to address the troops—the tourists, that is. Without periodic encouragement they tend to forget their objective, and settle down to gourmandizing."

"What *is* their objective?" Retief asked.

"Why, to reduce this miserable world to total inorganic sterility."

"Why?"

"Simple enough. By rendering it undesirable to inferior organisms, we make it available for ourselves. In a few decades with proper seeding of microorganisms, it will be ready for harvest again."

"What about the present population?" Retief asked.

"I'm not excessively finicky," Honk said. "We'll take them too, with no complaints. Candidly, we prefer the cows and those long-legged cows without horns, 'horses' I believe you term them in your barbaric dialect. And the dogs, of course, are quite succulent. Now, the young of your species are not at all bad, I'll concede, especially the small round ones, who merely squirm and gurgle as they're prepared for dinner."

"You're all heart, Honk," Retief said.

"One does one's best to give even the devil his due. Take these tourists of mine: they'd rise in a body and go home if I weren't here to flog their enthusiasm. Dull fellows. But as I'm always at the point of action, spurring them on, they pitch in and do their best."

"Suppose you ordered them all to back off and go away?" Retief asked.

"They'd comply with alacrity, of course. But it's no use, Retief. I have no intention, of course, of abandoning my prize. Do you realize I'm in line for promotion to AC of F after this victorious episode?"

"See that armor plate on the bugger?" Henry said to Retief. "Number eight just bounces off that."

"True enough, fellow," Honk said proudly. "Only at one point . . ." he indicated the juncture of the horny plates in the center of what, on a human being, would be the chest, "is my external integument permeable by sublight projectiles. But trivia aside, show me to a desk, fellow," he commanded, "where I may prepare my dispatches announcing imminent victory. Afterwards, you may prepare a repast of native specialities for me and make ready a suitable chamber for my night's repose."

"What's that? You expect me to give house-room to an alien that brags he's here to kill me and my family?"

"Of course, varlet. What choice have you?"

"Well," Henry said, "I don't rightly know, but I aim to find out." He doubled his fist and landed a straight right on Honk's facial plates that would have stunned an ox. Instead Henry yelled and drew back a bloodied fist, while Honk merely shook his head as if annoyed by a jelly-fly.

"I'll overlook that for the moment," he commented. "Later, I'll dismember you, slowly, in the presence of your squaw and pickaninnies. Or perhaps the reverse. But no matter; on to affairs of substance. Show me my office space!"

"Reckon I got no choice, like he said," Henry said apologetically to Retief, and led the way inside.

In a book-lined study he shoved the papers from a wide table and indicated to Honk that he could be seated.

"Bring paper, fellow, plus quills and a computer," the Basuran ordered. Finding the antique cherrywood chair somewhat confining, he ripped off the arms and threw them through the window. At the crash the door opened and Mellie appeared, looking agitated.

"Why, Henry, what . . .?" she started, but Honk uttered a yell and threw an ashtray at her. It struck her between the eyes; she cried out and retreated.

"Solitude!" Honk yelled. "I require togetherness with my own ineffable greatness in order to compose a dispatch adequate to capture the magnificence of my triumph!" He grabbed a ball-point and a sheet of pink paper and started scribbling.

"Before you commit yourself," Retief said, "how about discussing the matter?"

"No use!" Honk barked. "The die is cast! In any case, why trouble yourself about the fates of these rubes? Anyone can see they're of no importance whatever: no cash, no political pull, no organization, nothing! They'll never be missed! And my tourists are scheduled to engulf this spot within the hour. I don't wish to have my office devoured under me. Instead, I'll finish up this confounded paperwork and be off to the capital, where I'm to be guest of honor at a banquet given by His Excellency, the Chief Executive. Now, there's a reasonable man. When I pointed out that struggle would be futile, and that a cooperative attitude, while not essential, would be helpful, and would result in a handsome deposit of Groaci spruggs in his account in Zurich, he at once placed his personal copter at my disposal and began plans for the official request by Bliff for annexation by Basur. Practical fellow."

"Still, Honk, Terra can't stand by inertly while you and your tourists wipe out two million Terry colonists."

"But of course you can, dear fellow. I'll write you a little note that says you did your best even at the risk of irritating me, so your career won't suffer—and you can be on your way, while nature takes its course. You couldn't expect a ripe plum like Bliff to hang on the branch unnoticed forever."

"Honk, you're savvy enough to know that Terra could send a flotilla out here, any vessel of which could pick Basur up and toss it into your sun."

"Ah—but you *won't!* That's the curious fact I noticed in my studies of Terry history. You Terries are afflicted with an all-encompassing inhibition when push comes to shove. You've been trimmed time and again by upstarts, merely because of your curious and invariable reluctance to assert your power. Ergo—I shall do as I please."

"How about sparing the human population, then; go ahead and eat the topsoil, but leave the people. If you're interested in the public relations angle, that will make you smell a lot sweeter."

"PR and Galactic Public Opinion are the Terry bag. We Basurans couldn't care less. We want territory, not popularity."

"Maybe I could scrape up a few concessions, territorywise."

"Don't bother, Retief. My plans are made. My mind is made up. That's that!"

Retief found Henry and Mellie in the dining room surrounded by their brood. He shook his head. "No luck," he said. "I suggest you folks take Honk's flitter and get going."

"Nope, I'm not giving up, mister," Henry said flatly. "Somehow, I don't believe, when it gets right down to it, that Eety will actually try to kill us off."

At that moment Honk entered the room, splintering the door in the process.

"Ah, all gathered for dinner, I see," he said gaily. "Most considerate; much as I enjoy the small ones, it's a bit of a bore when one has to run them down. I recall one little devil day before yesterday, ran a good three miles, swam a river, threw rocks at my person, and at last I was forced to tear down a tree where he had naïvely taken refuge. But he was succulent; far better even than well-manured soil."

"Lookit here, Mr. Honk," Henry said in a strained tone. "You let my wife and kids go and I'll make it up to you someways."

"Ah, I require an agile body servant to fetch and carry, keep my plates polished, dispose of excreta and the like. Would you like to take the post in exchange for your very ordinary-looking dependents?"

"Dog robber to a junk pile," Henry muttered. "Never thought I'd see the day, but sure, if it'll keep them hooks of yours off my family."

"Done!" Honk exclaimed.

"That includes your tourists, of course," Retief said.

"As to that, one can't ever be quite sure what one's tourists, flushed with touring, may take it into their heads to do."

"I want an iron-bound guarantee," Henry said.

"What you want, and what you'll get may bear little resemblance each to other, fellow." Honk said loftily.

"I'll issue a memo on the matter, if I should happen to think of it. Meantime, go to my copter, remove my baggage, place it in my room and prepare the place for my occupancy. Move smartly, my man. I've no patience with dawdlers. You may as well help him, Retief," he added, offhandedly as Henry herded Mellie and the young ones from the room.

"I'd rather stay," Retief said. "I still think—"

"It's no use, Retief. You can talk all night and I'll not budge an inch. In a few moments I must be off to guide my tourists here and direct the line of march to engulf the capital, including that disgusting turncoat Burrsaddle and his banquet."

Henry came back in. "Honk, you don't mind if we eat a bite before you fellows get it all, do you?"

"No looting, Henry! Everything here belongs to me. Don't touch it!"

"Yeah, but the kids—"

"Just don't allow them to blat in earshot of my sleeping chamber. That's all, Henry."

"Wouldn't you like to be one of those magnanimous conquerors, Honk?" Retief asked.

"Not in the least," the Basuran replied. "Don't argue with me, Retief. I've indulged your persistence out of deference to your CDT affiliation. If all else fails, I may someday be relying on you chaps for a handout, so I like to keep matters chummy between us. But I warn you, I'm losing patience, and I shall be most surprised if you persuade me to change any detail of my program."

"Nice try, Retief," Henry said, and left the room.

"And now, if you'll excuse me," Honk said, and consumed a small wine glass. "My physician has cautioned me about snacks between meals." he confided guiltily. "So I'll simply continue eating, thus retroactively making these tidbits part of a regular meal." He snapped a plate in two and consumed the larger half, following that with a knife, fork, and spoon.

"Delicious," he said expansively. "So much tastier

than the hood ornaments on your Terry ground-cars—far too bland. Besides which, the chrome plating gets caught in my teeth."

"I think the time has come," Retief said, "to discuss the matter of our wager."

"Oh, that" Honk said shortly. "What were the details? I seem to recall some cheeky remark on your part."

"A square inch of your hide belongs to me," Retief said.

"Oh, indeed? But what a pity you won't be able to collect it. I place a high value on my hide, in its intact state. I must decline to hand your prize over to you voluntarily. Another race of beings, of course, might attempt to collect forcibly; but you Terries, of course, faced with such a situation, are forced by your perverse natures to simply whimper a platitude and abandon the point." Honk stared at Retief, then went on:

"A curious tribe, you Terries. By virtue of your superior endowments of intelligence, ingenuity and industry, you stand above the ordinary strife of galactic life. You could take whatever you want, organize the Arm to suit yourselves, but instead, you talk endlessly, nattering of Galactic Public Opinion and other superstitions, while practical-minded races with an eye on the main road push you around with no fear of effective reprisal. The present situation is a case in point. From the Terry viewpoint, I perceive that this was indeed an idyllic world, populated by successful, peaceful, and contented people. But because our Basuran Ultimate Ego happened to be in a conquistadorial mood one morning, you allow it to be snatched away from you. We're both aware that a single Peace Enforcer could eliminate Basur as an organized power and restore this planet to its legitimate owners, thereby preserving the lives of all these bucolics about whose welfare you seemed so exercised a moment ago. But instead, before nightfall, Henry and all his brood will be devoured, along with their lives' work. And by virtue of your own inhibitions, there is absolutely nothing you can do about it."

"I think I've picked out the square inch I want," Retief said. He extracted the power gun from its holster and aimed it at the center of Honk's thoracic plates. "That one, right there," he said. "Since it's mine, I'm sure you'll have no objection if I poke a hole in it."

Honk rose and stood staring at Retief. "For a moment," he muttered, "I almost thought—" His speech was interrupted as Retief fired. The alien staggered back and fell heavily, with a sound like two Japanese ground-cars colliding. A wisp of pungent smoke rose from the finger-sized hole in his chest.

Henry burst into the room. "What happened?" he demanded, eyeing the fallen Basuran chief.

"I think I succeeded in surprising him," Retief said.

"I'll do my best to put the best possible face on the affair," President Burrsaddle assured Retief as the latter stepped into his boat for the return trip to Terra. "Your finding anent the dust deposits will be helpful, of course," he added. "Over ninety-nine percent uranium, plutonium, radium, gold and chow mein. Zillions of tons of the stuff, in purified form, heaped at the center of the Basuran perimeter. Odd about the chow mein, I suppose, but late reports indicate that our chief Qual An man, Mao-Tse Leung, may have gotten part of his lunch mixed in with the sample. So we're taking steps to segregate the radioactives and insure that no one carelessly shovels up a critical mass. The price the stuff will bring on the open market should put us in the black again in short order."

"Fine," Retief said. "I'll give my regards to the numbered-account fellows in Zurich."

"Eh, what's that?" Burrsaddle yelped. "What envious rumormonger have you been listening to, sir?"

"You *don't* have a Swiss account?"

"Who, me? Of course not. How silly!"

"Then you won't mind if I see to it that account number Z47289 at the *Banque Suisse* is turned over to a fellow named Henry Suggs?"

"Of course not. What difference could that make to me? Ah . . . is anything troubling you?"

"Not really," Retief said. "It just occurred to me you might have a surprise coming to you, but I guess not. It might get to be a habit.

THE NEGOTIATORS

"Oh, Retief!" the reedy voice of First Secretary Magnan called anxiously. Retief turned to see the slight figure of the senior officer hurrying toward him across the slanting expanse of gray-tan rock where the little group of newly arrived Terran diplomats waited to be greeted by the appropriate officials of the local government.

"The Ambassador is most eager to have a word with you," Magnan panted, arriving at Retief's side. "Gracious, I've searched all over for you. I shouldn't wonder if this were a crucial point for you, career-developmentwise, Retief. His Excellency and I were chatting at lunch about possible new modes of approach to the problem. In that connection, I was able to bring up your name, quite casually, of course. I had no wish to seem to be thrusting you forward over the heads of senior officers, naturally."

"I'm three questions behind," Retief commented. "You've searched all over what? All there is is this three-fourths of an acre of exposed rock, surrounded by a few million square miles of unexplored ocean."

"To be sure," Magnan replied crisply. "It was this selfsame three-quarters acre of rock which I searched in quest of you."

"I've been luxuriating right here on the site of the future officers' lounge for the last couple of hours," Retief pointed out.

"Oh, indeed?" Magnan looked around with an expression of severity. "It's not like you, Retief, to idle away the working day in a bar, even an imaginary one."

"That comment has a rather cynical ring to it, Mr. Magnan—how can you term our luxurious facilities imaginary, when you've seen the actual programming documents which call for construction to begin within six months of funding of the project, which will no doubt take place within a year or two of the submission of the CDT construction program, which I'm sure will rank high on Ambassador Fullthrottle's agenda—as soon as he achieves full Embassy status for the Mission here on Sogood."

"Doubtless, Retief, please overlook the lapse. By the way, what have you been doing, here in the imaginary luxury of the hypothetical future club-room?"

"Drinking imaginary booze and watching theoretical bar girls, what else?"

"What else, indeed?" Magnan gazed around with an expression of disapproval at the bleak expanse of seaworn rock and the two dozen forlorn bureaucrats who wandered aimlessly or crouched tensely beside suitcases and crated forms, under the remote blue sun of Sogood. Sofar, the waterworld's sister planet, hung in the sky, a pale gray disc pitted with craters which formed a pattern resembling the leering visage of a plump sexual deviate.

"You said you'd mentioned my name to the Ambassador," Retief prompted. "In connection with new modes of approach, I believe you said. That has an ominous ring."

"Why, *au contraire*, Retief," Magnan twittered. "It's just that having been dispatched here as Terrestrial emissaries on the basis of exhaustive interstellar dialogues between the Department and the Soggies, with assurances that the latter enjoy a high level of technological competence, it was somewhat unsettling to His Excellency—as to us all—to arrive and find nothing but a bald knob of unadorned rock projecting above the surface of this unending ocean! In the absence of opposition negotiators, normal diplomatic gambitry is rendered nugatory in advance of the initial overture.

Why, after thirty-six hours of residence, we've not so much as met a representative of the people, to say nothing of members of the government to which we're accredited. It's unheard of, Retief. Something must be done! I suggest you hurry along before the Ambassador has cause to consider you dilatory."

"Sure. Where is he?"

"Why, in the Chancery, of course. The proposed Chancery, that is. But don't make mention of the illusory nature of His Excellency's present accomodations. He is a diplomat of great sensitivity in matters of protocol and RHIP, you know, though a natural democrat at heart. I sense that an effective performance now could well be the making of you, Retief. And in my assessment of His Excellency's present mood, you must recognize I bring to bear an encyclopedic familiarity with his highly complex character. I fancy I enjoy a rather unusual relationship with His Excellency, Retief; indeed, I think I may say that I enjoy the role of special confidant."

"Don't worry, I won't shatter his illusions." Retief went across toward the spot where a cluster of advancement-conscious functionaries surrounded the tall, lean figure of the Terrestrial Ambassador Extraordinary and Minister Plenipotentiary.

"What do you think, Retief? A hoax staged by the Groaci to make monkeys out of us Terries?" inquired a small, dapper Military Attaché, as Retief paused.

"Aha, got an angle working, eh, boy?" the Press Attaché said, falling in step beside Retief. "Let us in on it, huh? Don't hoard the news. What is it, a secret-invasion scheme, dumping us here on this crummy little island to distract 'em, while the Peace Enforcers hit 'em six ways from the ace on the mainland?"

"What mainland?" Retief asked. "This was the only patch of land visible on the screens as we came in."

"Oh, playing 'em close to the gravy stains, eh? OK, be like that." The fat newsman dropped back, muttering.

"Ah, there, my boy," Ambassador Fullthrottle cried

135

as he noticed Retief. He made shooing motions with his long knobby hands, scattering the other aspirants for ambassadorial attention. "Come right in." He rose from the Hip-U-Matic power swivel chair which had been uncrated for his use, and leaned on the nine-foot iridium desk (Field), Chief of Mission, for the exclusive use of.

"Now, that infernal little favor-currier, Magnan, was pestering me this morning, as usual," the great man said. "And he hinted that you, Retief, might well be the member of my staff most highly qualified to offer a useful proposal for placing this Mission on a somewhat less farcical footing. Ah, have a chair, my boy."

"There isn't one. OK if I have this rock instead?" Retief seated himself on a low, smoothly-eroded boulder.

"Of course, my boy. Smoke if you got 'em." The Ambassador beamed at Retief. "Now, in essence," he said, "our initial challenge appears to consist in the circumstance that I, we, that is, have been dispatched here, in good faith, to establish diplomatic relations with the local inhabitants—a consummation somewhat impeded by the apparent absence of local inhabitants— a circumstance which, unless nullified, will render impossible the conclusion of advantageous agreements between Terra and Sogood."

"If you mean we can't sell iceboxes to nonexistent Eskimos, I agree with you, Mr. Ambassador," Retief said.

"Just so," Fullthrottle said, placing his fingertips together and assuming a judicious expression. "It would appear to be essential to my career—to protection of Terran interests, that is to say—to turn up some sort of local authorities without further delay."

"What about that bunch of Soggies down on the beach?" Retief inquired, nodding toward a group of perhaps two dozen bulky, shiny-black creatures vaguely resembling flipperless seals slumped at the water's edge a hundred feet distant.

"Nothing doing there," Fullthrottle said, shaking his

head. "I dispatched Colonel Betterpart to open a dialogue with the creatures, and he reported that they seem unable to grasp the most elementary concepts of communication. Even friendly shouting didn't help."

"I wondered what the yelling was all about."

"Yes. So there they sprawl: some twenty gross and torpid creatures innocent of clothing, equipment or adornment, obviously bearing no conceivable relationship to the highly sophisticated biped beings with whom we've been in contact via screen for some months. So—what to do? I for one don't fancy sitting here in my office, waiting, while the initiative slips from my hands. Our handling of this initial contact will doubtless establish the pattern of Terry-Soggy relations for centuries to come. Ergo—*do* something, Retief! I have no wish to report to the Department utter failure on the part of my staff in meeting this emergency." The Ambassador leaned back, causing his Hip-U-Matic chair to groan in protest as he braced a foot against the effort of the power swivel attachment to rotate him to one side.

"I quite agree that we can't open peaceful relations with Sogood unless we can find someone to be peaceful with," Retief said. "It seems that bunch down on the beach is the only lead we have, so I'd better give it another try."

"As you will, my boy. If you succeed, I'll be the first to congratulate you. If you fail, I'm sure you won't be so naïve as to seek to imply that I authorized you to approach them. It's my personal conviction that these are a group of outcasts from whatever society may exist here—wherever it may be found in this wilderness of seawater."

Retief rose, inquired the way to the theoretical door, and walked down across the slope of rock toward a lone Soggy sprawled somewhat apart from his fellows.

"Heavens, Retief! Let me save you from a horrid blunder, disciplinewise," Magnan cried, hurrying to intercept Retief. "I had assumed you were conversant with the Ambassador's fiat anent fraternization with these casteless rejects. His Excellency has decided these chaps"—Magnan indicated the herd of Soggies at the water's edge—"are defectives or criminals culled from Soggy society and exiled here far from civilization, to die alone. Doubtless, any contact with them would contaminate the contactor with the same social stigma attaching to these unfortunates. A sad-looking lot, eh? Their degeneracy is apparent at a glance, now that Ambassador Fullthrottle has so perceptively pointed it out. Look at that fellow—" Magnan indicated the nearest Soggy, who sprawled some yards apart from the group. "He's apparently in the last stages of a loathsome disease. Note the lesions on his body. Great pustulent buboes at the point of bursting. Faugh!"

Retief glanced at the bulky form slumped on the rock like a mound of inert, shiny-black-skinned jelly. A number of prominent swellings marred the otherwise unadorned expanse of glossy hide. The only other visible surface feature of the creature was a ridiculously small tail into which the smooth curve of the baglike body tapered at one end. Magnan prodded the Soggy with a fastidious toe. "Go on, shoo, you obscene thing," he muttered. "Crawl into the water to die, can't you?"

"'Fraid not, chum," a moist voice came from somewhere. "And let's watch that footwork. Don't you dried-out foreigners have any respect for youth and beauty, if not for rank and dignity?"

Magnan recoiled, hopping on one foot as if to disassociate himself from the offending member. "Dear me" he choked, "for a moment, Retief, I almost imagined this formless hulk of protoplasm was speaking to us—to you, that is— in a tone of ill-natured reprimand."

"I thought it was *you* that kicked him," Retief said mildly.

"Hardly a kick, Retief! A mere good-natured prod, if that!"

"I heard Colonel Betterpart reported no luck in communicating with them," Retief said.

"So he did. Apparently he jumped to an erroneous conclusion."

"If you boys are talking about that little fancy pants in the hat who tried to pump me about Soggy defenses and armament," the wet voice came again from the general direction of the creature before them, "naturally I clammed up. I'm not spilling Soggy military secrets to the first clown that comes nosing around—and besides, I don't know what armaments and defenses are, such concepts being alien to the peace-loving and inoffensive nature of us Soggies."

"I see," Magnan sniffed. "Well, you could have at least answered the colonel when spoken to. Most rude of you to simply ignore him, thereby giving him an erroneous impression of your capabilities."

"It's legitimate technique to lead potential adversaries astray, according to a time-honored Soggy lore," the watery voice countered, "or it would be if us guileless natives had any history."

"See here, sir," Magnan said, "just how is it you're able to speak Terran, since I see no evidence of vocal apparatus on your person."

"Let's lay off the personal-type remarks, bud," the Soggy retorted. "You managed to get here from wherever you came from, but I don't see any rockets on you, now that you mention it."

"You would seem to imply, by analogy, that you employ technology to supplement your natural communicative endowments, if any!" Magnan stated with asperity. "However, this still ignores the question as to your knowledge of Terran."

"Easy, Jack. We've been in telecommunication with you Terries for months. If we hadn't doped out your language, that would have been kind of a waste of time, hey?"

"The fellow is insolent," Magnan adjudicated, and turning, strode away toward a gaggle of wide-eyed diplomats observing from a safe distance.

"You'll have to excuse Mr. Magnan," Retief said. "His career hasn't developed quite along the lines he dreamed of back in Peoria. It's made him a trifle bitter."

"What's his flavor got to do with it? Is he edible?"

"Only in an emergency."

"It looks like he's in a hurry to report the latest developments."

Retief turned; Magnan was engaged in an arm-waving conversation with half a dozen of his companions, pausing occasionally to point toward Retief and the alien.

"I'll give you odds he's up to no good," the Soggy stated in a voice like an underwater pipe organ. "Oh-oh, here he comes with fire in his eye."

Magnan, wearing an expression of Patience Outraged (721-b), was striding briskly back toward Retief.

"See here, Retief!" the First Secretary barked as he came up. "On behalf of His Excellency, and in consideration of his strict instructions, and in light of my own exalted position as Chief of the Political Section, I really must protest your hobnobbing with this loathsomely diseased outcast! The least you could do, if you insist on defying policy, is to strike up an acquaintance with those rather more clean-cut-appearing locals yonder."

"By the way, what's your name, chum?" the alien inquired in his gurgling voice. "I'm known as Sloonge to those privileged to address me by name."

"I'm Retief. This is Mr. Magnan."

"Never mind him; I got a feeling him and me will never be close."

"Not if I can avoid it," Magnan snapped, leaping back and flicking imaginary slime from his sleeve. "Very well, Retief, you have been cautioned." Magnan marched away yanking the overlapping lapels of his early midmorning hemi-semi-informal cutaway into line.

"That one is a pain in the third somite," Sloonge commented. "Look, Retief, I got to nip down to the pad to check on a couple of items. Want to come along?"

"Where's your pad located?" Retief asked, gazing out over the restless surface of the sea.

"About a quarter mile east and six hundred feet down."

"I'd like to go," Retief said, "if you'll give me a couple of minutes to make preparation."

"Yeah, sure. I guess your kind of metabolism don't work so hot once you get a few feet under water. Tough, chum, but I guess we all got our, like, drawbacks. No offense." With a rippling of his huge bulk, Sloonge flopped over. For the first time, Retief noted that at the end of the alien's six-foot ovoid body, opposite the undersized tail, there were two small protuberances which might have been eyes, plus a pair of small nostril-like perforations and a mouth as lipless as a saber wound. This, he deduced, represented the alien's face, which was otherwise undifferentiated from the rest of his rubbery bulk. With further ripplings, the ungainly creature slithered down the slope of rock and entered the water. Retief walked past the still-gossiping group standing nearby and made his way to a heap of baggage resting near the center of the island where the landing shuttle had dumped it a day and a half earlier. He lifted aside a large pigskin suitcase and extracted a metal-clad steamer trunk which he hoisted to his shoulder. Carrying the trunk, he went across to an unoccupied spot, lowered the trunk to the ground and opened it. From the items packed in the upper tray, he selected a pair of goggles and a heavy cylinder the size and shape of a beer bottle.

"Jerry, give me a hand will you, please?" he said to a slack-jawed youth passing by.

"Oh, going to break out the Poon gear, huh, Mr. Retief?"

"That's right, Jerry. Looks like everything's here," he added, examining the array of equipment laid out in the trunk.

"Sure, Mr. Retief, I'll help you get the stuff buckled on. Pretty smart bringing it out here, I guess. You going for a swim now, huh?"

"It looks that way. I was kind of hoping I wouldn't have to use this gear, but it seemed like a good idea to bring it, when I heard that the total visible land mass of Sogood was three-quarters of an acre, on a world bigger than Terra." Retief stripped off his late mid-morning utterly informal coverall, and began donning the gear.

"Lessee," Jerry mumbled, counting on his fingers: "propulsion, communication, lights, breather, emergency gear. Want me to help you with the water foils, Mr. Retief?"

"Thanks." Retief closed the trunk and sat on the lid, and the lad fitted large swim fins to his feet. Then he rose while Jerry rummaged in the trunk, then brought out a portable apparatus with a tank, compressor, and hose with a wide nozzle.

"OK, get set and I'll start squirting," Jerry said. He started up the compressor, twiddled the knobs, then directed a heavy spray of viscous gray fluid on Retief's chest, working it in a pattern that covered him to the knees, front and back; then he shut down and set about changing hoses and tanks.

"How about a special job, my own design, Mr. Retief? I call it a Hungry Jack."

"Better just give me a straight Big Mouth outfit, Jerry. I'm not sure what kind of appetites I might run into down there, and I'd just as soon look as noncompetitive as possible."

"Right, Mr. Retief." Jerry continued spraying, this time a garish yellow mixture with which he covered Retief's upper half, topping him off with a peaked crest. The soft, thick layer hardened quickly on his skin, forming a tough, seamless protective covering, with only the clear face mask exposed.

Jerry rummaged again, produced a light, short-barreled rifle from the muzzle of which a razor-edged spearhead protruded.

"I hope I don't need it," Retief said, "but I'll take it."

Furtive-eyed diplomats moved aside uneasily as

Retief, in his baroque costume, made his way through them and down to the water's edge. He slung the rifle on his back, waded out knee-deep, and dived forward into the clear water. A bulbous black shape rose up before him, executed a turn, and darted away toward the depths, propelled by rapid flagellations of its undersized tail. It was Sloonge; Retief recognized the outcast by the four painful-looking swellings marring the contour of his baglike body. In spite of his unwieldy bulk, the alien swam smoothly, propelled by undulations of his body and his inadequate-looking tail. Retief fell in behind him, and followed as they descended into increasingly green and opaque depths. Ahead, a sunken mountain peak loomed through the murk; simultaneously, Retief became aware of a dozen or so bulky, dark shapes rising from the depths to form a rough circle around him and his guide. More of the dark shapes appeared, emerging, Retief saw, from openings in the mountainous obstacle ahead. Sloonge quickened his pace, darting swiftly toward a dark spot in the side of the peak directly ahead, which, Retief saw as they approached, was a large orifice beyond which he could vaguely discern a grotto inside the rocky mass. The encircling forms drew close; Retief saw that they resembled the Soggies he had seen on the beach, except that each possessed four muscular limbs, two of which were arms, terminating in hands, which gripped efficient-looking guns. There was a sudden burst of bubbles from the weapon of the nearest of the ambushers. A two-foot spear with a barbed head emerged from the bubble cloud, lancing toward Sloonge. Retief put on a burst of speed, snatched the missile from midwater, and spun, bringing his gun to bear on the alien who had fired. The latter checked, wriggling frantically, and swam hastily away, paddling with all four limbs. Another alien appeared, holding his gun aimed at Retief, who, without hesitation, shifted aim and fired. The harpoon buried itself in the bulky body; an ochre stain leaked into the water from the wound. The stricken creature sank slowly away out of sight, and the others scattered. Retief resumed his previous path, followed Sloonge in through the opening into a spacious, colorfully walled chamber.

"Nice shooting, Retief," Sloonge burbled. "That will save the state the cost of tracking the miscreant down and executing him. By the way, how do you like the pad?"

Swimming close to the wall, Retief saw that the interior of the spacious chamber was entirely covered by skillfully executed mosaic murals, done in crystals of sparkling colored minerals. Sloonge moved past Retief to bump against a small white panel set in the wall. At once, soft light sprang up, emanating from the walls. Each point of color was now glowing with an internal illumination. There were a number of door-sized openings in the walls, each leading to an adjoining room. Retief glanced into a couple of them; each was decorated with glowing wall murals; one room was furnished with what appeared to be a gigantic gold-colored bathtub ornamented with grape-sized green pearls set in intricate patterns.

"Pretty fancy," Retief said.

"Sure, why not?" Sloonge replied cheerfully. "After all, it's the imperial palace."

"Maybe we'd better get out of here before the emperor gets back," Retief suggested.

"Oh, didn't I mention? I'm the emperor," Sloonge said. "Or I will be, as soon as a couple of minor details are cleared up, like that bunch of anarchists we ran into outside."

"Don't tell me I've stuck my nose into the middle of a revolution?" Retief said.

"Not really. Those guys are just troublemakers," Sloonge said. "Nobody can deny I'm the rightful heir, even if I am a little slow getting in shape."

"I take it you're referring to whatever ailment you have that's causing those swellings," Retief commented.

"Yeah, right. You're pretty perceptive for a foreigner." Sloonge said, and swam past Retief into the room

144

with the golden bathtub into which he settled himself with every appearance of luxurious ease.

"The condition looks highly uncomfortable," Retief said. "Can't anything be done to help it?"

"Just takes time," Sloonge said carelessly. Retief approached, studied the swellings nearest him; the glossy skin was bulged up to a height of several inches over an oval area of almost a square foot, and stretched to translucence.

"I'm no doctor," Retief said. "But I think that ought to be opened. It's been my experience that anytime there's a swelling like that, Mother Nature is trying to push something out."

"Maybe you're right," Sloonge said indifferently. "But what can I do about it?"

"If you'll hold still a minute, I'll try something," Retief said.

"Sure, go ahead."

Retief took the knife from its sheath at his hip, checked the edge with his thumb, then delicately stroked the keen blade across the bulge of the immense swelling, which instantly burst, releasing pale yellow fluid which quickly dissipated in the surrounding water. Inside the wound thus made lay a complicated dark shape, that twitched, unfolded and thrust out: it was a perfectly formed, muscular, knobby-kneed leg, terminating in a wide webbed foot.

"Say, that's a lot better!" Sloonge exclaimed, stretching the member out full length, and admiring the toes. "Pretty neat trick," he added. "The itch has been driving me balmy, to say nothing about cramps. If I could just get one more unlimbered, I'd be ready to take on that crowd outside, and show 'em who's head Soggy around here."

"Turn over," Retief said.

Ten minutes later, he and Sloonge, the latter now swimming briskly with four limbs, emerged into the deep-green gloom and headed for the surface.

"Well, those malcontents won't try anything now," Sloonge remarked. "Too bad my particular branch of the imperial dynasty is always a little slow in breaking through. I'll bet those deadbeats up on the beach are still lying around like the no-good bums they are, without a limb to show among 'em. Thought they were going to pull something fancy, I'll bet. Will they be surprised when they see me come ankling up the beach."

"Who are they?" Retief asked. "More rebels?"

"Not exactly," Sloonge said. "They're a bunch of relatives of mine, cousins and brothers and such. Nobody but the royal family is allowed on Imperial Rock, you know—at least, they weren't until you Terries came along and turned it into a hobo jungle. When I said I was coming up to catch a little air and sunshine, they came along on the pretext of attending to my wants while I waited to break through; but in the six weeks I was there, they never offered me so much as a drink of water. They're going to be a downhearted crowd of would-be usurpers. I guess they were playing the odds that one of them would break through ahead of me and ace me out of the imperial tub."

In shallow water, Retief rose to his feet and walked toward the shore. With a great deal of splashing and gasping, Sloonge tottered to his newfound limbs, and after staggering for a few steps, found his stride and walked along steadily at Retief's side, his bulky body balanced rather precariously on his long but skinny legs. At sight of them, the torpid Soggies heaped on the beach became agitated; the gurgling of their excited voices was audible from a hundred yards.

"That was pretty neat how you helped me along," Sloonge commented. "You put an end to the political crisis in a hurry."

"Nothing to it," Retief said casually. "Why didn't you arrange to have it done weeks ago, instead of just waiting around for nature to take its course?"

"On account of the, like, concept of the cutting edge is unknown among us Soggies. But if you'll leave me have that knife, I'll have it consecrated by Bishop Drooze and from now on, it'll be kept guarded, along

146

with the imperial crown and other treasures, to be used only for helping a new emperor to break through."

"Ah, there, Retief," Magnan said, falling in step beside him. "I really must caution you against fraternization with the local undesirable element. If you must hobnob with locals, why not pick one of those more clean-cut Soggies yonder?"

"Hey, Retief," Sloonge said, "tell this bird to shove off before he gets my ire working."

"By the way, sir, I meant to ask you," Magnan addressed the local: "You folks don't mind our calling you Soggies, I hope? No offense was intended, of course; it was just a convenient nickname—short for Sogooders—since we don't know your own word for yourselves."

"Heck, no, sport. Matter of fact, I think it's got a nice ring to it: it sounds sort of soft and juicy, you know; but you can call us by our native designation, if you like: *Vermin.*"

"On the whole, I think 'Soggies' has less unfortunate connotations," Magnan said.

As they came up to the group of Soggies lying on the beach, the aliens flopped about, arranging themselves in orderly rows aimed toward Sloonge. Most of them, Retief saw, exhibited the same sort of swellings which Sloonge had had, in varying degrees of development.

Retief drew Magnan aside. "I'd better tip you off," he said. "Sloonge is the emperor of this entire planet."

"Really? Not that I hadn't suspected something of the sort, of course," Magnan replied. "As you know, my knack for instant recognition of natural nobility is one of my most outstanding traits. Sloonge is as different from this crowd of idlers, for example, as I am from a herd of swine."

"They're all members of the imperial family," Retief pointed out.

"Really?" Magnan gasped.

"Yeah, but not a leg in the bunch!" Sloonge commented. "Ha! I wonder how they figured on knocking me off."

"You imply these fellows would have killed you?" Magnan said in a shocked tone.

"Sure. They were banking on breaking through ahead of me and then finishing me off. Of course they'd probably have gotten to squabbling among themselves about who had priority, and maybe only a couple of 'em would have lived to report my unfortunate demise by accident."

"Do you want me to operate on them?" Retief asked, drawing his knife.

"Cut their throats if you want to; I'll have to have 'em all executed anyway. In a way, it's kind of a shame; my big brother Glorb isn't a bad sort of fellow, and he plays a mean game of boof. I'm going to miss him."

"Then why not let him live?" Retief said in a reasonable tone.

"Nope. Glorb is an ambitious cuss; he'd never stop itching to slip into the imperial tub. He'd be a focal point for malcontents."

"You could turn his ambition to good account," Retief said. "By putting him in charge of your police force, with the job of nipping off revolution in the bud."

"Kind of a wild idea, Retief," Sloonge said. "The ruling emperor having a living relative. It's never been done; maybe I'll give it a try at that. Hey, Glorb! How does 'Field Marshal Prince Glorb' sound to you? I'm thinking about putting you in charge of the imperial security forces, with the job of stamping out treason in the realm."

One of the limbless Soggies, indistinguishable from his fellows, rippled his bulk and flopped forward a yard or two.

"As an alternative to being strangled to death with chuzz-weed, it might be OK," he gurgled. "My first official act will be to order half a ton of chuzz-weed to take care of this bunch of traitors." He nodded toward his former associates.

"Take it easy, Field Marshal," Sloonge said. "You

might be able to find spots for some of 'em in your organization."

"I'll find spots for 'em all right: I'll cement 'em into abandoned gimp holes at about two thousand fathoms."

"Ah, there you are, Retief!" the hearty voice of Ambassador Fullthrottle sounded from behind him. "For a moment I almost didn't recognize you in that outlandish Pupoony getup. Any progress to report on the matter I mentioned to you earlier?"

Retief turned. "I have one or two items of interest," he said.

"Shhh! Not in front of this local." Fullthrottle stared distastefully at Sloonge.

"It looks like a Soggy," he said in a stage whisper, "but where'd he get those limbs?"

"I grew 'em, sport," Sloonge called cheerfully. "Same as you, I guess, except maybe a little suddener. If you boys don't mind my asking, I'm kind of curious about you Terries. Except for Retief here, you aliens don't hardly look like you're equipped to survive in a normal environment. No gills, no tails, and you look sort of dried out and scratchy, and I haven't seen any of you even stick a toe in the water. Aren't you getting a little dehydrated? If so, you're welcome to jump in my ocean."

"Actually," Fullthrottle said, "on our native world, the majority of higher life forms live their entire lives on dry land."

"Sounds like a weird kind of place," Sloonge said. "Maybe your strange habits are on account of your whole planet is rock, without any ocean such as we Soggies are lucky enough to have covering approximately 99.44 percent of the planet, according to a quick mental calculation I just made."

"Why, no," chirped Magnan, who had come up beside the Ambassador, "as a matter of fact three-quarters of Terra—" He broke off abruptly as Retief trod on his foot.

"Say," Sloonge mused. "Now that you Terries have familiarized me with the concepts of space travel and alien worlds, and all, the thought comes to me: Maybe us Soggies could do with a little more marine real estate to help out our overpopulation problem. You don't know of a nice planet with plenty of ocean where we could maybe hatch out a few zillion tons of fertilized ova, do you?"

"Ugh!" Magnan cried. "Imagine the Atlantic teeming with giant polywogs!"

"See here, Magnan," Fullthrottle said testily, "it's hardly in consonance with the dignity of a Terran Ambassador, or even of you lesser ranks, to stand out in the wind nattering with a low-caste local."

"The wind, sir?" Magnan objected. "Why, we're right here in the handsomely appointed Embassy lounge, as designated by Your Excellency only yesterday."

"To be sure," the Ambassador conceded. "But that's hardly the point. The impudence of this untouchable in addressing me is the issue."

"Oh, didn't I tell you, Mr. Ambassador?" Magnan inquired. "This is His Imperial Highness, the Emperor Sloonge, hereditary sole and absolute ruler of Sogood."

"You jape at such a solemn moment as this, Magnan?" Fullthrottle responded indignantly. "My ability to instantly recognize true aristocracy is well-nigh a legend in the Corps. This fellow is quite obviously a reject of such primitive society as exists here on this benighted planet."

"Heck, I hate to appear to, like, contradict Your Excellency or anything, but I have it from a usually reliable source," Magnan eyed Retief bleakly, "that Sloonge is, indeed, the emperor."

"What about that, fellow?" Fullthrottle demanded, turning to eye Sloonge dubiously. "Do you have the temerity to put forth such a claim?"

"Them are the facts, sport," Sloonge said airily,

waving a hand to indicate the knob of rock on which they stood. "The whole thing's my realm."

"Well, Your Imperial Majesty," Fullthrottle said in a somewhat choked voice, glancing furtively around at what, to the uninitiated, would have appeared to be three-fourths of an acre of bare rock, "I'm sure that an individual of Your Majesty's sophistication won't take amiss my lighthearted remarks just now." He shot his cuffs and extended his right hand to be shaken.

Sloonge yawned, exposing the intimidating array of sharklike teeth lining his wide mouth.

"No, thanks," he said. "I never snack between meals. By the way, maybe you better present some credentials about now, just to keep matters on a correct footing."

"But of course, Your Majesty; I was about to propose a suitable ceremony as soon as possible."

"Yeah, hand 'em over," Sloonge said. "But don't bother unless you're ready to agree to my modest proposal for using your unused ocean worlds."

"I fear the matter will require study," Fullthrottle hedged.

"You got Terra," Sloonge cried. "Why not let us have the Atlantic?"

"We need it! And the Pacific too, to say nothing of the Indian and Arctic Oceans," Magnan sputtered. "We *don't* need annual plagues of seven-foot meat-eating Vermin croaking on the shores."

"Let's deal, Retief," Sloonge cried. "Sounds like you got four whole ocean worlds you ain't even using! But I guess you're holding out for an equal swap. How about it. Let's work out a trade: I'll swap you the entire land area of Verm, or Sogood, as you call it, namely Imperial Rock, a very high-class neighborhood, for your oceans. That's a square deal for you Terries and us Vermin, too!"

"I'm afraid we can't get together on that, Sloonge, but how about an alternate proposal? We've been having a little difficulty developing our marine resources, and perhaps instead of just hatchlings, you could supply us with a few thousand skilled craftsmen to build underwater structures, like that palace of yours; very fine workmanship!"

"Sure, I can supply all you need; but a few hundred thousand couldn't hardly build you a first-class privy. How about a couple hundred million to start with?"

"Would these be, er, spawn, or fully developed adults?" Magnan interposed.

"Trained workers, every one," Sloonge reassured him. "All they need is about a hundred pounds of fresh meat a day apiece."

"Heavens," Magnan cried. "I'm not sure we have enough fish in our seas to supply such a demand."

"No sweat, Mr. Magnan," Sloonge said easily. "They'll catch their own eats—even if they have to forage ashore—just so you got plenty of game on hand."

"Our only surviving land animal is man," Magnan said stiffly.

"OK, we ain't particular—leastways a bunch of hungry hard hats ain't," Sloonge said agreeably.

"Well, let me see," Magnan muttered. "Two hundred million, ah, Vermin—times one hundred pounds, times three hundred sixty-five, for the annual requirement. . . . Hm-m-m, I think perhaps we're on the verge of a solution to our overpopulation problem."

"Ah, Your Imperial Majesty will excuse Magnan for carelessly referring to your people as 'Vermin,' I trust," Fullthrottle put in quickly. "I'll personally see to it that he is appropriately dealt with at Departmental level." He turned to Magnan with a glacial expression. "I must say I'm surprised to hear a diplomat of your experience openly refer to these obnoxious creatures as Vermin," he whispered behind the symbolic privacy of a hand.

"Their own local name for themselves—or so I'm told," Magnan alibied, giving Retief an accusatory look.

"Don't waste a 729-t on me, Mr. Magnan," Retief

said. "Emperor Sloonge told us so himself, if you recall."

"Ah," Fullthrottle said dubiously to Magnan, "I fear I can never bring myself to openly call these creatures 'Vermin' to their faces, if any."

"Hey—what's wrong with our name?" Sloonge demanded. "I hope you Terries ain't figuring to, like, meddle in Soggy internal affairs and all!"

"Well—as to that," Fullthrottle gasped, "faced with a choice between referring to your people as, ah, 'Soggies' or—alternatively, as 'Vermin,' I'm not quite sure what CDT regs stipulate."

"What's wrong with 'Vermin'?"

"Ah, by a curious coincidence, the term has unfortunate connotations in Terran. It implies a certain lack of fastidiousness as well as various other disgusting traits."

"It figures," Sloonge commented thoughtfully. "Fits most Soggies like a glove. If you knew these no-goods like I do, you wouldn't be quibbling."

"Quite the contrary," the Ambassador objected, facing the Emperor squarely. "It's a time-honored truism of diplomacy that the most resented epithet is the one most accurately depicting the deficiencies of the recipient. Those who refuse to work, for example, dislike being called 'loafers,' while the industrious would merely be amused by the appellation."

"I get the idea; but I was talking about the lower classes, natch. Vermin they are, by anybody's definition."

"Your proposal for relocation of Soggies on Terra occasions certain grave difficulties, Your Majesty," Fullthrottle commented. "For example, provision for wives and families would constitute a problem. And then the details of vacations, recreational facilities, and pocket money—to say nothing of repatriation at the end of the term of contract."

"Don't sweat it, chum. Do like I do: work 'em till they drop, and if they start bitchin', I'll supply you with plenty of chuzz-weed. And if they *don't* bitch, give 'em the works anyway. And don't worry about returning 'em. I got plenty more; just let the sharks have 'em, if sharks' innards can handle Soggy-meat."

"How unfeeling!" Fullthrottle exclaimed. "Though this practical approach *does* simplify matters considerably. Still," he added, giving Magnan a glum look, "I trust none of my personnel will be so naïve as to suggest at any inquiry which might develop in future, that *I* in any way gave approval to any such scheme!" He walked away without further comment.

"I assume we may safely take that as authorization to go ahead," Magnan said briskly.

"You boys just fix up a title to all Terran oceans, and I'll see to it the work force is on hand for pickup in a week—*plus* a deed to Imperial Rock, here," Emperor Sloonge said, and headed for the surf.

"Just a minute," Retief demurred. "Before we give away three-fourths of a planet for three-fourths of an acre I think we ought to hold out for more consideration accruing to Terra."

"Why," Magnan gasped, "we mustn't appear greedy, Retief."

"Why not? Better greedy than suckers," Retief replied.

"Speaking of suckers, Retief," Sloonge said in a glutinous undertone, pausing beside Retief. "Let's you and me retire to the palace for a couple of quick ones and ditch all these nobodies, Terry and Soggy alike. We can work out a deal that includes some goodies for number one—and you, too."

"I take it that's an imperial command," Retief said, "that a mere bureaucrat has no option on."

"Right. Let's go—before Glorb gets into the act. He's a boy that's always got a hand out, even if he has to grow one special. And from the looks of him, this Mr. Ambassador of yours is the same type. They're both probably figuring an angle to ace you and me out of some legitimate graft—and after we earned it, too! I'll be expecting you, Retief."

Sloonge waved and waded into the breakers.

"Ah, excuse my interruption, Retief," Fullthrottle butted in, having reapproached from downwind. "I appreciate the potential benefits to accrue from your establishing a cordial relationship with His Imperial Majesty, by nattering informally of this and that. But, ah. . . ." He sidled closer, "Candidly, I was wondering if perhaps you and I might not, ah, draw aside and look more deeply into all aspects of the Terran posture *vis-à-vis* Sogood at this juncture . . . with a view to the possibility of so influencing the development of affairs as to enhance the professional profiles of those most instrumental in bringing about a Terran-Sogoodian accord. Between ourselves," he added, with a glance at the royal Soggies heaped nearby, "that chap Field Marshal Prince Glorb strikes me as being on the make, to employ the vernacular."

"Emperor Sloonge had the same idea, Mr. Ambassador," Retief said.

At that moment, Magnan tugged at his sleeve. "Er, Retief," he muttered, "if you can spare a moment . . . I've been wondering why you and I should do all the work, as usual, only to have the brass grab all the credit. Accordingly, I suggest we approach Glorb—he seems a reasonable chap—and see if a rapprochement can't be worked out more favorable to the interests of hard-working diplomats of intermediate rank than could be expected if finalization of the treaty and protocols are left to His Excellency and His Majesty."

"Seems like a popular idea," Retief said. "Just a moment, Mr. Magnan. Let's see what the Field Marshal has in mind." He nodded toward the Soggy inching his way toward the Terrans, wriggling awkwardly on his limbless torso.

"Look here, you Terries, I got pretty keen hearing—couldn't help overhearing some of your conversation. How about it, Retief?" Glorb said. "Let's get together on the practical end of this deal, what say? I always kind of hankered to get into the construction game; now's the chance to get my feet dry—you Terries will need a knowledgeable contractor to handle your imported labor. I've got the boys that will shape those loafers up in a hurry."

"Sounds reasonable, Your Imperial Highness," Magnan conceded. "How many extra personnel will your supervisory staff consist of?"

"Forget it, chum; just consider 'em as included in the original hundred zillion figure."

"But—I thought we'd agreed on a hundred *million,*" Magnan protested. "We mustn't exceed available transport capacity."

"A million, or a zillion, who cares?" Glorb said carelessly. "Let's get to the meat of the matter. Frankly, where I get well is supplying materials. Masonry specialties, plumbing fixtures—all that."

"Really, I must draw the line!" Magnan declared. "It's apparent, I fear, that Your Imperial Highness has no grasp of interstellar freight rates. Shipping concrete and lead pipes, indeed! Out of the question!" He retired to a distance of ten feet, turning his back, and radiated outrage. "I might have suspected a kickback arrangement," he mused. "Such gall! Retief, come along," he went on in a colorless tone. "Ambassador Fullthrottle will be getting restless unless we reassure him that no irretrievable indiscretions have been committed."

"First I have to make a duty call on the Emperor," Retief demurred.

"Look, Retief," Glorb said in the confidential tone employed by men of the world when discussing matters not understood by non-men of the world. "Your chum don't seem to realize our boys are pretty sensitive artistic types. They got to work in the familiar materials they know and love: gold, emeralds, diamonds, rubies, granite and stuff like that. You Terries need to supply the right stuff, or they go into a premature decline. And I can fix you up with everything you need to keep 'em happy, OK,"

"What kind of payment do you have in mind?" Retief asked.

"Why, Magnan let slip a mention of a minor

seaworld called Mediterranean," Glorb said. "How's about just deeding it to me as a modest personal estate. . . ."

"OK on the gold, diamonds, emeralds and rubies," Retief said. "Hold the granite."

"Say, that's big of you, Retief, accepting the stuff we got a surplus of, and foregoing the rare and expensive granite. I may make a small profit on this deal after all."

"Building materials!" Ambassador Fullthrottle exclaimed, eyeing Retief with an expression of Incredulous Indignation, a variation on the 291-x developed by the Ambassador himself in his youth, when a delegate to a Special Tribunal on Unsavory Prehistoric Events— a group which had been on the verge of a unanimous endorsement of a resolution introduced by young Fullthrottle condemning every mass migration in human prehistory as imperialistic protofascism—had mentioned the invasion of the European continent from Africa by *Homo Erectus* some 150,000 years B.C., an unfortunate piece of water-muddying which had nipped in the bud what might have been a valuable entry in the Fullthrottle dossier. In spite of this frustration of early hopes, Fullthrottle still looked back with a benign nostalgia on the days of STUPE, his first entry into the large arena of affairs, though he felt a pang of regret as he reflected that but for an unkind quirk of fate, his 291-y would today be officially listed in the CDT Career Officers Guide, with himself credited as originator, his name ranged alongside such giants of interstellar diplomacy as Crodfoller, Longspoon, Barnshingle, and Pruffy.

But, he recalled himself, back to the immediate problem.

"Is it possible, Retief," the great man continued, "that you are unaware of the costs of interstellar transport? I assure you there are better uses for Corps bottoms than hauling bricks and lead piping."

"Yes, sir" Retief replied. "But as Field Marshal

Prince Glorb pointed out, his craftsmen would work much more skillfully in their accustomed media."

"Ah, yes, a significant point, no doubt, my boy. Giving consideration to the personal preferences of these, er, Vermin, will, of course, look good in the 'Empathy and Involvement' column of your next ER, if I should happen to recall the matter when preparing it, which, I may as well point out, is unlikely in view of the sensation your proposal for massive waste of Corps funds will create in the Bureau of the Budget. So resign yourself to the realization that our Soggy labor corps will of necessity learn to lay Terry bricks and install native pipes and fittings, including bathtubs, which, I noted on your proposed schedule of cargoes, were specified most explicitly—as if the place of manufacture of a porcelain bathtub were a matter of vast concern in the conduct of interplanetary affairs!"

"I'm afraid I've committed myself on the tubs," Retief said. "Prince Glorb insisted on it."

"Hm-m-m," Fullthrottle mused. "I wonder just who is finessing whom in this negotiation. It was a most adroit gambit on my, ah, *our* part, I suppose I should say, to escalate Sloonge's request for breeding grounds into a solution to our marine development problem. But his arrogance in levying demands, bathtubwise, gives me pause. Perhaps there were nuances which I, that is, you and Magnan, missed. Still, I suppose it's too late now to abrogate the treaty of eternal chumship now that the Council has approved it, and made the appropriate notations in my 201 file."

"Too late, or too soon," Retief said. "The first shipload of bathtubs is in parking orbit now."

"So . . . well, matters have ripened somewhat precipitously, Retief. I fear you place me in a delicate position. CDT regs are quite explicit as to the proper handling of the matter, however. Inasmuch as you exceeded your approval authority in okaying these freight charges, I have no choice but to issue a Statement of Charges, permitting you the opportunity to salvage your career by merely paying these charges personally. I daresay the sum will be paid off within a few years."

"I understand, Mr. Ambassador. What about the two ships following, loaded to the gunwales with masonry specialties? No granite; I told Glorb he'd have to make do with Terry granite."

"Quite right!" Fullthrottle said firmly. "By the way, in accordance with Paragraph ninety-seven, Subsection B of the Manual, you'll of course be obligated to take personal title to these unauthorized cargoes. I suggest you make immediate arrangements for disposal to cut down on your demurrage."

"Oh, there you are," Magnan said brightly, peeking in the door at Retief. "Why, hi there, Mr. Ambassador, I just wanted to tip you off, sir; there's a fantastic rumor afoot to the effect that you've stuck poor Retief here with the bill for hauling bricks and so on all the way from Sogood. I suggest you scotch it, sir, before it goes any further. Just confidentially, sir," Magnan added furtively, "the Corps' image has already had its luster dimmed a trifle just by the terms of the treaty—you know how difficult it is for the public to distinguish between a diplomatic victory and a disaster. And socking it to one of our own will make very bad copy from a PR standpoint—nothing personal, of course—I quite understand that Retief is legally responsible."

"It's quite all right," Retief said. "I'll take my medicine without griping—just let me have it in writing."

GIANT KILLER

1

As Retief paid off his canal barge and stepped up on the jetty, Second Secretary Magnan pushed his way through the throng at the wharf entrance to the Royal Enclosure, his narrow face flushed with exertion. "There you are!" he cried as he spied his junior. "I've been searching everywhere! Ambassador Pinchbottle will be furious—"

"What's that on your head?" Retief eyed a half-inflated bladder of a sour yellow color which lolled over Magnan's left ear.

Magnan rolled an eye up at the varicolored cluster which bobbed with each movement, draggled feathers wagging and lengths of dirty string swaying, the entire assembly secured under his chin by a stained pink ribbon.

"Why, that's my ceremonial Rockamorra headdress; here . . ." He fumbled in his violet afternoon formal cutaway, brought out a bundle of puckered balloons and feathers, offered it. "Here's one for you: you'd better slip into it at once. I'm afraid a couple of the plumes are bent—"

"Where's the Ambassador?" Retief interrupted. There's something I have to tell him—"

"There are a number of things you'll be expected to tell him!" Magnan snapped. "Including why you're half an hour late for the Credentials Ceremony!"

"Oh-oh; there he goes with the staff, headed for the temple; excuse me, Mr. Magnan . . ." Retief pushed off through the crowd toward the wide doorless entry set in the high, blocky structure at the end of the courtyard. A long-legged, short-bodied, neckless local with immense flat feet, wearing an elaborate set of ruffles and holding a pike waved him through. The Ambassador and his four staff members were grouped in the gloom a few yards distant, before a gaudy backdrop of luminous plastic in slime green, dyspepsia pink and cirrhotic yellow.

". . . classic diplomatic coup," Pinchbottle was saying. "I should like to see the looks on the faces of our Groaci collegues when they learn we've stolen a march on them!"

"Mr. Ambassador," Retief started—

Pinchbottle spun, stared for an instant at a point just above Retief's belt-buckle, then tilted his spherical bald head back, gazed up at his junior.

"I've warned you about pussyfooting, Retief!" he yelped. "When you're around me, stamp your feet when you walk!"

"Mr. Ambassador, I'd like—"

The senior diplomat raised a small, plump-fingered hand. "Spare me a catalogue of your likes and dislikes, Mr. Retief! The ceremony is about to begin." He turned to include a wider audience. "Gentlemen, I trust you all observed my handling of protocol since our arrival here on Rockamorra this morning. Scarcely six hours, and we're about to become the first diplomatic mission ever to be accredited to this world! A world, I need not remind you, with a reputation for vigorous commercial activity and unrelenting hostility to diplomats; and yet I—"

"Before this goes any farther, Mr. Ambassador"—Retief cut in—"I think—"

"May I remind you, sir!" Pinchbottle shrilled. "I *am* talking! About a subject of vast importance, namely myself! Er, my contribution, that is, to diplomatic history—"

A pair of robed Rockamorrans bustled up waving elaborate candelabra which emitted clouds of pungent red and green smoke; they struck poses before the Terrans, intoned resonant–ritual phrases in sonorous tones, then stepped back, One pointed a thin, multi-jointed digit at Retief, made a sound like a saw blade dragged across a base-viol string.

"Where's your headdress, Retief?" Pinchbottle hissed.

"I don't have one; what I wanted to tell you—"

"Get one! Instantly! And take your place in my entourage!" the Ambassador screeched, moving off at the heels of the local officials. Magnan, rushing up at that moment, waved the bladders excitedly.

"Don't bother inflating it, just get it on!"

"Never mind that," Retief said, "I won't be needing it."

"What do you mean? We all have to wear them—"

"Not me; I won't be taking part in the ceremony; and I advise you to—"

"Crass insubordination!" Magnan gasped, and rushed off in the Ambassador's wake, as large bouncers moved in to bar the headdressless Retief from following.

2

It was a colorful ceremony, involving a vigorous symbolic beating of the diplomats with real laths, immersion in a pond which to judge from the expressions of the bathers when they surfaced, was considerably chillier than the bracing morning air, and finishing off with a brisk run around the compound—ten laps—during which the panting Terrans were spurred to creditable efforts by quirtwielding native dignitaries loping along behind them. Retief, observing the activities from a position among the curious at the sidelines, won ten credits in local currency on the Chief of Mission whose form he had correctly judged superior to that of his staff in the final event.

Amid a tolling of deep-toned gongs, the Rockamorran officials herded the wheezing Terrans together, read off a long speech from a scroll; then a small local stepped forward bearing a six-foot sword on a purple velvet cushion lettered MOTHER—a Terran import, Retief noted.

A tall Rockamorran in mauve and puce vestments strode up, lifted the sword; the Ambassador backed a step, said, "Look here, my good man—" and was prodded back into line. The sword-handler solemnly hung a beaded baldric over the stout diplomat's shoulderless frame and attached the scabbard to it.

The locals fell silent, staring at the Terran Envoy expectantly.

"Magnan, you're protocol officer; what am I supposed to do now?" the Ambassador muttered from the corner of his mouth.

"Why, I'd suggest that Your Excellency just sort of, ah, bow and then we all turn and leave, before they think up any more tortures—"

"All right, men: all together," Pinchbottle whispered hoarsely. "About face—" Magnan yelped as the two-yard-long cutlass connected solidly with his shin as the group turned; then they strode away, the Ambassador in the lead, drawn up to his full five feet, with the sword cutting a trail in the dust behind him. There was a happy mutter from the locals, then a swelling shout of joy; eager hands clapped the Terrans on the back, offered them sulphuretted dope sticks, proffered flasks of green liquid as the ceremony broke up into mutual rejoicing.

Retief made his way through the press, intercepted the Ambassador as he pushed through.

"Well, Retief!" the latter barked. "Absented yourself from the proceedings, I noted! Having sulked in your quarters during the voyage out, you now boycott official functions! I'll see you in my office as soon as I've seen to the safekeeping of this handsome ceremonial weapon I've been awarded—"

"That's what I wanted to tell you, Mr. Ambassador; it's not ceremonial. You're expected to use it."

"What? Me use this?" Pinchbottle smiled sourly. "I shall hang it on the wall as a symbol—"

"Possibly later, sir," Retief cut in. "Today you have a job to do with it."

"A job?"

"I think you misunderstood the nature of the ceremony. The Rockamorrans don't know anything about diplomacy. They thought you came here to help them—"

"As indeed we did," Pinchbottle snorted. "Now if you'll stand aside—"

"—so they're expecting you to make good on your promise."

"Promise? What promise?"

"That's what the ceremony was all about; the Rockamorrans are in trouble, but you've promised to get them out of it."

"Of course!" Pinchbottle nodded vigorously. "I've already planned an economic survey—"

"That won't do the job, Mr. Ambassador; there's a ninety-foot dinosaur named Crunderthush loose in the area—"

"Dinosaur?" Pinchbottle's voice rose to a squeak.

Retief nodded. "And you've just sworn to kill him before sundown tomorrow."

3

"Look here, Retief," First Secretary Whaffle said in an accusing tone, "how is it you appear to understand the proceedings, conducted as they were in this barbaric local patois?"

"I didn't; they talked too fast. But I picked up a smattering of the language studying tapes on the way out, and I had a nice chat with the boatman—"

"I dispatched you to arrange for lodging and servants, not natter with low-caste locals!" Pinchbottle chirped.

"I had to do a little nattering in order to rent rooms; the locals don't understand sign language—"

"Impertinence, Mr. Retief? You may consider yourself under suspension—"

A group of Rockamorran officials had gathered, a column of pikemen behind them, stolid and menacing in green-scaled breastplates and greaves.

"Ah—before you confine yourself to quarters, Retief," Pinchbottle added, "just tell these chaps we won't be available for monster-killing. However, I think I can promise them a nice little Information Service Library, well-stocked with the latest CDT pamphlets—"

One of the Rockamorrans stepped forward, ducked his head, addressed the Ambassador:

"Honorable sir, I have pleasure of to be Haccop, interpretator of Terry mouth-noise learn from plenty Japanee, Dutch, Indian, and Hebrew Terry trader. We had nice chin-chin via telescreen before you-chap hit beach. . . ."

"Ah, to be sure! Pity you weren't standing by during the ceremony. Now we'll get to the bottom of this nonsense!" The Ambassador shot Retief a withering look. "I have heard . . . ah . . . rumors, to the effect that there's some sort of ha ha dinosaur roaming the countryside—"

"Yes, yes, excellent sir! Damm decent you-chap come along us, under circumstances!"

Pinchbottle frowned. "Perhaps I'd better clarify our position, just in case there was any confusion in translation. I am, of course, accredited by the *Corps Diplomatique Terrestrienne* as Ambassador Extraordinary and Minister Plenipotentiary to your government, with full authority to—"

"Hkkk! With title like that, how can you miss?" Haccop exulted. "You want few our boys along for pick up pieces, or you handle Crunderthush alone, catch more glory?"

"Here, I'm a diplomat! My offer was to assist your poor backward nation—"

"Sure; swell gesture of interplanetary chumship—"

"Just a moment!" Pinchbottle thrust out his lower lip, pointing a finger heavenward. "I deal in words and paper, sir, not deeds! That is, I am empowered to promise you anything I deem appropriate, but the actual performance is up to lesser persons—"

Haccop arranged his wide features in what was obviously a frown. "Around this end Galaxy, chum say, chum do—"

"Surely; and I'll speak to Sector HQ early next month when my vessel returns; I imagine something can be arranged—"

"Crunderthush on rampage *now!* No catchem wait next month! You owner genuine Japanese-made sword; you use!"

The Ambassador's chins quivered. "Sir! You forget yourself! I am the Terrestrial Ambassador, not a confounded exterminator service!"

"You-chap violate Rockamorran tradition number six-oh-two, passed two hours ago by Council of Honorable Dotards!"

Pinchbottle unbuckled the sword, tossed it aside. Retief lunged, caught it before it hit the dirt. Arms folded, the Ambassador glared at the Rockamorran.

"Let me state unequivocally, at once, that I have no intention of attacking a dinosaur!"

Haccop's face fell—an effect like a mud-pack slipping. "Is final decison?"

"Indeed it is, sir!"

The Rockamorran turned, spoke to the pikeman in glottal Rockamorran; they closed in, pikes aimed at Pinchbottle and the four diplomats who had participated in the oath-taking ceremony.

"Here, what's going on?" the Ambassador yelped.

"It seems they're taking you away to the local lockup, sir," Retief said.

"They can't do this to me! And why aren't you included?"

I didn't take the oath—"

"You-chap move along," Haccop said. "Rockamorran got no time be patience with oath-busters."

"H-how long will we be incarcerated?" First Secretary Whaffle bleated.

"One day," Haccop said.

"Well, that's not too bad, Your Excellency," Magnan pointed out. "We can spend the time figuring out an alibi—I mean, of course, composing a despatch to Sector Headquarters explaining how this is really a sort of diplomatic victory, in reverse,"

"Tomorrow, my good man," the Ambassador barked, "I can assure you I shall take drastic steps—"

"Have honor of to doubt that, faithless one," Haccop said. "Pretty neat trick take steps with head off."

4

Ambassador Pinchbottle glared at Retief through the barred window of his cell.

"I hold you fully responsible, sir, for not warning me of this barbaric custom! I trust you've established communication with the Corps Transport and ordered their instant return?"

"I'm afraid not; the local transmitter doesn't have the range—"

"Are you out of your mind? That means . . ." Pinchbottle sagged against the bars. "Retief," he whispered. "They'll lop our heads off. . . ."

A squad of Rockamorran pikemen rounded a corner, marched up to the Terrans' cell; Haccop produced a large key.

"Well, you-chap ready to take part in execution?"

"Just a minute," Retief said. "They promised to kill Crunderthush by sundown tomorrow. That's still a full day away."

"True; but always had head-cutting after lunch; pack in better house that way, at one credit per ticket."

Retief shook his head. "Highly illegal procedure. Killing off a few diplomats is perfectly understandable, but it has to be done in accordance with protocol or you'll have a squadron of Peace Enforcers in here revising Rockamorran traditions before you can say 'interference with internal affairs.'"

"Hmmm. You might have point there. OK, we hold off until tomorrow night, have torchlight execution, very colorful."

"Retief?" Magnan gasped, pushing up against the bars. "Isn't there some way to prevent this ghastly miscarriage of justice?"

"Only way, you-chap change mind, kill Crunderthush," Haccop said cheerfully.

Retief looked thoughtful. "Do these gentlemen have to do the job personally?"

"Posilutely! Can't have every Tom, George and Meyer getting into act. After all, killers of Crunderthush not only national heroes, win plenty refrigerator and green stamp too!"

"How about it, sir?" Whaffle addressed his chief. "Have a go, eh? Not much to lose. . . ."

"How? I can't kill the beast by firing off a despatch!"

"Maybe we could dig a hole and let him fall in—"

"Do you have any idea what size excavation would be required to inconvenience a ninety-foot behemoth, you idiot!"

"Suppose the Ambassador had a little help; would that be cricket?"

Haccop cocked his wide head. "Is good questioning; have to check with Ministry of Tradition on that point."

"I'd *love* to help, of course," Magnan said brightly. "It's just that I have this cough—"

"Yes, kaff kaff," Whaffle said. "Must be the damp air, all these confounded canals—"

"Will you let them out of the cell to scout the area and plan some strategy for the kill?" Retief asked.

Haccop shook his head. "Nix. Oath-breakers incarcerated by order of Big Shots. Release also have to clear through same. But glad to check up after nap-time."

"When will that be?"

"Nap over late tomorrow afternoon; maybe Midget-with-shiny-head and pals have just time turn trick before deadline."

"How can we kill a dinosaur while we're locked in here?" Pinchbottle demanded.

"Should have think of this before break oath," Haccop said briskly. "Interesting problem; interesting see how comes out."

5

Outside, Retief drew Haccop aside. "I don't suppose there's any objection to my taking a look around? I'd like to see what this monster looks like."

"Sure; do what you like, not charge for look at Crunderthush, see free any time—just so you got money pay way."

"I see. I don't suppose you'd lend me an official guide?"

"Correct. Rockamorran great tightwad, don't lend nothing, especially to foreigner."

"All I have is pocket change; I don't suppose you'd cash a check?"

"Hey, you skillful guesser, Terry, you like gamble?"

"I can see it's going to be a bit difficult to get around, without funds—"

"Oh-oh, guess wrong that time, spoil record. Better find answer, though; you run out of cash, you automatically slave."

"I get the feeling you don't much care whether this monster menace is removed or not."

"Is correct assumption. Big tourist drawing card. Also more fun this way, have something to bet on. Odds ten to one against Terries now."

169

"Meanwhile, he goes on eating people."

"Sure, few peasants got devour, but so long Crunderthush avoid eat me, is no scales off my stiz-plats, in word of immortal bard."

"Shakespeare?"

"No. Egbert Hiesenwhacker, early Terran trader introduce cards and dice to Rockamorra."

"Cards and dice, eh?"

"Sure; you like play? Come on, have fun, forget troubles, help kill time up to big affair tomorrow."

"That's a good idea, Haccop; lead the way. . . ."

6

It was dawn when Retief emerged from the Rockamorran gambling hell; Haccop followed him at the end of a light chain attached to a steel ring rivetted to his ankle, carrying a large basket of Rockamorran currency.

"Hey, Retief-master, lousy trick fill up when I got three ladies of ill repute—"

"I warned you about those inside straights, Haccop. Now tell me something; all that information the boys gave me about Crunderthush's habits. Was that all the straight dope?"

"Sure, Retief: pukka information—"

"All right, next stop the Ministry of Tradition. Lead on, Haccop."

7

An hour later, Retief emerged from the Ministry, frowning.

"It's not the best deal in the world, Haccop, but I suppose it's better than nothing."

"Should have offered bigger bribes, boss."

"I'm on a tight budget. Still I think we have a fighting chance. I'm going to need a heli and a good pair of binoculars. See to it at once, and meet me at the Grand Canal in half an hour."

"Boss, why worry about small-timers back in hoosegow? Look, I got plan; we be partners. You deal, and I circulate around behind opposition and signal with trick sunglasses—"

"We can discuss business later. Get going, before I report you to the Slave Relations Board for insubordination."

"Sure, chief, chop-chop!" Haccop set off at a lope, and Retief headed for the nearest sporting-goods shop.

8

Half an hour later, Haccop dropped a second-hand float-mounted heli in beside the quay where Retief waited beside a heap of goods. The Terran caught the mooring rope, pulled the light machine close, handed in his purchases and stepped aboard.

"They say Crunderthush is foraging a mile or two east of town; let's buzz over that way and size him up."

The heli lifted above the fernlike palms, beat its way across the gleaming pattern of canals and dome-shaped dwellings of Rockamorra City, gaining altitude; beyond the tilled paddies at the edge of the town a vast swamp stretched to distant smudges of jungle.

"That's him, boss!" Haccop called, pointing. Retief used the binoculars, picked out a towering shape almost invisible among the tall trees rising in clumps from the shallow water.

"He's big, all right. But he seems to be eating treetops; I thought he was a meat-eater."

"Sure, meat-eater, master. Dumb peasant climb tree get away, Crunderthush not have to bend neck."

The heli approached the browsing dinosaur at three hundred feet, circled him while Retief observed. The giant saurian, annoyed by the buzzing interloper, raised his great-jawed head, emitted a bellow like a blast on a giant tuba. Retief caught a vivid glimpse of a purple throat wide enough to drive a ground car through, studded with fangs like stalactites.

"Friendly-looking fellow. Is it possible to predict his course?"

"Maybe; Crunderthush always take it easy, graze village over pretty good before move on to next. About done here, I estimation. By lunchtime start toward next stop, half mile south."

"Let's cruise over that way."

Haccop dropped the heli to a fifty-foot altitude, buzzed across the flat water, leaving behind a pattern of blastripples, bending the scattered reeds in the wind of its passage.

"How deep is the water here?" Retief called.

"Knee-deep at low tide."

"When's low tide?"

"Hour before sunset tonight."

"What's the bottom like?"

"Exquisite soft mud. Hey, master, you like go down scroonch around in mud awhile? Is good for what ails you—"

"Sorry, we Terries aren't amphibians, Haccop."

"Oops, big excuses, chief; not mean draw attention to racial deficiencies."

"Will Crunderthush follow a straight course across the swamp?"

The heli was over the mud walls of the next village now. Retief could see the inhabitants going about their business as usual, appartently undisturbed by their position next on the menu.

"No telling, boss; might get distracted by juicy fisherman or unwary swimming party."

"Can we hire boats down there, and a few helpers?"

"Retief-master, you got enough cash to hire whole town." Haccop signed. "That pot before last; I never figured you for eagles back to back—"

"No post-mortems," Retief admonished. "Land there, in the marketplace."

Haccop dropped the flier in, grinned at the quickly gathering crowd of curious locals.

"I tell hicks go away, give Retief-boss room walk around, do little shopping?" he suggested.

"Absolutely not; we're going to need them. Listen carefully, Haccop; here's what I have in mind . . ."

9

It was late afternoon when Retief, wet and plastered to the hips with black mud, signaled to Haccop to land at the northernmost point of the village, a narrow finger of land edged by a baked-mud retaining wall. Half a mile away, wading ponderously across the shallows, Crunderthush rumbled softly to himself.

"The sound carries well, across the water," Retief commented. "It sounds as though he's right on top of us."

"And will be, plenty chop-chop," Haccop pointed out. "Retief-master think rope across water make big fella fall down?" The Rockamorran waved a hand at the taut one-inch nylon cable stretch two feet above the surface of the water across the oncoming monster's path.

"He won't get that far, if everything works out all right. How much time do we have? Another hour?"

"Crunderthush stop now to scratch—"

Retief observed the dinosaur sinking to his haunches, bringing up a massive hind leg to rake at the armored hide with two-foot talons, amid a prodigious splashing. "Maybe have hour, hour and half before dinnertime." Haccop concluded judiciously.

"OK, let's get moving! Get the hauling crew over here on the double. Have them attach a line to the center of the cable, and winch it this way until they can hook it over the trigger." Retief pointed to a heavy timber construction consisting of an eighteen-inch pile projecting a yard from the ground with a toggle mounted atop it.

"Retief-chief, humble slave bushed from all day stringing wires to trees—"

"We'll be through pretty soon. How's the axe-crew doing with that pole?"

"Top hole, sahib. Pretty near get nice point on one end, notch on other—"

"Get it set up here as soon as they're finished; prop it in the two forked saplings the boys are supposed to set in the bottom out there."

"Too many thing do all one time," Haccop complained. "Bwana Retief have strange hobby—"

"I'm taking the heli into town; I'll be back in half an hour. Have everything ready just the way I explained it, or it won't be just Terry heads rolling around here."

10

The great pale sun of Rockamorra, with its tiny blue-white companion close behind, was just sinking in a glory of purple and old rose as Retief returned to ground the heli at the village.

"Ohio, Retief-san!" Haccop called. "All set, accordingly to plan! Now we hit trail, plenty quick! Crunderthush too close for maximizing adjustment!"

"Look at the creature!" Whaffle quavered, descending from the heli. "As big as a Yill Joss Palace—and coming this way!"

"Why have you brought us here, Retief?" Pinchbottle demanded, his jowls paler than usual. "I prefer beheading to serving as hors d'oeuvre to that leviathan!"

"It's quite simple, Mr. Ambassador," Retief said soothingly, leading the stout diplomat across to where

Haccop stood beaming beside the completed apparatus. "You merely use this mallet to hit the trigger; this releases the cable, which drives the lance—"

"R-R-R-R-Retief! Are you unaware that-that-that—"

"I know: he looks pretty big at a hundred yards, doesn't he, Mr. Magnan? But he moves slowly. We have plenty of time—"

"We? Why include *us* in this mad venture?" the portly envoy demanded.

"You heard what Haccop said, sir. You gentlemen have to personally kill the creature. I think I have it arranged so that—"

"Oh-oh, Master!" Haccop pointed. "Look like distraction! Couple drunks going fishing!"

Retief followed the Rockamorran's gaze, saw a dugout pushing off with two staggering locals singing gaily as they took up paddles, steered for deep water on a course that would take them within fifty feet of the dinosaur.

"Try to stop them, Haccop! If he changes course now, we're out of luck!"

Haccop splashed out a few yards into the mud, floundering, cupped his hands and bellowed. The fishermen saw him, waved cheerfully, kept going.

"No use, boss." Haccop waded back to shore. "Look, better you and me make tracks, hit town farther up archipelago; swell floating crap game going—"

"Mr. Ambassador, stand by!" Retief snapped. "I'll have to bait him in. When I give the word, hit that trigger, and not a second before!" He sprinted to the small wharf nearby, jumped into a tethered boat, slipped the painter, plied quickly out toward Crunderthush. The monster was poised now, mouth open, gazing toward the fishermen. He emitted a rumbling growl, turned ponderously, took a step to intercept them. Retief, cutting in front of the dinosaur, waved his paddle and shouted. The giant reptile hesitated, turned to stare at Retief, rumbled again. Then, at a burst of song from the happy anglers, swung back their way. Retief stopped, plucked a rusty fishing weight from the bottom of his skiff, hurled it at Crunderthush. It struck the immense leathery chest with a resounding *whop!* at which the monster paused in mid-swing, brought its left eye to bear on Retief. It stared, cocked its head to bring the right eye into play, then, its tiny mind made up, raised a huge foot from the mud with a sucking sound, started for Retief. He eased the boat back with quick strokes of the paddle; the dinosaur, tantalized by the receding prey, lunged, gained thirty feet, sending up a swell which rocked the tiny craft violently. Retief grabbed for balance, dropped the paddle.

"Retief-boss!" Haccop boomed. "This no time to goof!"

"Somebody do something!" Magnan's voice wailed.

"He'll be devoured!" Whaffle yelped.

The dinosaur lunged again; his power-shovel jaws gaped, snapped to with a clash of razor-edged crockery a yard short of the boat. Retief, standing in the stern, gauged the range, then turned and raised an arm, brought it down in a chopping motion.

"Let her go, Mr. Ambassador!" he called, and dived over the side. Ambassador Pinchbottle, standing transfixed beside the trigger apparatus of the oversized arbalest, gaped as Crunderthush raised his long neck twenty feet above the water, streaming mud, emitted an ear-splitting screech, and struck at Retief, swimming hard for shore. At the last instant, Retief twisted, kicked off to the left. The monster, confused, raised his head for another look; his eye fell on the diplomats on shore, now only fifty feet distant. At his glance, Pinchbottle dropped the heavy mallet, turned and sprinted for the heli. Three other Terrans gave sharp cries and wheeled to follow. As the stout mission chief bounded past Secretary Magnan he tripped, dived face-down in the soft dirt. The mallet skidded aside; Magnan sprang for it, caught it on the second bounce, leaped to the trigger, and brought the hammer over and down in an overarm swing—

There was a deep, musical *boing!* The sharpened twelve-foot hardwood pole leaped forward as the taut nylon sprang outward. Crunderthush, just gathering himself for the final satisfying snap at the morsel in the water before him, rocked back as the lance buried half its length full in his chest. Retief surfaced in time to see the dinosaur totter, fall sideways with a tremendous splash that swamped the sea wall, sent a tide of mud-and-blood-stained water washing around the frantic Terrans fighting for position at the heli hatch. Pinchbottle staggered to his feet sputtering, as the flood receded from his position. Magnan sat down hard, fumbled out a hanky and daubed mud from his lapels, watching the stricken monster kicking spasmodically. Haccop whooped delightedly, plunged into the water to assist Retief ashore.

"Nice going, Sidi! Plenty meat here for barbecue for whole town! Dandy substitute event for disappoint of not to see Terry head-chopping after all!"

11

Dabbing at his mud-caked shirt front, Ambassador Pinchbottle nodded curtly at Retief.

"Having gotten me into this awkward situation, young man, I'm glad to see that you carried on to rectify matters. Naturally, I could have extricated myself and my staff at any time, merely by a skillful word in the right quarter, but I felt it would be valuable experience for you to work this out for yourself—"

"Hey, Retief-master, I form Terries up in column of ducks, go get fitted for leg irons?"

"No, I don't think that will be necessary, Haccop—"

"What's that? Leg irons?" Pinchbottle whirled on the Rockamorran. "See here, you nincompoop, I've slain your monster, as required by your barbaric code! Now I demand—"

"Slave not demand nothing," Haccop said. "Slave

hold mouth right, work hard, hope for escape beating—"

The Ambassador spun to face Retief. "What, may I ask, is the meaning of this idiot's driveling?"

"Well, Mr. Ambassador, the Rockamorrans have very rigid rules about this sort of thing, However, I managed to work out a deal with them. Ordinarily, you couldn't have any assistance in carrying out your oath—"

"Assistance? I seem to recall that you were disporting yourself in the swamp yonder when I—er, ah—a member of my staff, that is—dispatched the brute!"

"True; but the Rockamorrans seem to think I had something to do with it. Under the circumstances they agreed to commute your sentence to slavery for life."

"Slavery!"

"Fortunately, I was able to buy up an option on your contracts—provided you still had heads—"

"Buy up . . . ? Well, in that case, my boy, I suppose I can overlook the irregularity. If you'll just run along and see to my baggage—"

"I'm afraid it's not quite that simple, sir. You see, I still have to pay your upkeep, and since I've spent all my money buying you—"

Pinchbottle sputtered incoherently.

". . . I've had to hire you out to earn enough to cover living expenses until the ship gets back."

"But—but—that will be weeks—"

"OK, Terries; I, Haccop, am slave foreman. First job, strip out blubber from dead monster. Good job, take maybe two weeks, keep you in ration with maybe little left over for pack of Camels once a week—"

"But—but—Retief! What will you be doing in the meantime?"

"Haccop tells me there's another dinosaur operating a few miles east. If I can bag it, that will give you another two weeks' work after this job's finished. With a little luck, I can keep you going until the ship arrives."

"Hey, Retief . . ." Haccop came close, whispered

behind his hand, "Maybe better bring thin-face slave name Magnan along you, me. Got idea Midget-with-bad-temper hold grudge, Magnan trip him and make him lose number one position in dash for heli. . . ."

"Good idea, Haccop, bring him along. . . ."

12

Two hours later, Retief, Haccop, and Magnan, bathed and clad in new Rockamorran hose and doublets, sat on a tiled roof terrace, dining on a delicately spiced casserole of whitefish and sea vegetables. The view out over the town and the water to the east was superb; the brilliant light of the three moons showed the silvery waterways, the island-villages, and, distantly, the great hulk of the dead dinosaur, its four legs in the air, and four tiny figures crawling over it like fleas. Their arms, wielding machetes, could be clearly discerned.

"Retief, no time linger over succulent native dishes," Haccop said. "Plenty big game of Red Eye just getting under way at Tavern of Golden Ale Keg. . . ."

"Don't rush me, Haccop. Order us a second round of drinks—but none for Mr. Magnan. He doesn't indulge. The Ambassador doesn't approve of booze."

Magnan blinked at him thoughtfully.

"Ah, Retief, knowing your skill with the pasteboards and the, er, galloping dominoes, why couldn't you secure sufficient capital to provision Ambassador Pinchbottle and the others without the necessity for their stripping all that blubber?"

Retief sampled the fresh drink the waiter put before him, nodded appreciatively.

"Mr. Magnan, the ship won't arrive for at least six weeks, possibly longer. Would you recommend that a nonaccredited diplomat with Ambassador Pinchbottle's personality be permitted to run loose among the Rockamorrans for that length of time?"

Magnan looked grave, swallowed hard. "I see what you mean, Retief; but if he finds out, he'll be furious. . . ."

"I don't intend to burden him with the knowledge, Mr. Magnan. Do you?"

Magnan pursed his lips. "No," he said. "What he doesn't know won't hurt him, eh?" He managed a tentative smile. "Speaking of which, I think I'll have that drink after all."

THE FOREST
IN THE SKY

1

As Second Secretary of Embassy Jame Retief stepped from the lighter which had delivered the Terran Mission to the close-cropped turquoise sward of the planet Zoon, a rabbit-sized creature upholstered in deep blue-violet angora bounded into view from behind an upthrust slab of scarlet granite. It sat on its oddly arranged haunches a few yards from the newcomers, twitching an assortment of members as though testing the air for a clue to their origin. First Secretary Magnan's narrow face registered apprehension as a second furry animal, this one a yard-wide sphere of indigo fuzz, came hopping around the prow of the vessel.

"Do you suppose they bite?"

"They're obviously grass-eaters," Colonel Smartfinger, the Military Attaché, stated firmly. "Probably make most affectionate pets. Here, ah, kitty, kitty." He snapped his fingers and whistled. More bunnies appeared.

"Ah—Colonel." The Agricultural Attaché touched his sleeve. "If I'm not mistaken—those are immature specimens of the planet's dominate life-form!"

"Eh?" The colonel pricked up his ears. "These animals? Impossible!"

"They look just like the high-resolution photos the Sneak-and-peek teams took. My, aren't there a lot of them!"

"Well, possibly this is a sort of playground for them. Cute little fellows—" Smartfinger paused to kick one which had opened surprising jaws for a nip at his ankle.

"That's the worst of these crash operations," the Economic Officer shied as a terrier-sized fur-bearer darted in close and crunched a shiny plastic button from the cuff of his mauve late-midmorning semi-informal hip-huggers. "One never knows just what one may be getting into."

"Oh-oh." Magnan nudged Retief as a technician bustled from the lock, heavy-laden. "Here comes the classified equipment the Ambassador's been sitting on since we left Sector HQ."

"Ah!" Ambassador Oldtrick stepped forward, rubbing his small, well-manicured hands briskly together. He lifted an article resembling a Mae West life jacket from the stack offered.

"Here, gentlemen, is my personal contribution to, ahem, high-level negotiations!" He smiled proudly and slipped his arms through a loop of woven plastic. "One-man, self-contained, power-boosted aerial lift units," he announced. "With these, gentlemen, we will confront the elusive Zooner on his home ground!"

"But—the post report said the Zooners are a sort of animated blimp!" the Information Officer protested. "Only a few have been seen, cruising at high altitude! Surely we're not going after *them!*"

"It was inevitable, gentlemen." Oldtrick winced as the technician tugged the harness strap tight across his narrow chest. "Sooner or later man was bound to encounter lighter-than-air intelligence—a confrontation for which we of the *Corps Diplomatique Terrestrienne* are eminently well qualified!"

"But, Your Excellency," First Secretary Magnan spoke up, "couldn't we have arranged to confront these, er, gaseous brains here on solid land—"

"Nonsense, Magnan! Give up this superb opportunity to display the adaptabality of the trained diplomat? Since these beings dwell among the clouds of their native world, what more convincing evidence of good will could we display than to meet them on their own ground, so to speak?"

182

"Of course," the corpulent Political Officer put in, "we aren't actually *sure* there's anyone up there." He squinted nervously up at the lacy mass of land-coral that reached into the Zoonian sky, its lofty pinnacles brushing a seven-thousand-foot stratum of cumulonibus.

"That's where we'll steal a march on certain laggards," Oldtrick stated imperturbably. "The survey photos clearly show the details of a charming aerial city nestled on the peak. Picture the spectacle, gentlemen, when the Mission descends on them from the blue empyrean to open a new era of Terran-Zoon relations!"

"Yes—a striking *mise-en-scène* indeed, as Your Excellency points out." The Economic Officer's cheek gave a nervous twitch. "But what if something goes wrong with the apparatus? The steering mechanism, for example, appears a trifle insubstantial—"

"These devices were designed and constructed under my personal supervision, Chester," the Ambassador cut him off coolly. "However," he continued, "don't allow that circumstance to prevent you from pointing out any conceptual flaws you may have detected."

"A marvel of light-weight ingenuity," the Economic Officer said hastily. "I only meant . . ."

"Chester's point was just that maybe some of us ought to wait here, Mr. Ambassador," the Military Attaché said hastily. "In case any, ah, late despatches come in from Sector, or something. Much as I'll hate to miss participating, I volunteer—"

"Kindly rebuckle your harness, Colonel," Oldtrick said through thinned lips, "I wouldn't dream of allowing you to make the sacrifice."

"Good Lord, Retief," Magnan said in a hoarse whisper behind his hand. "Do you suppose these little tiny things will actually work? And does he really mean . . ." Magnan's voice trailed off as he stared up into the bottomless sky.

"He really means," Retief confirmed. "As for His Excellency's invention, I suppose that given a large-diameter, low-density planet with a standard mass of 4.8 and a surface G of .72, plus an atmospheric pressure of 27.5 P.S.I. and a superlight gas—it's possible."

"I was afraid of that," Magnan muttered. "I don't suppose that if we all joined together and took a firm line . . .?"

"Might be a savings at that," Retief nodded judiciously. "The whole staff could be court-martialed as a group."

". . . and now," Ambassador Oldtrick's reedy voice paused impressively as he settled his beret firmly in place. "If you're ready, gentlemen—inflate your gasbags!"

A sharp hissing started up as a dozen petcocks opened as one. Bright-colored plastic bubbles inflated with sharp popping sounds above the shoulders of the Terran diplomats. The Ambassador gave a little spring and bounded high above the heads of his staff, where he hung, supported by the balloon, assisted by a softly snorting battery of air jets buckled across his hips. Colonel Smartfinger, a large bony man, gave a half-hearted leap, fell back, his toes groping for contact as a gust of air bumbled him across the ground. Magnan, lighter than the rest, made a creditable spring, rose to dangle beside the Chief of Mission. Retief adjusted his bouyancy indicator carefully, jumped off as the rest of the staff scrambled to avoid the distinction of being the last man airborne.

"Capital, gentlemen!" Oldtrick beamed at the others as they drifted in a ragged row, roped together like alpinists, five yards above the surface. "I trust each of you is ready to savor the thrill of breaking new ground!"

"An unfortunate turn of phrase," Magnan quavered, looking down at the rocky outcropping below. The grassy plain on which the lighter had deposited the mission stretched away to the horizon, interrupted only by the upthrusting coral reefs dotted across it like lonely castles in the Daliesque desert, and a distant smudge of smoky green.

"And now—onward to what I hope I may, without charges of undue jocularity, term a new high in diplomacy," Oldtrick cried. He advanced his jet control lever and lifted skyward, trailed by the members of his staff.

2

Five hundred feet aloft, Magnan clutched the arm of Retief, occupying the adjacent position in the line.

"The lighter is lifting off!" He pointed to the slim shape of the tiny Corps vessel, drifting upward from the sands below. "It's abandoning us!"

"A mark of the Ambassador's confidence that we'll meet with a hospitable reception at the hands of the Zooners," Retief pointed out.

"Frankly, I'm at a loss to understand Sector's eagerness to accredit a Mission to this wasteland." Magnan raised his voice above the whistling of the sharp wind and the polyphonous huffing of the jato units. "Retief, you seem to have a way of picking up odd bits of information; any idea what's behind it?"

"According to a usually reliable source, the Groaci have their eyes—all five of them—on Zoon. Naturally, if they're interested, the Corps has to beat them to it."

"Aha!" Magnan looked wise. "They must Know Something. By the way," he edged closer. "Who told you? The Ambassador? The Undersecretary?"

"Better than that; the bartender at the Departmental snackbar."

"Well, I daresay our five-eyed friends will receive a sharp surprise when they arrive to find us already on a cordial basis with the locals. Unorthodox though Ambassador Oldtrick's technique may be, I'm forced to concede that it appears the only way we could have approached these Zooners." Magnan craned upward at the fanciful formation of many-fingered rock past which they were rising. "Odd that none of them have sallied forth to greet us."

Retief followed his gaze. "We still have six thousand feet to go," he said. "I suppose we'll find a suitable reception waiting for us at the top."

Half an hour later, Ambassador Oldtrick in the lead, the party soared above the final rampart to look down on a wonderland of rose and pink and violet coral, an intricacy of spires, tunnels, bridges, grottos, turrets, caves, avenues, as complex and delicately fragile as spun sugar.

"Carefully, now, gentlemen." Oldtrick twiddled his jato control, dropped in to a gentle landing on a graceful arch spanning a cleft full of luminous gloom produced by the filtration of light through the translucent coral. Other members of his staff settled in around him, gazing with awe at the minarets rising all around them.

The Ambassador, having twisted a knob to deflate his gasbag and laid aside his flying harness, was frowning as he looked about the silent prospect.

"I wonder where the inhabitants have betaken themselves?" he lifted a finger, and six eager underlings sprang to his side.

"Apparently the natives are a trifle shy, gentlemen," he stated. "Nose around a bit, look friendly, and avoid poking into any possibly taboo areas such as temples and public comfort stations."

Leaving their deflated gasbags heaped near their point of arrival, the Terrans set about peering into caverns and clambering up to gaze along twisting alleyways winding among silent coral palaces. Retief followed a narrow path atop a ridge which curved upward to a point of vantage. Magnan trailed, mopping at his face with a scented tissue.

"Apparently no one's at home," he puffed, coming up to the tiny platform from which Retief surveyed the prospect spread below. "A trifle disconcerting, I must say. I wonder what sort of arrangements have been laid on for feeding and housing us?"

"Another odd thing," Retief said. "No empty beer bottles, tin cans, old newspapers, or fruit rinds. In fact, no signs of habitation at all."

"It rather appears we've been stood up," the Economic Officer said indignantly. "Such cheek! And from a pack of animated intangibles, at that!"

"It's my opinion the town's been evacuated," the Political Officer said in the keen tones of one delivering an incisive analysis of a complex situation. "We may as well leave."

"Nonsense!" Oldtrick snapped. "Do you expect me to trot back to Sector and announce that I can't find the government to which I'm accredited?"

"Great heavens!" Magnan blinked at a lone dark cloud drifting ominously closer under the high overcast. "I thought I sensed something impending! Oh, Mr. Ambassador . . . !" he called, starting back down. At that moment, a cry from an adjacent cavern focused all eyes on the Military Attaché, emerging therefrom with a short length of what appeared to be tarred rope, charred at one end.

"Signs of life, Your Excellency!" he announced. "A dope stick butt!" He sniffed it. "Freshly smoked."

"Dope sticks! Nonsense!" Oldtrick prodded the exhibit with a stubby forefinger. "I'm sure the Zooners are far too insubstantial to indulge in such vices."

"Ah, Mr. Ambassador," Magnan called. "I suggest we all select a nice dry cave and creep inside out of the weather—"

"Cave? Creep? Weather? What weather?" Oldtrick rounded on the First Secretary as he came up. "I'm here to establish diplomatic relations with a newly discovered race, not set up houskeeping!"

"*That* weather," Magnan said stiffly, pointing at the giant cloud sweeping swiftly down on them at a level which threatened to shroud the party in fog in a matter of minutes.

"Eh? Oh . . ." Oldtrick stared at the approaching thunderhead. "Yes, well, I was about to suggest we seek shelter—"

"What about the dope stick?" The Colonel tried to recapture the limelight. "We hadn't finished looking at my dope stick when Magnan came along with his cloud."

"My cloud is of considerably more urgency than your dope stick, Colonel," Magnan said loftily. "Particularly since, as His Excellency has pointed out, your little find couldn't possibly be the property of the Zooners."

"Ha! Well if it isn't the property of the Zooners, then whose is it?" The officer looked at the butt suspiciously, passed it around. Retief glanced at it, sniffed it.

"I believe you'll find this to be of Groaci manufacture, Colonel," he said.

"What?" Oldtrick clapped a hand to his forehead. "Impossible!" Why I myself hardly know—that is, they couldn't—I mean to say, drat it, the location of the town is Utter Top Secret!"

"Ahem." Magnan glanced up complacently at his cloud, now a battleship-sized shape only a few hundred feet distant. "I wonder if it mightn't be as well to hurry along now before we find ourselves drenched."

"Good Lord!" The Political Officer stared at the gray-black mass as it moved across the hazy sun, blotting it out like an eclipse. In the sudden shadow, the wind was abruptly chill. The cloud was above the far edge of the reef now; as they watched, it dropped lower, brushed across a projecting digit of stone with a dry *squeee!*, sent a shower of tiny rock fragments showering down. Magnan jumped and blinked his eyes hard, twice.

"Did you see . . . ? Did *I* see . . . ?"

Dropping lower, the cloud sailed between two lofty minarets, scraped across a lower tower topped with a series of sharp spikes. There was a ripping sound, a crunch of stone, a sharp *pow!*, a blattering noise of escaping gas. A distinct odor of rubberized canvas floated across to the diplomats, borne by the brisk breeze.

"Ye Gods!" the Military Attaché shouted. "That's

no cloud! It's a Trojan Horse! A dirigible in camouflage! A trick—" He cut off and turned to run as the foundering four-acre balloon swung, canted at a sharp angle, and thundered down amid gratings and crunchings, crumbling bridges, snapping off slender towers, settling in to blanket the landscape like a collapsed circus tent. A small, agile creature in a flared helmet and a black hip-cloak appeared at its edge, wading across the deflated folds of the counterfeit cloud, cradling a formidable blast gun in its arms. Others followed, leaping down and scampering for strategic positions on the high ground surrounding the Terrans.

"Groaci shock troops!" the Military Attaché shouted. "Run for your lives!" He dashed for the concealment of a shadow canyon; a blast from a Groaci gun sent a cloud of coral chips after him. Retief, from a position in the lee of a buttress of rock, saw half a dozen of the Terrans skid to a halt at the report, put up their hands as the invaders swarmed around them, hissing soft Groaci sibilants. Three more Terrans, attempting flight, were captured within forty feet, prodded back at gunpoint. A moment later a sharp *oof!* and a burst of military expletives announced the surrender of Colonel Smartfinger. Retief made his way around a rock spire, spotted Ambassador Oldtrick being routed from his hidingplace behind a cactus-shaped outcropping.

"Well, fancy meeting *you* here, Hubert." A slightly built, splendidly dressed Groaci strolled forward, puffing at a dope stick held in silver tongs. "I regret to submit you to the indignity of being trussed up like a gerp-fowl in plucking season, but what can one expect when one commits aggravated trespass, eh?"

"Trespass? I'm here in good faith as Terran envoy to Zoon!" Oldtrick sputtered. "See here, Ambassador Shish, this is an outrage! I demand you order these bandits to release me and my staff at once—"

"Field Marshal Shish, if you please, Hubert," Shish whispered. "These are a duly constituted constabulary.

If you annoy me, I may just order them to exercise the full rigor of the law which you have so airily disregarded!"

"What law? Your confounded dacoits have assaulted peaceful diplomats in peaceful pursuit of their duties!"

"Interplanetary law, my dear sir," Shish hissed. "That section dealing with territorial claims to uninhabited planets."

"But—but the Zooners inhabit Zoon!"

"So? An exhaustive search of the entire planetary surface by our Scouting Service failed to turn up any evidence of intelligent habitation."

"Surface? But the Zooners don't occupy the surface—"

"Exactly. Therefore we have assumed ownership. Now, about reparations and damages in connection with your release; I should think a million credits would be about right—paid directly to me, of course, as Planetary Military Governor, *pro tem.* . . ."

"A million?" Oldtrick swallowed hard. "But . . . but . . . see here!" He fixed Shish with a desperate eye. "What is it you fellows are after? This isn't the kind of sandy, dry real estate you Groaci prefer—and the world has no known economic or strategic value. . . ."

"Hmmm." Shish flicked his dope stick butt aside. "No harm in telling you, I suppose. We intend to gather a crop."

"Crop? There's nothing growing here but blue grass and land coral!"

"Wrong again, Hubert. The crop that interests us is this . . ." He fingered the edge of his shaggy violet cape. "A luxury fur, light, colorful, nonallergic . . ." He lowered his voice and leered with three eyes. "And with reportedly fabulous aphrodisiac effects; and there are millions of credits worth of it, leaping about the landscape below, free for the harvesting!"

"But—surely you jest, sir! Those are—"

There was a sudden flurry as one of the Terrans broke free and dashed for a cave. The Groaci constabulary gave chase. Shish made an annoyed sound and hurried away to oversee the recapture. Oldtrick, left momentarily alone, eyed the flying harness lying in a heap ten yards from him. He took a deep breath, darted forward, snatched up a harness. As he turned to sprint for cover, a breathy cry announced his discovery. Desperately, the Chief of Mission struggled into his straps as he ran, twisted the valve, fired his jato units, and shot into the air over the heads of a pair of fleet-footed aliens who had been about to lay him by the heels. He passed over Retief's head at an altitude of twenty feet, driven smartly by the brisk breeze. Retief ducked his head, hugged the shadows as Groaci feet pounded past at close range, pursuing the fleeing Terran. Retief saw half a dozen marksmen taking aim at the airborne diplomat as the wind swept him out over the reef's edge. Shots rang. There was a sharp report as a round pierced the gasbag. With a despairing wail, the Ambassador sank swiftly out of sight.

Retief rolled to his feet, ran to the pile of flight harnesses, grabbed up two, whirled and sprinted for the edge over which Oldtrick had vanished. Two Groaci, turning to confront the new menace descending on their rear, were bowled aside by Retief's rush. Another sprang to intercept him, bringing his gun around. Retief caught the barrel in full stride, swung the gun with its owner still clinging desperately to it, slammed the unfortunate alien into the faces of his astounded comrades. Shots split the air past Retief's ear, but without slowing, he charged to the brink and dived over into seven thousand feet of open air.

4

The uprushing wind shrieked past Retief's ears like a typhoon. Gripping one of the two harnesses in his teeth, he pulled the other on as one would don a vest, buckled the straps. He looked down, squinting against the rush of air. The Ambassador, falling free now with his burst balloon fluttering at his back, was twenty feet below. Retief tucked his arms close, kicked his heels up to assume a diver's attitude. The distance between the two men lessened. The rock face flashed past, dangerously close. Retief's hand brushed Old-trick's foot. The Ambassador twisted convulsively to roll a wild eye at Retief, suspended above him in the hurtling airstream. Retief caught the senior diplomat's arm, shoved the spare harness into his hand. A moment later Oldtrick had shed his ruined gasbag and shrugged into the replacement. With a twist of the petcock, he inflated his balloon and at once slowed, falling behind Retief, who opened his own valve, felt the sudden tug of the harness. A moment later, he was floating lightly a hundred feet below the Ambassador.

"Quick thinking, my boy . . ." Oldtrick's voice came faintly. "As soon as I'm back aboard the transport, I shall summon a heavy PE Unit to deal with those ruffians! We'll thwart their inhuman scheme to massacre helpless infant Zooners, thus endearing ourselves to their elders!" He was close now, dropping as Retief rose. "You'd better come along with me," he said sharply as they passed, ten feet apart. "I'll want your corroborative statements, and—"

"Sorry, Mr. Ambassador," Retief said. "I seem to have gotten hold of a heavy-duty unit. It wants to go up, and the valve appears to be stuck."

"Come back," Oldtrick shouted as he dropped away below the younger man. "I insist that you accompany me . . ."

"I'm afraid it's out of my hands now, sir," Retief called. "I suggest you stay out of sight of any colonist who may have settled in down below. I have an idea they'll be a little trigger happy when they discover their police force is stranded on the reef; and a dangling diplomat will make a tempting target."

5

The southwest breeze bore Retief along at a brisk twenty-mile-per-hour clip. He twisted the buoyancy control lever both ways, to no avail. The landscape dwindled away below him, a vast spread of soft aquamarine hills. From this height, immense herds of creatures were visible, ranging in color from pale blue to deep grapejuice. They appeared, Retief noted, to be converging on a point not far from the base of the coral reef, where a number of black dots might have been small structures. Then the view was obscured, first by whipping streamers of fog, then by a dense, wet mist which enveloped him like a cool Turkish bath.

For ten minutes he swirled blindly upward; then watery sunshine penetrated, lighting the vapor to a golden glow; a moment later he burst through into brilliance. A deep blue sky arched above the blinding white cloud-plain. Squinting against the glare, he saw a misty shape of pale green projecting above the clouds at a distance he estimated at five miles. Using steering jets, he headed for it.

Fifteen minutes later, he was close enough to make out thick, glossy yellow columns, supporting masses of chartreuse foliage. Closer, the verdure resolved into clusters of leaves the size of tablecloths, among which gaudy blossoms shone scarlet and pink. In the leafy depths, the sun striking down from zenith was filtered to a deep, green-gold gloom. Retief maneuvered toward a sturdy-looking branch, only at the last moment saw the yard-long thorns concealed in the shadow of the spreading leaves. He ducked, twisted aside from the savage stab of a needlepoint, heard the rip and *ker-pow!* as his gasbag burst, impaled; then he slammed hard against a thigh-thick, glass-smooth branch, grabbed with both hands and both legs, and braked to a halt inches from an upthrust dagger of horny wood.

6

All around, life swarmed, humming, buzzing, chattering in a hundred oddly euphonious keys. There were fluffy, spherical bird-things in vivid colors; darting scaled runners like jeweled ferrets; swarms of tiny golden four-winged butterflies. Once something hooted, far away, and for a moment the chorus was stilled, to resume a moment later.

Looking down, Retief could see nothing but level after level of leafy branches, blotting out the swirling clouds two hundred feet below. The ground, he estimated, was a mile and a half farther—not what could be described as an easy climb. Still, it looked like the only way. He divested himself of the ruined altitude harness, picked a route and started down.

Retief had covered no more than fifty feet when a sudden flurry of motion caught his eye through the foliage. A moment later, a clump of leaves leaned aside, pushed by a gust of wind, to reveal a bulky, ghost-pale creature, its body covered with short white bristles, its head a flattened spheroid. Its multiple shiny black limbs threshed wildly against the restraint of a web of silky, scarlet threads, stretched between limbs in an intricate spiral pattern. A flat pouch, secured by a flat strap, bobbed against the trapped creature's side. The web, Retief saw, was constructed at the very tip of a pair of long boughs which leaned in a deep curve under the weight of the victim—and of something else.

Peering into the shadows, he saw a foot-long claw like a pair of oversized garden shears poised in the air two feet from the trapped being; then he noted that the claw was attached to an arm like a six-foot length of stainless-steel pipe, which was attached, in turn, to a body encased in silvery-blue armor-plate, almost invisible in the leafy gloom.

As Retief watched, the arm lunged, sheared through a cluster of awning-sized leaves, snipped off a tuft of stiff white hairs as the snared one made a desperate bound sideways. The aggressor, it appeared, had advanced as far along the fragile support as possible; but it was only a matter of time until the murderous pincer connected with its target.

Retief checked his pockets, produced a pocketknife with a two-inch blade, useful chiefly for cutting the tips from hand-rolled Jorgensen cigars. He used it to saw through a half-inch-thick vine drooping near him. He coiled the rope over his shoulder and started back up.

7

From a branch far above, Retief peered down through the leafy shadows at the twelve-foot monstrosity clinging, head down, from a six-inch stem. The predator had stretched itself out to its utmost length in its effort to reach its victim trapped below.

Retief slid down to a crouch within touching distance of the monster's hind leg. He flipped out the lariat he had fashioned hastily from the length of pliable vine, passed its end under the massive ankle joint, whipped it quickly into a slip knot which would tighten under pressure. He tied the other end of the rope to a sturdy bole at his back, pulling it up just short of taut. Then he slid around the trunk and headed back for the scene of the action, paying out a second rope, the end of which was secured to a stout limb.

The trapped creature, huddled at the extreme extent of the rein given it by the binding strands of silk, saw Retief, gave a convulsive bound which triggered another snap of the giant claw hovering above.

"Stand pat," Retief called softly. "I'll try to distract his attention." He stepped out on a slender branch, which sagged but held. Holding the end of the rope in his free hand, he made his way to within ten feet of the web.

Above, the claw-creature, sensing movement near-by, poked out a gliterring eye at the end of a two-foot rod, studied Retief from a distance of five yards. Retief watched the claw, which hovered indecisevely, ready to strike in either direction.

A baseball-sized fruit was growing within easy reach. Retief plucked it, took aim, and pitched it at the monster's eye. It struck and burst, spattering the surrounding foliage with a sticky yellow goo and an odor of overripe melon. Quick as thought, the claw struck out at Retief as he jumped, gripping the vine, and swung in a graceful Tarzan-style arc across toward a handy landing platform thirty feet distant. The armored meat-eater, thwarted, lunged after him. There was a noisy rasping of metal-hard hooks against wood, a frantic shaking of branches; then the barrel-shaped body halted in mid-spring with a tremendous jerk as the rope lashed to its leg came up short. Retief, safely lodged in his new platform, caught a momentary glimpse of an open mouth lined with ranks of multi-pronged teeth; then, with a sharp *zong!* the rope supporting the monster parted. The apparition dropped away, smashing its way downward with a series of progressively fainter concussions until it was lost in the depths below.

8

The bristled Zoonite sagged heavily in the net, watching Retief with a row of shiny eyes like pink shirt buttons as he sawed through the strands of the web with his pocketknife. Freed, it dipped into its hip-pouch with a four-fingered hand encased in a glove ornamented with polished, inch-long talons, brought out a small cylinder which it raised to its middle eye.

"*Hrikk*," it said in a soft rasp. A mouth like Jack Pumpkinhead's gaped in an unreadable expression.

There was a bright flash which made a green after-image dance on Retief's retinas. The alien dropped the object back in the pouch, took out a second artifact resembling a footlong harmonica, which it adjusted on a loop around its neck. At once, it emitted a series of bleeps, toots and deep, resonant thrums, then looked at Retief in a way which seemed expectant.

"If I'm not mistaken, that's a Groaci electronic translator," Retief said. "Trade goods like the camera, I presume?"

"Correct," the device interpreted the small alien's rasping tones. "By George, it works!"

"The Groaci are second to none, when it comes to miniaturized electronics and real estate acquistion," Retief said.

"Real estate?" the Zoonite inquired with a rising inflection.

"Planetary surfaces," Retief explained.

"Oh, that. Yes, I'd heard they'd settled in down below. No doubt a pre-germination trauma's at the root of the matter. But, every being to his own form of self-destruction, as Zerd so succinctly put it before he dissolved himself in fuming nitric acid." The alien's button eyes roved over Retief. "Though I must say your own death wish takes a curious form."

"Oh?"

"Teasing a vine-jack for a starter," The Zoonite amplified. "That's dangerous, you know. The claw can snip through six inches of *gilv* as though it were a zoob-patty."

"Actually, I got the impression the thing was after you," Retief said.

"Oh, it was, it was. Almost got me, too. Hardly worth the effort. I'd make a disappointing meal." The Zoonite fingered its translator, the decorative claws clicking tinnily on the shiny plastic. "Am I to understand you came to my rescue *intentionally*?" it said.

Retief nodded.

"Whatever for?"

"On the theory that one intelligent being should

keep another from being eaten alive, whenever he conveniently can."

"Hmmm. A curious concept. And now I suppose you expect me to reciprocate?"

"If it doesn't inconvenience you," Retief replied.

"But you look so, so edible . . ." Without warning, one of the alien's ebon legs flashed out, talons spread, in a vicious kick. It was a fast stroke, but Retief was faster; shifting his weight slightly, he intercepted the other's shin with the edge of his shoe, eliciting a sharp report. The Zooner yelped, simultaneously lashed out, left-right, with a pair of arms, to meet painful interceptions as Retief struck upward at one, down at the other. In the next instant, a small hand gun was pressing into the alien's paunch-bristles.

"We Terries are handy at small manufacturing, too," Retief said easily. "This item is called a crater gun. You'll understand why when you've seen it fired."

". . . but appearances can be so deceiving," the Zooner finished its interrupted sentence, wringing its numbed limbs.

"A natural mistake," Retief commiserated. "Still, I'm sure you wouldn't have found me any more nourishing than the vine-jack would have found you: incompatible body chemistry, you know."

"Yes. Well, in that case, I may as well be off." The Zooner backed a step.

"Before you go," Retief suggested, "there are some matters we might discuss to our mutual profit."

"Oh? What, for example?"

"The invasion of Zoon, for one. And ways and means of getting back down to *Zoona Firma* for another."

"You *are* a compulsive—and it's a highly channelized neurosis: a vine-jack or my humble self won't do; it has to be the hard way."

"I'm afraid your translator is out of adjustment," Retief said. "That doesn't seem to mean anything."

"I find your oblique approach a trifle puzzling, too,"

the alien confided. "I sense that you're trying to tell me something, but I can't for the life of me guess what it might be. Suppose we go along to my place for an aperitif, and possibly we can enlighten each other. By the way, I'm known as Qoj, the Ready Biter."

"I'm Retief, the Occasional Indulger," the Terran said. "Lead the way, Qoj, and I'll do my best to follow."

9

It was a breathtaking thirty-minute journey through the towering treetops. The alien progressed by long, curiously dream-like leaps from one precarious rest to another, while Retief made his way as rapidly as possible along interlacing branches and bridges of tangled vine, keenly aware of the bottomless chasm yawning below.

The trip ended at a hundred-foot spherical space where the growth had been cleared back to create a shady, green-lit cavern. Bowers and leafy balconies were nestled around its periphery; tiny, fragile-looking terraces, hung suspended under the shelter of sprays of giant fronds. There were several dozen Zooners in sight, some lounging on the platforms or perched in stem-mounted chairs which swayed dizzyingly to the light breeze; others sailed gracefully from one roost to another, while a few hung by one or more limbs from festooning vines, apparently sleeping.

"I'll introduce you around," the Zooner said. "Otherwise the fellows will be taking experimental cracks at you and getting themselves hurt. I'm against that, because an injured Zooner is inclined to be disagreeable company." He flipped a switch on the translator and emitted a sharp cry. Zooner heads turned. Qoj spieled off a short speech, waved a hand at Retief, who inclined his head courteously. The locals eyed the

Terran incuriously, went back to their previous activities. Qoj indicated a tiny table mounted atop a ten-foot rod, around which three small seats were arranged, similarly positioned. Retief scaled the support, took up his seat like a flagpole sitter. Qoj settled in opposite him, the stem quivering and swaying under his weight. He whistled shrilly, and a black-spotted gray creature came sailing in a broad leap, took orders, bounded away, returned in a moment with aromatic flagons.

"Ah," Qoj leaned back comfortably with two pairs of legs crossed. "Nothing like a little bottled Nirvana, eh?" He lifted his flask and poured the contents in past a row of pronged teeth rivaling those of the vine-jack.

"Quite an interesting place you have here." Retief unobtrusively sniffed his drink, sampled it. The fluid evaporated instantly on his tongue, leaving a fruity aroma.

"It's well enough, I suppose," Qoj assented, "under the circumstances."

"What circumstances are those?"

"Not enough to eat. Too many predators—like that fellow you dispatched. Cramped environment—no place to go. And of course, cut off as we are from raw materials, no hope for technological advancement. Let's face it, Retief: we're up the tree without a paddle."

Retief watched a bulky Zooner sail past in one of the feather-light leaps characteristic of the creatures.

"Speaking of technology," he said. "How do you manage that trick?"

"What trick?"

"You must weigh three hundred pounds—but when you want to, you float like a dandelion seed."

"Oh, that. Just an inherent knack, I guess you'd call it. Even our spore-pods have it; otherwise, they'd smash when they hit the ground."

"Organic antigravity," Retief said admiringly. "Or perhaps teleportation would be a better name."

"The gland responds to mental impulses" Qoj said.

"Fortunately, our young have no mentality to speak of, so they're grounded. Otherwise, I suppose we'd never have a moment's peace."

"He tossed another shot down his throat, lounging back in his chair as it swayed past Retief, rebounded to swing in the opposite direction, while Retief's perch waved in a gentle counterpoint, a motion which tended to cross the eyes and bring a light sweat to the forehead.

"I wondered why there were no little ones gamboling about your doorstep," Retief said.

"Doorstep?" Qoj jerked upright and stared in alarm toward the shaded entrance to his bower. "Great slaving jaws, Retief, don't give me a start like that! The little monsters are down on the surface where they belong!"

"Unattended?"

Qoj shuddered. "I suppose we really ought to be doing something about them, but frankly—it's too dangerous."

Retief raised an eybrow in polite inquiry.

"Why, the little fiends would strip the very crust off the planet if they weren't able to assuage their voracity by eating each other."

"So that's why you don't occupy the surface."

"Um. If our ancestors hadn't taken to the trees, we'd be extinct by now—devoured by our own offspring."

"And I suppose your apparent indifference to the arrival of the Groaci is based on the same reasoning."

"Feeding season's about to begin," Qoj said offhandedly. "Those fellows won't last a day. Not much juice in them, though—at least not in the one I met—"

"That would be the previous owner of the camera and the translator?"

"Correct. Interesting chap. He was buzzing about in an odd little contrivance with whirling vanes on top, and ran afoul a loop of string vine. My, wasn't he full of plans . . ." The Zooner sipped his flask, musing.

"The Groaci, individually, don't look like much, I'll agree," Retief said. "But they have a rather potent subnuclear arsenal at their command. And it appears they're about to launch a general offensive against your young."

"So? Maybe they'll clear the little nuisances out. Then we can descend to the ground and start living like gentlebeings."

"What about the future of the race?"

"*That* for the future of the race," Qoj made a complicated gesture with obscure biological implications. "We're only concerned about ourselves."

"Still," Retief countered, "you were young once—"

"If you're going to be crude," the Zooner said with inebriated dignity, "you may leave me."

"Sure," Retief said. "But before I go, would you mind describing these little fellows?"

"In shape, they're not unlike us adults; they come in all sizes, from this"—Qoj held two taloned fingers an inch apart—"to this." He indicated a yard and a half. "And of course, the baby fur. Ghastly blue fuzz a foot long."

"You did say . . . blue?"

"Blue."

Retief nodded thoughtfully. "You know, Qoj, I think we have the basis for a cooperative undertaking after all. If you'll give me another five minutes of your time, I'll explain what I have in mind. . . ."

10

Flanked by Qoj and another Zooner named Ornx the Eager Eater, Retief dropped down through the cloud layer, propelled by a softly hissing steering jet salvaged from his punctured lift harness.

"That's it, dead ahead," he pointed to the towering coral reef, pale rose-colored in the distance.

"Wheee!" Qoj squealed with delight as he pulled up abreast of Retief with a shrill whistling of his borrowed jet. "Capital idea, Retief, these little squirt-bottles! You know, I never dreamed flying could be such fun! Always lived in dread of getting out of reach of a branch and just drifting aimlessly until one of the boys or some other predator got me. With these, a whole new dimension opens up! I can already detect a lessening of sibling rivalry drives and inverted Oedipus syndromes!"

"Don't let your released tensions go to your head, Qoj," Retief cautioned. "The Groaci may still take a little managing. You hang back while I go in to check the lie of the land."

Minutes later, Retief swept in above the convoluted surface of the coral peak. No Groaci were to be seen, but half a dozen Terrans were wandering aimlessly about their lofty prison. They ran forward with glad cries as Retief landed.

"Good show, my boy!" Colonel Smartfinger pumped his hand. "I knew you wouldn't leave us stranded here! Those rascally Groaci commandeered our harnesses—"

"But—where are the reinforcements?" the Political Officer demanded, staring around. "Where's the lighter? Where's His Excellency? Who are *these* creatures?" He eyed the Zooners, circling for a landing. "Where have you been, Retief?" He broke off, staring. "And where's your harness?"

"I'll tell you later," Retief motioned the diplomats toward the deflated Groaci gasbag now draped limply across the rocks. "There's no time to dally, I'm afraid. All aboard."

"But—its punctured!" Smartfinger protested. "It won't fly, man!"

"It will when our new allies finish," Retief reassured the colonel.

The Zooners were already busy, bustling about the ersatz cloud, stuffing fistfuls of seed-pods inside. A corner of the big bag stirred lazily, lifted to flap gently in the breeze. One side curled upward, tugging gently.

"You know what to do," Retief called to Qoj. "Don't waste any time following me down." He jumped into the air, thumbed the jet control wide open, and headed for the next stop at flank speed.

11

Two thirds of the way down the sheer wall of the coral reef, a small figure caught Retief's eye, perched disconsolately in a crevice in the rock. He swung closer, saw the spindly shanks and five-eyed visage of a Groaci, his once-splendid raiment in tatters.

"Well, Field Marshal Shish," he called. "What's the matter, conditions down below not to your liking?"

"Ambassador Shish, if you please," the castaway hissed in sorrowful Groaci. "To leave me in solitude, Soft One; to have suffered enough."

"Not nearly enough," Retief contradicted. "However, all is not yet lost. I take it your valiant troops have encountered some sort of difficulty below?"

"The spawn of the pits fell upon us while I was in my bath!" the Groaci whispered, speaking Terran now. "They snapped up a dozen of my chaps before I could spring from the tub of hot sand in which I had been luxuriating! I was fortunate to escape with my life! And then your shoddy Terran-made harness failed and dropped me here. Alack! Gone are the dreams of a procuratorship."

"Maybe not." Retief maneuvered in close, held out a hand. "I'll give you a piggyback, and explain how matters stand. Maybe you can still salvage something from the wreckage."

Shish canted his eye-stalks. "Piggyback? Are you insane, Retief? Why, there's nothing holding you up! How can it hold *two* of us up?"

"Take it or leave it, Mr. Ambassador," Retief said. "I have a tight schedule."

"I'll take it." Shish gingerly swung his scrawny frame out and scrambled to a perch on Retief's back, four of his eyes sphinctered tight shut. "But if I hadn't already been contemplating suicide, nothing would have coaxed me to it!"

12

Five minutes later, Retief heard a hail; he dropped down, settled onto a narrow ledge beside the slight figure of Ambassador Oldtrick. The senior diplomat had lost his natty beret, and there was a scratch on his cheek. His flight harness, its gasbag flat, hung on a point of the rock behind him.

"What's this?" he blurted. "Who's captured whom? Retief, are you—did he . . ."

"Everything's fine, Your Excellency," Retief said soothingly. "I'll just leave His Groacian Excellency here with you. I've had a little talk with him, and he has something he wants to tell you. The staff will be along in a moment."

"But—you can't—" Oldtrick broke off as a dark shadow flitted across the rock. "Duck! It's that confounded cloud back again!"

"It's all right," Retief called as he launched himself into space. "It's on our side now."

13

At the long table in the main dining room aboard the heavy Corps transport which had been called in to assist in the repatriation of the Groaci Youth Scouts marooned on Zoon after the local fauna had devoured their ship, encampment, equipment, and supplies, Magnan nudged Retief.

"Rather a surprising about-face on the part of Ambassador Shish," he muttered. "When that fake cloud dumped us off on the rock ledge with him, I feared the worst."

"I think he'd had a spiritual experience down below that made him see the light," Retief suggested.

"Quite an equitable division of spheres of influence the Ambassadors agreed on," Magnan went on. "The Groaci seem quite pleased with the idea of erecting blastproof barriers to restrain those ferocious little eaters to one half the planet, and acting as herdsmen over them, in return for the privilege of collecting their hair after moulting season."

"I wouldn't be surprised if they didn't sneak out a few pelts beforehand," Colonel Smartfinger leaned to contribute. "Still, the Zooners don't seem to mind, eh, Ornx?" He cocked an eye at his neighbor.

"No problem," the Zooner said airily. "We're glad to wink at a few little violations in return for free access to our own real estate."

There was a sharp dinging as Ambassador Oldtrick tapped his glass with a fork and rose.

"Gentlemen—gentlebeings, I should say—" he smirked at the Groaci and Zooners seated along the board. "It's my pleasure to announce the signing of the Terran-Zoon accord, under the terms of which we've been ceded all rights in the coral reef of our choice on which to place our chancery, well out of reach of those nasty little—that is, the untutored—I mean, er, playfully inclined . . ." he quailed under the combined glares of a dozen rows of pink eyes.

"If he brings those abominations into the conversation again, I'm walking out," Qoj said loudly.

"So we're going to be relegated to the top of that dreadful skyscraper?" Magnan groaned. "I suppose we'll all be commuting by patent gasbag—"

"Ah!" Oldtrick brightened, glad of a change of subject. "I couldn't help overhearing your remark, Magnan. And I'm pleased to announce that I have just this afternoon developed a startling new improvement to my flight harness. Observe!" All eyes were on the

Ambassador as he rose gently into the air, hung, beaming down from a height of six feet.

"I should mention that I had some assistance from Mr. Retief in, ah, working out some of the technicali-5ties," he murmured as the Terrans crowded around, competing for the privilege of offering their congratulations.

"Heavens! And he's not even wearing a balloon!" Magnan gasped as he rose to join the press. "How do you suppose he does it?"

"Easy," Qoj grunted. "He's got a pocketful of prime-quality Zooner spore-pods."

Beside him, Ambassador Shish gave an annoyed hiss. "Somehow, I can't escape the conviction that we Groaci have been had again." He rose and stalked from the room.

"Hmph," Magnan sniffed, "he got what he wanted, didn't he?"

"True," Retief said. "But it's some people's ill luck to always want the wrong thing."

TRICK OR TREATY

1

A large green-yolked egg splattered across the flexglas panel as it slammed behind Retief. Across the long, narrow lobby, under a glare-sign reading HOSTELRY RITZKRUDLU, the Gaspierre room clerk looked up, then came quickly around the counter. He was a long-bodied, short-legged creature, wearing an expression as of one detecting a bad odor on his flattened, leathery-looking face. He spread six of the eight arms attached to his narrow shoulders like a set of measuring spoons, twitching the other two in a cramped shrug.

"The hotel, he is fill!" he wheezed. "To some other house you convey your custom, yes?"

"Stand fast," Retief said to the four Terrans who had preceded him through the door. "Hello, Strupp," he nodded to the agitated clerk. "These are friends of mine. See if you can't find them a room."

"As I comment but now, the rooms, she is occupy!" Strupp pointed to the door. "Kindly facilities provide by management to place selves back outside use!"

A narrow panel behind the registration desk popped open; a second Gaspierre slid through, took in the situation, emitted a sharp hiss. Strupp whirled, his arms semaphoring an unreadable message.

"Never mind that, Strupp," the newcomer snapped in accentless Terran. He took out a strip of patterned cloth, mopped under the breathing orifices set in the sides of his neck, looked at the group of Terrans, then back at Retief. "Ah, something I can do for you, Mr. Retief?"

"Evening, Hrooze," Retief said. "Permit me to introduce Mr. Julius Mulvihill, Miss Suzette la Flamme, Wee Willie, and Professor Fate, just in from out-system. There seems to be a room shortage in town. I thought perhaps you could accommodate them."

Hrooze eyed the door through which the Terrans had entered, twitched his nictating eyelids in a nervous gesture.

"You know the situation here, Retief!" he said. "I have nothing against Terries personally, of course, but if I rent to these people—"

"I was thinking you might fix them up with free rooms, just as a sort of good-will gesture."

"If we these Terries to the Ritz-Krudlu admit, the repercussions political out of business us will put!" Strupp expostulated.

"The next ship out is two days from now," Retief said. "They need a place to stay until then."

Hrooze looked at Retief, mopped his neck again. "I owe you a favor, Retief," he said. "Two days, though, that's all!"

"But—" Strupp began.

"Silence!" Hrooze sneezed. "Put them in twelve-oh-three and -four!"

He drew Retief aside as a small bellhop in a brass-studded harness began loading baggage on his back.

"How does it look?" he inquired. "Any hope of getting that squadron of Peace Enforcers to stand by out-system?"

"I'm afraid not; Sector HQ seems to feel that might be interpreted by the Krultch as a warlike gesture."

"Certainly it would! That's exactly what the Krultch can understand—"

"Ambassador Sheepshorn has great faith in the power of words," Retief said soothingly. "He has a reputation as a great verbal karate expert; the Genghis Khan of the conference table."

"But what if you lose? The cabinet votes on the

Krultch treaty tomorrow! If it's signed, Gaspierre will be nothing but a fueling station for the Krultch battle fleet! And you Terries will end up as mess-slaves!"

"A sad end for a great oral athlete," Retief said. "Let's hope he's in good form tomorrow."

2

In the shabby room on the twelfth level, Retief tossed a thick plastic coin to the baggage slave, who departed emitting the thin squeaking that substituted in his species for a jaunty whistle. Mulvihill, a huge man with a handlebar mustache, looked around, plumped his vast, bulging suitcase to the thin carpet, mopped at the purple-fruit stain across his red plastiweve jacket.

"I'd like to get my hands on the Gasper that threw that," he growled in a bullfrog voice.

"That's a mean crowd out there," said Miss La Flamme, a shapely redhead with a tattoo on her left biceps. "It was sure a break for us the Ambassador changed his mind about helping us out. From the look the old sourpuss gave me when I kind of bumped against him, I figured he had ground glass where his red corpuscles ought to be."

"I got a sneaking hunch Mr. Retief swung this deal on his own, Suzy," the big man said. "The Ambassador's got bigger things on his mind than out-of-work variety acts."

"This is the first time the Marvelous Merivales ever been flat out of luck on tour," commented a whiskery little man no more than three feet tall, dressed in an old-fashioned frock coat and a checkered vest. His voice was like the yap of a Pekinese. "How come we got to get mixed up in politics?"

"Shut up, Willie!" the big man said. "It's not Mr. Retief's fault we came here."

"Yeah," the midget conceded. "I guess you fellows in the CDT got it kind of rough, too, trying to pry the Gaspers outa the Krultch's hip pocket. Boy, I wish I could see the show tomorrow when the Terry Ambassador and the Krultch brass slug it out to see whose side the Gaspers'll be neutral on."

"Neutral, ha!" the tall, cadaverous individual looming behind Wee Willie snorted. "I caught a glimpse of that ferocious war vessel at the port, openly flying the Krultch battle flag! It's an open breach of interworld custom—"

"Hey, Professor, leave the speeches to the CDT," the girl said.

"Without free use of Gaspierre ports, the Krultch plans for expansion through the Gloob cluster would come to naught. A firm stand—"

"Might get 'em blasted right off the planet," the big man growled. "The Krultch play for keeps."

"And the Gaspers aim to be on the winning side," the midget piped. "And all the smart money is on the Krultch battlewagon to put up the best argument."

"Terries are fair game around here, it looks like, Mr. Retief," Mulvihill said. "You better watch yourself going back."

Retief nodded. "Stay close to your rooms; if the vote goes against us tomorrow, we may all be looking for a quick way home."

3

Outside, on the narrow elevated walkway that linked the gray slablike structures of the city, thin-featured Gaspierre natives shot wary looks at Retief, some skirting him widely, others jostling him as they crowded past. It was a short walk to the building where the Terrestrial delegation occupied a suite. As Retief neared it, a pair of Krultch sailors emerged from a grogshop, turned in his direction. They were short-coupled centauroid quadrupeds, with deep, narrow chests, snouted faces with business-like jaws and fringe beards, dressed in the redstriped livery of the Krultch Navy, complete with sidearms and short swagger sticks. Retief altered course to the right to give them passing room; they saw him, nudged each other, spaced themselves to block the walk. Retief came on without slowing, started between them. The Krultch closed ranks. Retief stepped back, started around the sailor on the left. The creature sidled, still blocking his path.

"Oh-hoh, Terry loose in street," he said in a voice like sand in a gear box. "You lost, Terry?"

The other Krultch crowded Retief against the rail. "Where you from, Terry? What you do—?"

Without warning, Retief slammed a solid kick to the shin of the Krultch before him, simultaneously wrenched the stick from the alien's grip, cracked it down sharply across the wrist of the other sailor as he went for his gun. The weapon clattered, skidded off the walk and was gone. The one whom Retief had kicked was hopping on three legs, making muffled sounds of agony. Retief stepped quickly to him, jerked his gun from its holster, aimed it negligently at the other Krultch.

"Better get your buddy back to the ship and have that leg looked at," he said.

A ring of gaping Gaspierre had gathered, choking the walk. Retief thrust the pistol into his pocket, turned his back on the Krultch, pushed through the locals. A large coarse-hided Gaspierre policeman made as if to block his way; Retief rammed an elbow in his side and kept going. A mutter was rising from the crowd behind him. The Embassy was just ahead now. Retief turned off toward the entry; two yellow-uniformed Gaspierre moved into sight under the marquee, eyed him as he came up.

"Terran, have you not heard of the curfew?" one demanded in shrill but accurate Terran.

"Can't say that I have," Retief replied. "There wasn't any, an hour ago."

"There is now!" the other snapped. "You Terries are not popular here. If you insist on inflaming the populace by walking abroad, we cannot be responsible for your safety—" he broke off as he saw the Krultch pistol protruding from Retief's pocket.

"Where did you get that?" he demanded in Gaspierran, then switched to pidgin Terran: "Where you-fella catchum bang-bang?"

"A couple of lads were playing with it in the street," Retief said in the local dialect. "I took it away from them before someone got hurt." He started past them.

"Hold on there," the policeman snapped. "We're not finished with you, fellow. We'll tell you when you can go. Now . . ." He folded his upper elbows. "You're to go to your quarters at once. In view of the tense interplanetary situation, all you Terries are to remain inside until further notice, I have my men posted on all approaches to, ah, provide protection—"

"You're putting a diplomatic mission under arrest?" Retief inquired mildly.

"I wouldn't call it that. Let's say that it wouldn't be safe for foreigners to venture abroad—"

"Threats too?"

"This measure is necessary in order to prevent unfortunate incidents—!"

"How about the Krultch? They're foreigners; are you locking them in their bedrooms?"

"The Krultch are old and valued friends of the Gaspierre," the police captain said stiffly. "We—"

"I see now; ever since they set up an armed patrol just outside Gaspierran atmosphere, you've developed a vast affection for them. Of course, their purchasing missions help too."

The captain smirked. "We Gaspierre are nothing if not practical." He held out his clawlike two-fingered hand. "You will now give me the weapon."

Retief handed it over silently.

"Come, I will escort you to your room," the cop said.

Retief nodded complacently, followed the Gaspierre through the entry cubicle and into the lift.

"I'm glad you've decided to be reasonable," the cop said. "After all, if you Terries *should* convince the cabinet, it will be much nicer all around if there have been no incidents."

"How true," Retief murmured.

He left the car at the 20th floor.

"Don't forget, now," the cop said, watching Retief key his door. "Just stay inside and all will yet be well." He signaled to a policeman standing a few yards along the corridor.

"Keep an eye on the door, Klosta. . . ."

Inside, Retief picked up the phone, dialed the Ambassador's room number. There was a dry buzz, no answer. He looked around the room. There was a tall, narrow window set in the wall opposite the door, with a hinged section that swung outward. Retief opened it, leaned out, looked down at the dizzying stretch of blank facade that dropped sheer to the upper walkway seventy yards below. Above, the wall extended up twenty feet to an overhanging cornice. He went to the closet, yanked a blanket from the shelf, ripped it into four wide strips, knotted them together, tied one end to a chair which he braced below the window.

Retief swung his legs outside the window, grasped the blanket-rope, and slid down.

4

The window at the next level was closed and curtained. Retief braced himself on the sill, delivered a sharp kick to the panel; it shattered with an explosive sound. He dropped lower, reached through, released the catch, pulled the window wide, knocked the curtain aside, scrambled through into a darkened room.

"Who's there?" a sharp voice barked. A tall, lean man in a ruffled shirt with an unknotted string tie hanging down the front gaped at Retief from the inner room.

"Retief! How did you get here? I understood that none of the staff were to be permitted—that is, I agreed that protective custody—er, it seems . . ."

"The whole staff is bottled up here in the building, Mr. Ambassador. I'd guess they mean to keep us here until after the Cabinet meeting. It appears the Krultch have the fix in."

"Nonsense! I have a firm commitment from the Minister that no final commitment will be made until we've been heard—"

"Meanwhile, we're under house arrest—just to be sure we don't have an opportunity to bring any of the cabinet around to our side."

"Are you suggesting that I've permitted illegal measures to be taken without a protest?" Ambassador Sheepshorn fixed Retief with a piercing gaze which wilted, slid aside. "The place was alive with armed gendarmes," he sighed. "What could I do?"

"A few shrill cries of outrage might have helped," Retief pointed out. "It's still not too late. A fast visit to the Foreign Office—"

"Are you out of your mind? Have you observed the temper of the populace? We'd be torn to shreds!"

Retief nodded. "Quite possibly; but what do you think our chances are tomorrow, after the Gaspierre conclude a treaty with the Krultch?"

Sheepshorn made two tries, then swallowed hard. "Surely, Retief, you don't—"

"I'm afraid I do," Retief said. "The Krultch need a vivid symbol of their importance—and they'd also like to involve the Gaspierre in their skulduggery, just to ensure their loyalty. Packing a clutch of Terry diplomats off to the ice-mines would do both jobs."

"A great pity," the Ambassador sighed. "And only nine months to go till my retirement."

"I'll have to be going now," Retief said. "There may be a posse of annoyed police along at any moment, and I'd hate to make it too easy for them."

"Police? You mean they're not even waiting until after the Cabinet's decision?"

"Oh, this is just a personal matter; I damaged some Krultch naval property and gave a Gaspierre cop a pain in the neck."

"I've warned you about your personality, Retief," Sheepshorn admonished. "I suggest you give yourself up, and ask for clemency; with luck, you'll get to go along to the mines with the rest of us. I'll personally put in a good word—"

"That would interfere with my plans, I'm afraid," Retief said. He went to the door. "I'll try to be back before the Gaspierre do anything irrevocable. Meanwhile, hold the fort here. If they come for you, quote regulations at them; I'm sure they'll find that discouraging."

"Plans? Retief, I positively forbid you to—"

Retief stepped through the door and closed it behind him, cutting off the flow of ambassadorial wisdom. A flat policeman posted a few feet along the corridor came to the alert, opened his mouth to speak—

"All right, you can go home now," Retief said in brisk Gaspierran. "The chief changed his mind; he decided violating a Terran Embassy's quarters was just asking for trouble. After all, the Krultch haven't won yet."

The cop stared at him, then nodded. "I wondered if this wasn't kind of getting the rickshaw before the coolie . . ." he hesitated. "But what do *you* know about it?"

"I just had a nice chat with the captain, one floor up."

216

"Well, if he let you come down here, I guess it's all right."

"If you hurry, you can make it back to the barracks before the evening rush begins." Retief waved airily and strolled away along the corridor.

5

Back at ground level, Retief went along a narrow service passage leading to the rear of the building, stepped out into a deserted-looking courtyard. There was another door across the way. He went to it, followed another hall to a street exit. There were no cops in sight. He took the sparsely peopled lower walkway, set off at a brisk walk.

6

Ten minutes later, Retief surveyed the approaches to the Hostelry Ritz-Krudlu from the shelter of an interlevel connecting stair. A surging crowd of Gaspierre blocked the walkway, with a scattering of yellow police uniforms patrolling the edge of the mob. Placards lettered TERRY GO HOME and KEEP GASPIERRE BROWN bobbed above the sea of flattened heads. Off to one side, a heavily braided Krultch officer stood with a pair of age-tarnished locals, looking on approvingly.

Retief retraced his steps to the debris-littered ground level twenty feet below the walkway, found an eighteen-inch-wide air space leading back between the buildings. He inched along it, came to a door, found it locked. Four doors later, a latch yielded to his touch. He stepped inside, made out the dim outlines of an empty storage room. The door across the room was locked. Retief stepped back, slammed a kick against it at latch level; it bounced wide.

217

After a moment's wait for the sound of an alarm which failed to materialize, Retief moved off along the passage, found a rubbish-heaped stair. He clambered over the debris, started up.

At the twelfth level, he emerged into the corridor. There was no one in sight. He went quickly along to the door numbered 1203, tapped lightly. There was a faint sound from inside; then a bass voice rumbled, "Who's there?"

"Retief. Open up before the house dick spots me."

Bolts clattered and the door swung wide; Julius Mulvihill's mustached face appeared; he seized Retief's hand and pumped it, grinning.

"Cripes, Mr. Retief, we were worried about you. Right after you left, old Hrooze called up here and said there was a riot starting up—"

"Nothing serious; just a few enthusiasts out front putting on a show for the Krultch."

"What's happened?" Wee Willie chirped, coming in from the next room with lather on his chin. "They throwing us out already?"

"No, you'll be safe enough right here. But I need your help."

The big man nodded, flexed his hands.

Suzette la Flamme thrust a drink into Retief's hand. "Sit down and tell us about it."

"Glad you come to us, Retief," Wee Willie piped.

Retief took the offered chair, sampled the drink, then outlined the situation.

"What I have in mind could be dangerous," he finished.

"What ain't?" Willie demanded.

"It calls for a delicate touch and some fancy footwork," Retief added.

The professor cleared his throat. "I am not without a certain dexterity—" he started.

"Let him finish," the redhead said.

"And I'm not even sure it's possible," Retief stated.

The big man looked at the others. "There's a lot of things that look impossible—but the Marvelous Merivales do 'em anyway. That's what made our act a wow on a hundred and twelve planets."

The girl tossed her red hair. "The way it looks, Mr. Retief, if somebody doesn't do something, by this time tomorrow this is going to be mighty unhealthy territory for Terries."

"The ones the mob don't get will be chained to an oar in a Krultch battlewagon," Willie piped.

"With the Mission pinned down in their quarters, the initiative appears to rest with us," Professor Fate intoned. The others nodded.

"If you're all agreed then," Retief said, "here's what I have in mind . . ."

7

The corridor was empty when Retief emerged, followed by the four Terrans.

"How are we going to get out past that crowd out front?" Mulvihill inquired. "I've got a feeling they're ready for something stronger than slogans."

"We'll try the back way—"

There was a sudden hubbub from the far end of the corridor; half a dozen Gaspierre burst into view, puffing hard from a fast climb. They hissed, pointed, started for the Terrans at a short-legged trot. At the same moment, a door flew wide at the opposite end of the hallway; more locals popped into view, closed in.

"Looks like a necktie party," Wee Willie barked. "Let's go get 'em Julie!" He put his head down and charged. The oncoming natives slowed, skipped aside. One, a trifle slow, bounced against the wall as the midget rammed him at knee level. The others whirled, grabbing at Wee Willie as he skidded to a halt. Mulvihill roared, took three giant steps, caught two Gaspierre by the backs of their leathery necks, bounced them off the wall.

The second group of locals, emitting wheezes of

excitement, dashed up, eager for the fray. Retief met one with a straight right, knocked two more aside with a sweep of his arm, sprinted for the door through which the second party of locals had appeared. He looked back to see Mulvihill toss another Gaspierre aside, pluck Wee Willie from the melee.

"Down here, Julie!"

The girl called, "Come on, Professor!"

The tall, lean Terran, backed against the wall by three hissing locals, stretched out a yard-long arm, flapped his hand. A large white pigeon appeared, fluttered, squawking, into the faces of the attackers; they fell back, slapping and snorting. Professor Fate plunged through them, grabbed the bird by the legs as he passed, dashed from the door where Retief and the girl waited.

There was a sound of pounding feet from the stairwell; a fresh contingent of locals came charging into view on stub legs. Retief took two steps, caught the leader full in the face with a spread hand, sent him reeling back down among his followers, as Mulvihill appeared, Wee Willie over his shoulder, yelling and kicking.

"There's more on the way," Retief called. "We'll have to go up."

The girl nodded, started up, three steps at a time. Mulvihill dropped the midget, who scampered after her. Professor Fate tucked his bird away, disappeared up the stairs in giant strides, Mulvihill and Retief behind him.

8

On the roof, Retief slammed the heavy door, shot the massive bolt. It was late evening now; cool blue air flowed across the unrailed deck; faint crowd sounds floated up from the street twenty stories below.

"Willie, go secure that other door," Mulvihill commanded. He went to the edge of the roof, looked down, shook his head, started across toward another side. The redhead called to him.

"Over here, Julie . . ."

Retief joined Mulvihill at her side. A dozen feet down and twenty feet distant across a narrow street was the slanted roof of an adjacent building. A long ladder was clamped to brackets near the ridge.

"Looks like that's it," Mulvihill nodded. Suzette unlimbered a coil of light line from a clip at her waist, gauged the distance to a projecting ventilator intake, swung the rope, and let it fly; the broad loop spread, slapped the opposite roof, encircling the target. With a tug, the girl tightened the noose, quickly whipped the end around a four-inch stack. She stooped, pulled off her shoes, tucked them in her belt, tried the taut rope with one foot.

"Take it easy, baby," Mulvihill muttered. She nodded, stepped out on the taut, down-slanting cable, braced her feet, spread her arms, and in one smooth swoop, slid along the line and stepped off the far end, turned and executed a quick curtsy.

"This is no time to ham it up," Mulvihill boomed.

"Just habit," the girl said. She went up the roof, freed the ladder, released the catch that caused an extensible section to slide out, then came back to the roof's edge, deftly raised the ladder to a vertical position.

"Catch!" she let it lean toward Mulvihill and Retief; as it fell both men caught it, lowered it the last foot.

"Hey, you guys," Willie called. "I can't get this thing locked!"

"Never mind that now," Mulvihill rumbled. "Come on, Prof," he said to the lean prestidigitator. "You first."

The professor's Adam's apple bobbed as he swallowed. He peered down at the street far below, then threw his shoulders back, clambered up onto the ladder, and started across on all fours.

"Don't look down, Professor," Suzie called. "Look at me."

"Let's go, Willie!" Mulvihill called over his shoulder. He freed the rope, tossed it across, then stepped up on the ladder, started across, one small step at a time. "This isn't my strong suit," he muttered, teeth together. The professor had reached the far side. Mulvihill was half way. There was a sudden yelp from Willie. Retief turned. The midget was struggling against the door, which was being forced open from inside.

"Hey!" Mulvihill boomed. Suzie squealed. Retief sprinted for the embattled midget, caught him as he was hurled backward as the door flew open, disgorging three Gaspierre who staggered for balance, went down as Retief thrust out a foot. He thrust Wee Willie aside, picked up the nearest native, pitched him back inside, followed with the other two, then slammed the door, tried the bolt.

"It's sprung," he said. "Let's go, Willie!" He caught up the small man, ran for the ladder where Mulvihill still stood, halfway across.

"Come on, Julie!" the girl cried. "It won't hold both of you!"

There were renewed breathy yells from the site of the scuffle. The door had burst open again, and more Gaspierre were spilling from it. Mulvihill snorted, finished the crossing and scrambled for footing on the slanting roof. Retief stepped out on the limber ladder, started across, Willie under his arm.

"Look out!" Suzette said sharply. The rungs jumped under Retief's feet. He reached the roof in two jumps, dropped the midget, turned to see a huddle of Gaspierre tugging at the ladder. One, rendered reckless in his zeal, started across. Retief picked up the end of the ladder, shook it; the local squeaked, scrambled back. Retief hauled the ladder in.

"Up here," the girl called. Retief went up the slope, looked down at an open trap door in the opposite slope. He followed the others down through it into a musty loft, latched it behind him. The loft door opened into an empty hall. They followed it, found a lift, rode it down to ground level. Outside in a littered alley, the crowd noises were faint.

"We appear to have out-foxed the ruffians," Professor Fate said, adjusting his cuffs.

"The Gaspers ain't far behind," Wee Willie shrilled. "Let's make tracks!"

"We'll find a spot and hide out until dark," Retief said. "Then we'll make our try."

9

A faint gleam from Gaspierre's three bright star-sized moons dimly illuminated the twisting alley along which Retief led the four Terrans.

"The port is half a mile from the city wall," he said softly to Mulvihill at his side. "We can climb it between watchtowers, and circle around and hit the ramp from the east."

"They got any guards posted out there?" the big man asked.

"I think the Krultch will have a few sentries out."

"Oh-oh, here's the wall . . ." The barrier loomed up, twelve feet high, Suzette came forward, looked it over.

"I'll check the top," she said. "Give me a boost, Julie." He lifted her, raised her to arm's length. She put a foot on the top of his head, stepped up. Mulvihill grunted. "Watch out some Gasper cop doesn't spot you!"

"Coast is clear." She pulled herself up. "Come on, Willie, I'll give you a hand." Mulvihill lifted the midget, who caught the girl's hand, scrambled up. Mulvihill bent over, and Retief stepped in his cupped hands, then to the big man's shoulders, reached the top of the wall. The girl lowered her rope for Mulvihill. He clambered up, swearing softly, with Retief's help hoisted his bulk to the top of the wall. A moment later the group was moving off quietly across open ground toward the south edge of the port.

10

Lying flat at the edge of the ramp, Retief indicated a looming, light-encrusted silhouette.

"That's her," he said. "Half a million tons, crew of three hundred."

"Big enough, ain't she?" Wee Willie chirped.

"Hsst! There's a Krultch . . . !" Mulvihill pointed.

Retief got softly to his feet. "Wait until I get in position behind that fuel monitor . . ." he pointed to a dark shape crouching fifty feet distant. "Then make a few suspicious noises."

"I better go with you, Retief," Mulvihill started, but Retief was gone. He moved forward silently, reached the shelter of the heavy apparatus, watched the Krultch sentinel move closer, stepping daintily as a deer on its four sharp hooves. The alien had reached a point a hundred feet distant when there was a sharp *ping!* from behind Retief. The guard halted; Retief heard the *snick!* of a power gun's action. The Krultch turned toward him. He could hear the cli-clack, cli-clack of the hooves now. At a distance of ten feet, the quadruped slowed, came to a halt. Retief could see the vicious snout of the gun aimed warily into the darkness. There was another sound from Mulvihill's position. The guard plucked something from the belt rigged across his chest, started toward the source of the sound. As he passed Retief, he shied suddenly, grabbed for his communicator. Retief leaped, landed a haymaker on the bony face, caught the microphone before it hit the pavement. The Krultch, staggering back from the blow, went to his haunches, struck out with knife-edged forefeet. Retief ducked aside, chopped hard at the collarbone. The Krultch collapsed with a choked cry. Mulvihill appeared at a run, seized the feebly moving guard, pulled off the creature's belt, trussed his four legs together, then used other straps to bind the hands and gag the powerful jaws as the others joined the group.

"Now what?" Wee Willie inquired. "You gonna cut his throat?"

"Shove him back of the monitor," Mulvihill said.

"Now let's see how close we can get to the ship without getting spotted," Retief said.

11

The mighty Krultch war vessel was a black column towering into the night, ablaze with varicolored running and navigation lights. Giant floods mounted far up on the ship's sleek sides cast puddles of blue-white radiance on the tarmac; from the main cabin amidships, softer light gleamed through wide view-windows.

"All lit up like a party," Mulvihill growled.

"A tough party to crash," Wee Willie said, looking up the long slant of the hull.

"I think I see a route, Mr. Retief," the girl said. "What's that little square opening up there, just past the gun emplacement?"

"It looks as though it might be a cargo hatch. It's not so little, Miss La Flamme; it's a long way up—"

"You reckon I could get through it?"

Retief nodded, looking up at the smooth surface above. "Can you make it up there?"

"They used to bill me as the human ladybug. Nothing to it."

"If you get in," Retief said, "try to find your way

back down into the tube compartment. If you can open one of these access panels, we're in."

Suzette nodded, took out her rope, tossed a loop over a projection fifteen feet above, clambered quickly up the landing jack to its junction with the smooth metal of the hull. She put her hands flat against the curving, slightly inslanting wall before her, planted one crepe-soled shoe against a tiny weld seam and started up the sheer wall.

Ten minutes passed. From the deep shadow at the ship's stern, Retief watched as the slim girl inched her way up, skirting a row of orange glare panels spelling out the name of the vessel in blocky Krultch ideographs, taking advantage of a ventilator outlet for a minute's rest, then going on up, up, thirty yards now, forty, forty-five . . .

She reached the open hatch, raised her head cautiously for a glance inside, then swiftly pulled up and disappeared through the opening.

Julius Mulvihill heaved a sigh of relief. "That was as tough a climb as Suzie ever made," he rumbled.

"Don't get happy yet," Wee Willie piped up. "Her troubles is just starting."

"I'm sure she'll encounter no difficulty," Professor Fate said anxiously. "Surely there'll be no one on duty aft, here in port. . . ."

More minutes ticked past. Then there was a rasp of metal, a gentle clatter. A few feet above ground, a panel swung out; Suzie's face appeared, oil streaked.

"Boy, this place needs a good scrubbing," she breathed. "Come on; they're all having a shindig up above, sounds like."

Inside the echoing, gloomy vault of the tube compartment, Retief studied the layout of equipment, the placement of giant cooling baffles, the contour of the bulkheads.

"This is a Krultch-built job," he said. "But it seems to be a pretty fair copy of an old Concordiat cruiser of the line. That means the controls are all the way forward."

"Let's get started!" Wee Willie went to the wide-runged catwalk designed for goatlike Krultch feet, started up. The others followed. Retief glanced around, reached for the ladder. As he did, a harsh Krultch voice snapped, "Halt where you are, Terrans!"

12

Retief turned slowly. A dirt-smeared Krultch in baggy coveralls stepped from the conceal-ment of a massive ion-collector, a grim-looking power gun aimed. He waited as a second and third sailor followed him, all armed.

"A nice catch, Udas," one said admiringly in Krultch. "The captain said we'd have Terry labor to do the dirty work on the run back, but I didn't expect to see 'em volunteering."

"Get 'em down here together, Jesau," the first Krultch barked. His partner came forward, motioned with the gun.

"Retief, you savvy Fustian?" Mulvihill muttered.

"Uh-huh," Retief answered.

"You hit the one on the left; I'll take the bird on the right. Professor—"

"Not yet," Retief said.

"No talk!" the Krultch barked in Terran. "Come down, plenty quick-quick!"

The Terrans descended to the deck, stood in a loose group.

"Closer together!" the sailor said; he poked the girl with the gun to emphasize the command. She smiled at him sweetly. "You bat-eared son of a goat, just wait till I get a handful of your whiskers—"

"No talk!"

Professor Fate edged in front of the girl. He held out both hands toward the leading Krultch, flipped them over to show both sides, then twitched his wrists, fanned two sets of playing cards. He waved them under the astounded nose of the nearest gunman, and with a flick they disappeared.

The two rearmost sailors stepped closer, mouths open. The professor snapped his fingers; flame shot from the tip of each pointed forefinger. The Krultch jumped. The tall Terran waved his hands, whipped a gauzy blue handkerchief from nowhere, swirled it around; now it was red. He snapped it sharply, and a shower of confetti scattered around the dumbfounded Krultch. He doubled his fists, popped them open; twin puffs of colored smoke whoofed into the aliens' face. A final wave, and a white bird was squawking in the air.

"Now!" Retief said, and took a step, uppercut the leading sailor; the slender legs buckled as the creature went down with a slam. Mulvihill was past him, catching Krultch number two with a roundhouse swipe. The third sailor made a sound like tearing sheet metal, brought his gun to bear on Retief as Wee Willie, hurtling forward, hit him at the knees. The shot melted a furrow in the wall as Mulvihill floored the hapless creature with a mighty blow.

"Neatly done," Professor Fate said, tucking things back into his cuffs. "Almost a pity to lose such an appreciative audience."

13

With the three Krultch securely strapped hand and foot in their own harnessess, Retief nudged one with his foot.

"We have important business to contract in the control room," he said. "We don't want to disturb anyone, Jesau, so we'd prefer a nice quiet approach via the back stairs. What would you suggest?"

The Krultch made a suggestion. Retief tsked. "Professor perhaps you'd better give him a few more samples."

"Very well," Professor Fate stepped forward, waved his hands; a slim-bladed knife appeared in one. He tested the edge with his thumb, which promptly dripped gore. He stroked the thumb with another finger; the blood disappeared. He nodded.

"Now, fellow," he said to the sailor. "I've heard you rascals place great store by your beards; what about a shave?" He reached—

The Krultch made a sound like glass shattering. "The port catwalk!" he squalled. "But you won't get away with this!"

"Oh, no?" The professor smiled gently, made a pass in the air, plucked a small cylinder from nowhere.

"I doubt if anyone will be along this way for many hours," he said. "If we fail to return safely in an hour, this little device will detonate with sufficient force to distribute your component atoms over approximately twelve square miles." He placed the object by the Krultch, who rolled horrified eyes at it.

"O-on second thought, try the service catwalk behind the main tube," he squeaked.

"Good enough," Retief said. "Let's go."

14

The sounds of Krultch revelry were loud in the cramped passage.

"Sounds like they're doing a little early celebrating for tomorrow's big diplomatic victory," Mulvihill said. "You suppose most of them are in there?"

"There'll be a few on duty," Retief said. "But that sounds like a couple of hundred out of circulation for the moment—until we trip something and give the alarm."

"The next stretch is all right," Professor Fate said, coming back dusting off his hands. "Then I'm afraid we shall have to emerge into the open."

"We're not far from the command deck now," Retief said. "Another twenty feet, vertically, ought to do it."

The party clambered on up, negotiated a sharp turn, came to an exit panel. Professor Fate put his ear against it.

"All appears silent," he said. "Shall we sally forth?"

Retief came to the panel, eased it open, glanced out; then he stepped through, motioned the others to follow. It was quieter here; there was deep-pile carpeting underfoot, an odor of alien food and drug smoke in the air.

"Officers' country," Mulvihill muttered.

Retief pointed toward a door marked with Krultch lettering. "Anybody read that?" he whispered.

There were shakes of the head and whispered negatives.

"We'll have to take a chance," Retief went to the door, gripped the latch, yanked it suddenly wide. An obese Krultch in uniform but without his tunic looked up from a brightly colored magazine on the pages of which Retief glimpsed glossy photos of slender-built Krultch mares flirting saucy derriers at the camera. The alien stuffed the magazine in a desk slot, came to his feet, gaping, then whirled and dived for a control panel across the narrow passage in which he was posted. He reached a heavy lever, hauled it down just as Retief caught him with a flying tackle. Man and Krultch hit the deck together; Retief's hand chopped; the Krultch kicked twice and lay still.

"That lever—you suppose—" Wee Willie started.

"Probably an alarm," Retief said, coming to his feet. "Come on!" he ran along the corridor; it turned sharply to the right. A heavy door was sliding shut before him. He leaped to it, wedged himself in the narrowing opening, braced himself against the thrust of the steel panel. It slowed, with a groaning of machinery. Mulvihill charged up, grasped the edge of the door, heaved. Somewhere, metal creaked. Together, Retief and the strong man strained. There was a loud *clunk!* and a clatter of broken mechanism. The door slid freely back.

"Close," Mulvihill grunted. "For a minute there—" he broke off at a sound from behind him. Ten feet back along the passage a second panel had slid noiselessly out, sealing off the corridor. Mulvihill jumped to it, heaved against it.

Ahead, Retief saw a third panel, this one standing wide open. He plunged through it; skidded to a halt. A braided Krultch officer was waiting, a foot-long purple cigar in his mouth, a power gun in each hand. He kicked a lever near his foot. The door whooshed shut behind Retief.

"Welcome aboard, Terran," the captain grated. "You can be the first of your kind to enjoy Krultch hospitality."

15

"I have been observing your progress on my inspection screen here," the captain nodded toward a small panel which showed a view of the four Terrans pushing fruitlessly against the doors that had closed to entrap them.

"Interesting," Retief commented.

"You are surprised at the sophistication of the equipment we Krultch can command?" the captain puffed out smoke, showed horny gums in a smilelike grimace.

"No, anybody who can steal the price can buy a Groaci spy-eye system," Retief said blandly. "But I find it interesting that you had to spend all that cash just to keep an eye on your crew. Not too trustworthy, eh?"

"What? Any of my crew would die at my command!"

"They'll probably get the chance, too," Retief nodded agreement. "How about putting one of the guns down—unless you're afraid of a misfire."

"Krultch guns never misfire." The captain tossed one pistol aside. "But I agree: I am overprotected against the paltry threat of a single Terran."

"You're forgetting—I have friends."

The Krultch made a sound like fingernails on a blackboard. "They are effectively immobilized," he said. "Now, tell me: what did you hope to accomplish by intruding here?"

"I intend to place you under arrest," Retief said. "Mind if I sit down?"

The Krultch captain made laughing noises resembling a flawed drive bearing; he waved a two-fingered claw-hand.

"Make yourself comfortable—while you can," he said. "Now, tell me; how did you manage to get your equipment up to my ship without being seen? I shall impale the slackers responsible, of course."

"Oh, we have no equipment," Retief said breezily. He sniffed. "That's not a Lovenbroy cigar, is it?"

"Never smoke anything else," the Krultch said. "Care for one?"

"Don't mind if I do," Retief admitted. He accepted an eighteen-inch stogie, lit up.

"Now, about the equipment," the captain persisted. "I assume you used fifty-foot scaling ladders, though I confess I don't see how you got them onto the port—"

"Ladders?" Retief smiled comfortably. "We Terrans don't need ladders; we just sprouted wings."

"Wings? You mean?"

"Oh, we're versatile, we Terries."

The captain was wearing an expression of black disapproval now. "If you had no ladders, I must conclude that you broached my hull at ground level," he snapped. What did you use? It would require at least a fifty K-T/Second power input to penetrate two inches of flintsteel—"

Retief shook his head, puffing out scented smoke. "Nice," he said. "No, we just peeled back a panel barehanded. We Terrans—"

"Blast you Terrans! Nobody could . . ." The captain clamped his jaws, puffed furiously. "Just outside, in the access-control chamber, you sabotaged the closure mechanism. Where is the hydraulic jack you used for this?"

"As I said, we Terrans—"

"You entered the secret access passage almost as soon as you boarded my vessel!" the captain screeched. "My men are inoculated against every talk-drug known! What did you use on the traitor who informed you—"

Retief held up a hand. "We Terrans can be very persuasive, Captain. At this very moment, you yourself, for example, are about to be persuaded of the futility of trying to outmaneuver us."

The Krultch commander's mouth opened and closed. "Me!" he burst out. "You think that you can divert a Krultch officer from the performance of his duty?"

"Sure," a high voice piped from above and behind the captain. "Nothing to it."

The Krultch's hooves clattered as he whirled, froze at the sight of Wee Willie's small, round face smiling down at him from the ventilator register above the control panel. In a smooth motion, Retief cracked the alien across the wrist, twitched the gun from his nerveless hand.

"You see?" he said as the officer stared from him to the midget and back. "Never underestimate us Terrans."

16

The captain dropped in his chair, mopping at his face with a polka-dotted hanky provided by Wee Willie.

"This interrogation is a gross illegality!" he groaned. "I was assured that all your kind did was talk—"

"We're a tricky lot," Retief conceded. "But surely a little innocent deception can be excused, once you understand our natures. We love strife, and this seemed to be the easiest way to stir up some action."

"Stir up action?" the Krultch croaked.

"There's something about an apparently defenseless nincompoop that brings out the opportunist in people," Retief said. "It's a simple way for us to identify troublemakers, so they can be dealt with expeditiously. I think you Krultch qualify handsomely. It's convenient timing, because we have a number of new planet-wrecking devices we've been wanting to field-test—"

"You're bluffing!" the Krultch bleated.

Retief nodded vigorously. "I have to warn you, but you don't have to believe me. So if you still want to try conclusions—"

There was a sharp buzz from the panel; a piercing yellow light blinked rapidly. The captain's hand twitched as he eyed the phone.

"Go ahead, answer it," Retief said. "But don't say anything that might annoy me. We Terrans have quick tempers."

The Krultch flipped a key.

"Exalted One," a rapid Krultch voice babbled from the panel. "We have been assassinated by captives! I mean, captivated by assassins! There were twelve of them—or perhaps twenty! Some were as high as a hundred-year Fufu tree, and others smaller than hoofnits! One had eyes of live coals, and flames ten feet long shot from his hands, melting all they touched, and another—"

"Silence!" the captain roared. "Who are you? Where are you? What in the name of the Twelve Devils is going on here!" He whirled on Retief. "Where are the rest of your commandos? How did they evade my surveillance system? What—"

"Ah-ah," Retief clucked. "I'm asking the questions now. First, I'll have the names of all Gaspierre officials who accepted your bribes."

"You think I would betray my compatriots to death at your hands?"

"Nothing like that; I just need to know who the cooperative ones are so I can make them better offers."

A low *brackk!* sounded; this time a baleful blue light winked. The Krultch officer eyed it warily.

"That's my outside hot line to the local Foreign Office," he said. "When word reaches the Gaspierre government of the piratical behavior you alledgedly peaceful Terries indulge in behind the façade of diplomacy—"

"Go ahead, tell them," Retief said. "It's time they discovered they aren't the only ones who understand the fine art of the triple-cross."

The Krultch lifted the phone. "Yes?" he snapped. His expression stiffened. He rolled an eye at Retief, then at Wee Willie.

"What's that?" he barked into the communicator. "Flew through the air? Climbed where? What do you mean, giant white birds!"

"Boy," Wee Willie exclaimed, "them Gaspers sure exaggerate!"

The captain eyed the tiny man in horror, comparing his height with Retief's six-three. He shuddered.

"I know," he said into the phone. "They're already here . . ." He dropped the instrument back on its hook, glanced at his panel, idly reached—

"That reminds me," Retief said. He pointed the gun at the center of the captain's chest. "Order all hands to assemble amidships," he said.

"They—they're already there," the Krultch said unsteadily, his eyes fixed on the gun.

"Just make sure."

The captain depressed a key, cleared his throat.

"All hands to the central feeding area, on the double," he said.

There was a moment's pause. Then a Krultch voice came back: "All except the stand-by crews in power section and armaments, I guess you mean, Exalted One?"

"I said all hands, damn you!" the officer snarled. He flipped off the communicator. "I don't know what you think you'll accomplish with this," he barked. "I have three hundred fearless warriors aboard this vessel; you'll never get off this ship alive!"

Two minutes passed. The communicator crackled. "All hands assembled sir."

"Willie, you see that big white lever?" Retief said mildly. "Just pull it down, and the next one to it."

The captain made as to move. The gun jumped at him. Willie went past the Krultch, wrestled the controls down. Far away, machinery rumbled. A distinct shock ran through the massive hull, then a second.

"What was that?" the midget inquired.

"The disaster bulkheads, sliding shut," Retief said. "The three hundred fearless warriors are nicely locked in between them."

The captain slumped, looking stricken. "How do you know so much about the operation of my vessel?" he demanded. "It's classified. . . ."

"That's the result of stealing someone else's plans; the wrong people may have been studying them. Now, Willie, go let Julius and the rest of the group in; then I think we'll be ready to discuss surrender terms."

"This is a day that will live in the annals of treachery," the captain grated hollowly.

"Oh, I don't think it needs to get into the annals," Retief said. "Not if we can come to a private understanding, just between gentlemen. . . ."

17

It was an hour past sunrise when the emergency meeting of the Gaspierre Cabinet broke up. Ambassador Sheepshorn, emerging from the chamber deep in amiable conversation with an uncomfortable-looking Krultch officer in elaborate full dress uniform, halted as he spied Retief.

"Ah, there, my boy! I was a trifle concerned when you failed to return last evening, but as I was just pointing out to the captain here, it was really all just a dreadful misunderstanding. Once the Krultch position was made clear—that they really preferred animal husbandry and folk dancing to any sort of warlike adventures, the Cabinet was able to come to a rapid and favorable decision on the Peace-and-Friendship Treaty."

"I'm glad to hear that, Mr. Ambassador," Retief said, nodding to the stony-faced Krultch commander. "I'm sure we'd all rather engage in friendly competition than have to demonstrate our negotiating ability any further."

There was a stir at the end of the corridor; a harried-looking Krultch officer with a grimy Krultch yeoman in tow appeared, came up to the captain, saluted.

"Exalted One, this fellow has just escaped from some sort of magical paralysis—"

"It was that one," the sailor indicated Retief. "Him and the others." He looked reproachfully at Retief. "That was a dirty trick, telling us that was a bomb you were planting; we spent a rough night waiting for it to go off before we found out it was just a dope stick."

"Sorry," Retief said.

"Look, Exalted One," the sailor went on in a stage whisper. "What I wanted to warn you about, that Terry—the long one, with the pointed tail and the fiery breath; he's a warlock; he waves his hands and giant white flying creatures appear—"

"Silence, idiot!" the captain bellowed. "Have you no powers of observation? They don't merely *produce* birds; any fool could do *that!* They transform themselves! Now get out of my sight! I plan to enter a monastery as soon as we return home, and I want to get started on my meditating!" He nodded curtly and clattered away.

"Odd sort of chap," Sheepshorn commented. "I wonder what he was talking about?"

"Just some sort of in-group joke, I imagine," Retief said. "By the way, about that group of distressed Terrans I mentioned to you yesterday—"

"Yes; I may have been a bit abrupt with them, Retief; but of course I was busy planning my strategy for today's meeting. Perhaps I was hasty. I hereby authorize you to put in a good word for them."

"I took the liberty of going a little further than that," Retief said. "Since the new treaty calls for Terran cultural missions, I signed a six-months contract with them to put on shows here on Gaspierre."

Sheepshorn frowned. "You went a bit beyond your authority, Retief," he snapped. "I'd thought we might bring in a nice group or two to read classic passages from the Congressional Record, or perform some of the new silent music, and I had halfway promised the Groaci Minister I'd have one of his nose-flute troupes—"

"I thought it might be a good idea to show Terran solidarity, just at this juncture," Retief pointed out. "Then, too, a demonstration of sword-swallowing, prestidigitation, fire-eating, juggling, tight-rope walking, acrobatics, and thaumaturgics might be just the ticket for dramatizing Terran versatility."

Sheepshorn considered with pursed lips, then nodded. "You may have a valuable point there, my boy; we Terrans *are* a versatile breed. Speaking of which, I wish you'd been there to see my handling of the negotiation this morning! One moment I was all fire and truculence; the next, as smooth as Yill silk."

A brilliant performance, I daresay, Mr. Ambassador."

"Yes, indeed." Sheepshorn rubbed his hands together, chuckling. "In a sense, Retief, diplomacy itself might be thought of as a branch of show business, eh? Thus, these performers might be considered colleagues of a sort."

"True; but I wouldn't mention it when they're within earshot."

"Yes; it might go to their heads. Well, I'm off, Retief. My report on this morning's work will become a classic study of diplomatic subtlety."

He hurried away. A Gaspierre with heavy bifocal lenses edged up to Retief.

I'm with the *Gaspierre Morning Exhalation*," he wheezed. "Is it true, sir, that you Terries can turn into fire-breathing dragons at will . . . ?"

A second reporter closed in. "I heard you read minds," he said. "And about this ability to walk through walls—"

"Just a minute, boys," Retief held up a hand. "I wouldn't want to be quoted on this of course, but just between you and me, here's what actually happened, as soon as the Ambassador had looked into his crystal ball . . ."